**'Why can...
Miss Cran...**

Even the worst of enemies is usually forgiven when he truly tries to make amends. And it's inevitable that we'll see something of one another during your stay in London. I know it would grieve Aunt Lydia if she thought you and I were at loggerheads.'

Rosalind gave Felix back the slightest smile.

'That sounds suspiciously like a kind of black-mail, Captain Holden.'

'I think you could call it that.'

Dear Reader

Sally Blake gives us all the glamour and humorous mistakes of Queen Victoria's coronation in A ROYAL SUMMER while the hero and heroine try to solve their problems, and Stephanie Laurens launches in Masquerade with her first Regency, TANGLED REINS, in which the gorgeous hero manipulates a delightful heroine, only to have his wiles rebound! What more could you ask?

See you next month. . .

The Editor

Sally Blake was born in London but now lives in Weston-super-Mare. She started writing when her three children went to school and has written many contemporary and historical novels using various pen-names. She loves the research involved in writing historical novels, finding it both exciting and addictive. Conscious of the way that circumstances can change people, she applies this maxim to her fictional characters, providing them with an emotive background in which to grow and develop.

Recent titles by the same author:

FAR DISTANT SHORES
LADY OF SPAIN

A ROYAL SUMMER

Sally Blake

*First published in Great Britain 1992
by Mills & Boon Limited*

© Sally Blake 1992

*Australian copyright 1992
Philippine copyright 1992
This edition 1992*

ISBN 0 263 77847 9

*Masquerade is a trademark published by
Mills & Boon Limited, Eton House,
18–24 Paradise Road, Richmond, Surrey, TW9 1SR.*

*Set in 10 on 11 pt Linotron Baskerville
04-9209-79390*

*Typeset in Great Britain by Centracet, Cambridge
Made and printed in Great Britain*

CHAPTER ONE

'NATURALLY, if Sir George Greville proposes marriage to you, Rosalind, I shall expect you to give the gentleman a favourable answer,' Miles Cranbourne said, far too casually for it to be a genuine afterthought.

The atmosphere among the three people in the drawing-room of Cranbourne Hall suddenly seemed charged. Miles poured himself an after-dinner brandy and folded his arms determinedly as he awaited his daughter's reaction. His wife continued to stitch at her embroidery, stabbing at the canvas with the needle and pricking her fingers a dozen times. But she barely noticed the pin-pricks, concentrating instead on mentally pleading with her daughter not to be too outraged by the statement her father had just made.

Rosalind Cranbourne studied them both with a growing anger fit to rival her father's. She wasn't the daughter of good Sussex stock for nothing, and during her childhood days her father had always said arrogantly that, if he couldn't have a son, then Rosalind was the next best thing, riding and hunting as well as any boy . . .she remembered that now and faced him angrily, aware of her fast-beating heart.

'Father, you know I don't mean to displease you——' She tried not to let her voice shake with either anger or distress at that moment, for, although she meant what she said, she knew how unlikely it was!

'But you know you often *do* displease me, my dear!' Miles unfolded his arms and placed both hands behind his head in an attitude of implacability. 'You know how important it is for you to make a good marriage, and I want to see you happily settled before I die.'

His daughter looked back at him, her exasperated eyes exactly the same honey-brown hue as her father's. The tawny bronze of their hair was identical too, though in Rosalind's case it was glossy and luxurious, while Miles Cranbourne's was a mere ginger whisper covering the bald patch, which was shining with rage by now.

'Father, you're no more about to die than I am, and I wish you wouldn't blackmail me with such suggestions,' she said more heatedly. 'And you know very well that my visit to London has nothing to do with my being courted by Sir George! It was his mother who invited me to London, not the gentleman!'

Her mother laid down her embroidery, looking uneasily at her daughter.

'Rosalind, dear, please don't speak to your father in that way. We all know it's quite true that Lady Greville was most taken with you——'

'I apologise if I upset you, Mother.' The girl moved with unconscious grace to her mother and sat down beside her in a rustle of lavender skirts and petticoats. 'But surely you understand? If I thought the real reason behind the invitation was to have me paraded for Sir George's inspection like a—a prize cow, I'd refuse to go at all! And how can you sanction the possibility of my marrying someone I don't love?'

'You can learn to love,' her mother murmured, cheeks tinged with red at this frank conversation. 'Love often grows after marriage, and it's not always necessary to be filled with a blind passion to make a successful union.'

'And a happy one?' Rosalind said, failing to find the support she had hoped for in her mother, and wondering just how this innocent invitation to spend a season in London at the elegant Greville home had suddenly turned into something quite different—at least, as far as her father was concerned.

Miles Cranbourne stood up.

'Enough of this shilly-shallying, Rosalind, I'm convinced Sir George Greville intends to make an offer for your hand, and you'd do well to accept. He'll be a fine politician one of these days. Why, I'm told he even had an audience with the Queen recently. If he's starting to move in those circles, you may be included in a royal invitation for the coronation in June! This year of 1838 looks truly blessed, with the young Queen coming to the throne, and Mr Brunel's *Great Western* setting a record speed for steamships across the Atlantic!'

Engrossed as he so often was in the doings of the great engineer, he spoke of him with all the vicarious pride of a less ambitious shipping man. But even more so, Rosalind could see him preening himself like a peacock at the unlikely thought of her marriage to a titled gentleman.

Miles Cranbourne's modest shipping business was successful enough, but to imagine that his daughter could be invited to the pomp and circumstance surrounding the coronation of the young Queen Victoria was obviously turning his head! It would all be surreptitiously reported to the local news journal, Rosalind thought, and the squire of Cranbourne Hall would be famous by proxy.

'What do I care for royal invitations?' she said now, her eyes suddenly diamond-bright with tears. 'Sometimes I think the only reason you want to marry me off is for the prestige it will bring you, Father. Am I such an embarrassment to you to be still unmarried at twenty years old? I'm hardly in my dotage!'

'It'll be a wonder to me if anybody's ever willing to take you on, knowing the way you argue, my lady,' Cranbourne said caustically. 'In any case, I'm not pushing you into marriage right away, ninny. I've simply agreed to let you spend the summer months at Sir George Greville's home under his mother's patronage. You and her son will have ample opportunity to get to know one another better during that time, and if anything should come of it I wanted you to know it has my full blessing. Good God, any other young country girl would be ecstatic at the thought of spending a season in London!'

But Rosalind was not a docile country girl, and, since she'd been given too free a rein as a child, she now had a mind and a will of her own. She sat in silence while her father ranted on.

'Sir George is away in France on business at the present time, so it's been arranged that his cousin will escort you and your maid to London in a few days from now. After that, I expect you to be the young lady your mother has endeavoured to make you, and to consider any marriage proposal with all due grace.'

The slight on her mother's teachings almost diverted Rosalind from the real issue, but only for a moment. Her throat was full, and she knew her father would never relent. Besides, what real objections did she have? It wasn't as if George Greville was old, or ugly, or grossly deformed. . .he was a most personable man, tall and upright, late of Her Majesty's Guards until a hip injury had forced him to abandon any further equestrian plans, retire early and take up a political career.

It was while he and his mother were on a protracted holiday in Sussex last summer that the Cranbournes had made their acquaintance, resulting in the invitation from Lady Lydia Greville for Rosalind to spend a season at their London home.

But Rosalind was still full of objections, seeing past her father's eagerness to send her off.

'If I must go to London, why can't I stay with Aunt

May? Don't you think she'll be affronted that I'm in town and staying somewhere else?'

'Your aunt May's much too infirm to relish the thought of having a boisterous young woman in the house,' Miles said, clearly having anticipated this. 'Naturally, I shall expect you to visit her, but you will obey me in all else, Rosalind.'

And if she didn't, what option would there be? To remain in the country, where life went on at a leisurely pace, until she agreed to marry some worthy farmer's son or contemporary of her parents'? Or to take a position as governess to someone else's child, since there was little other option for the daughter of a comfortably middle-class family that still didn't *quite* have the status of being somebodies in the county. Or not to marry at all, which sometimes seemed to be more of a stigma to one's parents than marrying a totally unsuitable man!

Rosalind wasn't so eager to make any changes in her life. She hadn't yet met a man who could stir her beyond normal friendship, and marriage must surely involve more than friendship and mere tolerance. The wilder streak in her nature, which her father alternately admired and deplored, was privately tempered by a softer, romantic side that even she hadn't explored as yet.

But it was her father, with his undeniable snobbery, who had seemingly just recognised that his girl was stagnating. He had begun insisting that she must get out and about and meet people and be more of a social butterfly, when she'd far rather be racing her horse over the Sussex Downs on a frosty morning or sun-drenched afternoon, and feeling as free as the birds wheeling above. She was a country girl and happy to be so.

In his own way, Miles had been responsible for her being the way she was. Although they lived in reasonable proximity to London, the Cranbournes were an insular family apart from Miles's business transactions, rarely moving far from their own fireside. Miles had always treated his young daughter as the son he'd never had, and when he'd realised he had a tomboy on his hands he'd tried too late to turn her into a graceful swan. He couldn't understand just how much she had adored the freedom of her early years, and revelled so much in being a part of nature.

And now it was all to come to an end. There was no doubt of her father's hopes for her in this prolonged visit to London, and an eventual marriage with Sir George Greville would change everything. She turned abruptly away from her father's wary eyes, and her mother's troubled ones.

'May I go to my room now, please? I'm very tired this evening.'

'Providing you think on everything I've said, my dear.'

'Yes, I will, Father,' she said, suddenly resigned. 'I shall think of nothing else! Goodnight to you both.'

It wasn't done for a well-brought-up young lady to question her parents' wishes. Rosalind had had the fact drummed into her by the stern-faced tutor who had taught her to read and write and draw, discovering an artistic talent in herself she'd never known she had. She was an eager pupil, immensely interested in the recent history of their own country: the mad King George; then the era that became known so fashionably as the Regency; especially the fateful and enchanting way that a young girl of eighteen years old became a Queen overnight. To any romantic, it was a fairy-tale. . .

But she had no wild desire to gawp at the coronation of that same Queen, especially if it meant being there at the invitation of a man she didn't care about in the slightest. She hadn't been unaware of his interest in her when he was visiting Sussex. It had been his charming mother whom Rosalind had felt most warmly towards, despite Sir George's bold declaration that she was the most comely young lady in these parts. . .

Rosalind scowled into her dressing-table mirror now, and heard the amused laugh of the maid-cum-companion who had been with her for ten years, and was a good deal older than herself.

'You know what they say, Miss Rosalind. If the wind changes while you're making such a face, it will stay like it.'

'I wouldn't care if it did. I wish I was the ugliest person in the world!'

The plain-faced Margaret looked shocked.

'It's wicked to say such a thing, miss, and you know it. The good Lord made us what we are, and you should be grateful for them lovely looks of yours.'

She plumped up the pillows on the bed, clearly ruffled, and Rosalind was instantly contrite.

'I'm sorry, Margaret, but you know what's being planned for me, and I can't help being resentful at the thought of being courted by a man I don't love.'

'I dare say that's true, but there's a long way to go yet between thinking about marriage and actually tying the knot, so don't go wasting your time by fretting about it. Anyway, you might change your mind about him when you get to know him properly.'

And she might not. Rosalind unpinned her long hair and began to brush the tangles out of it, until Margaret came and lovingly took over.

'Were you ever in love, Margaret?' she said suddenly.

The woman paused in her task, used to her mistress's change of tactics.

'I was once, long ago,' she said, lost in memory. 'He were a young wheelwright, but he got the lust for the sea in his veins and his boat went down in a storm. And that was the end of falling in love for me!'

The brush-strokes resumed with some vigour until Rosalind protested.

'But how did it feel?' she persisted. 'How did you *know*?'

It didn't seem at all incongruous to be asking the maid these questions, for they were things she could never ask her mother. Some subjects were taboo, even the most fundamental ones.

Margaret laughed. 'It felt like I were walking on air, Miss Rosie. And when it happens to you, you'll know!'

And since that was all she would say on the subject, Rosalind had no option but to allow her to help her undress and slip into her cambric nightgown and into bed. It was spring, but the nights were still cool, and she was glad to find the warm comfort of the stone water bottle, wrapped carefully in a blanket to stop her feet from burning.

When it happened to her, she would know. . . Rosalind tried to recall George Greville's handsome face and willed such a feeling to come to her. Perhaps if he courted her in earnest, instead of the rather roundabout way he'd arranged for his mother to invite her to their Hampstead home, she would warm towards him. And perhaps she would not. Rosalind turned restlessly in the bed, innocently believing that something as wonderful as love shouldn't need to be worked upon. It should surely just happen.

Sir George Greville's letter to her father had arrived at the end of April. It stated that since he was presently obliged to travel abroad for a few weeks arrangements had been made for his cousin to take Rosalind and her maid to London, and he hoped the young lady would do him the honour of leaving with Felix as soon as she felt inclined. His mother was looking forward very much to receiving her. It was as cold and formal a letter as it was possible to write, Rosalind thought, feeling more uneasy by the minute at the thought of allying her life to this man.

But during the next days, when Margaret oversaw the laundering and ironing and packing of her clothes into boxes and trunks for the journey, Rosalind made herself believe that, in the end, her father wouldn't really force her into it, and that thoughts of a romantic connection between the two of them was all in her father's imagination after all.

And, because she was young and alive, by now the thought of staying in London for the summer was beginning to stir her. By focusing her thoughts on that, she could at least feel some excitement coursing through her veins. More than she did at the prospect of marrying Sir George Greville!

She knew the Greville cousin must arrive any day now, and each afternoon she rode her favourite horse over the Downs in a kind of desperation, feeling almost traitorous at the prospect of abandoning him to her groom. She leaned low over the reins, hugging the horse's neck and feeling the power in the animal beneath her. In her green velvet riding habit, she rode astride like a man, for on this empty stretch of land there was no one to see her, except for a rider in the far distance behind her, whom she was sure she could easily outstrip.

She was so distressed at the thought that this would be one of her last rides on Hunter that she didn't see the tree-stump in front of her until it was too late. Hunter apparently didn't see it either, because the next minute she was flung from his back and landing in a heap in a hollow, all the breath knocked out of her. She didn't move for some minutes, wondering whether anything was broken, and then she carefully flexed every part of herself, relieved to find she was still intact except for a few bruises. And almost uncaring at the thought that it would be a fine way to greet this city cousin if she was black and blue. . .

'Are you hurt?' a man's voice said beside her. Rosalind looked up, startled. She hadn't heard the other rider approach, and had assumed that the sound of pawing hoofs had belonged to Hunter. She squinted into the sun now, and saw the outline of a man, seated on a horse and dressed in military uniform. From her undignified seat in the hollow, he looked enormous, and might have been threatening if she'd been made of lesser stuff. There was concern in his voice, but with the sun in her eyes she couldn't see his face fully, shadowed as it was beneath his officer's cap.

'Thank you, but I think not,' she said at once, feeling very foolish at being found sprawled on the grass like this.

'Allow me to help you,' the officer said, sliding down from the horse in one easy movement. She saw at once that he was tall and lithe, and he helped her to her feet as she brushed the bracken off her green velvet in some confusion. She wasn't usually confused by a man, but neither was she used to being thrown from a horse and rescued by a handsome stranger.

'I'm perfectly all right, really,' she said quickly. 'Nothing's broken, and I'm quite able to re-mount.'

She stepped carefully out of the hollow with the man's hand still firmly on her arm. She looked around, but there was no sign of Hunter, and she could only think he had taken fright, cantered off and found his own way home. She fumed inwardly, since it was a good three miles across the undulating Downs to the Hall.

'It looks as if your nag has bolted. If you'll allow me,

I'll see you safely home, ma'am,' the stranger said casually, and Rosalind's face went scarlet.

'I'm sure I can manage perfectly well!' she said, with some of her usual spirit. 'Forgive me, sir, but I don't know you, and I'm quite able to get home by myself.'

Even as she said it, her heart quailed at the thought of walking so far in the cumbersome riding habit. It was one thing to be riding a horse suitably dressed in velvet. It was quite another to be covering three miles on foot with the warm spring sunshine beating down overhead.

'Then allow me to introduce myself, and, once you do the same, we will know one another, and can proceed,' the officer said with what seemed to Rosalind like maddening military efficiency.

She looked at him properly. He was a good-looking man, with clear brown eyes, the dark hair beneath his cap ruffled by the small breeze to give him a youthful look. Not that he was old. She'd guess he would be no more than five or six years older than herself.

She'd never seen him before, and she couldn't place his accent. It was oddly clipped, and slightly flat and businesslike, but its attraction lay in its rich timbre. As his smile widened in his tanned face, she realised she had been staring, and felt herself blush again. She wasn't usually nonplussed by a young man, and she didn't like the feeling.

'My name is Captain Holden,' he said, saluting formally. 'And whom do I have the honour of addressing?'

He was so—so—she couldn't find the word for it. It was arrogance and pride and masculine self-assurance all rolled up in one. At that moment some little devil of mischief made Rosalind tilt back her head and look at him boldly.

'I'm called Margaret—Margaret Wood,' she invented, giving him her maid's name.

He made a small bow, accompanied by a low laugh. 'Then if Margaret Wood will give me her hand, I'll assist her on to my horse and take her home.'

Rosalind felt an unexpected giggle begin inside her. She had only been winded from her fall, and she was beginning to feel a kind of exhilaration now. This meeting was turning into something of an adventure, and once the captain deposited her at the gates of Cranbourne Hall and went on his way she would have quite a tale to tell the real Margaret. Though her maid would no doubt admonish her roundly for being so foolish as to mount a stranger's horse in this isolated place, and even more so for telling him untruths. But Rosalind was in a reckless mood, knowing her days of freedom were so soon to come to an end, and, besides, it seemed such a harmless little adventure. . .

She gave up arguing, and chose to be seated side-saddle now, demure as a lady was expected to be, even one who gave her full name so readily to a stranger. When the captain mounted behind her, his arms necessarily went around her to take up the reins. She was aware of the piquant scent of his wool uniform and the warmth of his body as she was obliged to be pressed against it, and it was surprisingly difficult to remain detached from the sensations such closeness evoked.

'This is a most delightful encounter, Miss Margaret Wood,' he said softly in her ear, suddenly smiling at her in such a wickedly disarming way that her heart began to beat very fast.

'I'm not a miss. I'm a—a widow,' Rosalind said recklessly, adding another untruth to the first in the sudden confusion of feelings as she glanced back at the face so close to hers. Apart from the elegant dark moustache he was slightly unshaven, as if he had travelled some distance, and it gave him a somewhat rakish air. Rosalind was suddenly finding it quite hard to breathe properly, as if all the air in her lungs was being compressed.

'A widow! But you're far too young to be deprived of a husband! Must I address you as Widow Wood, or just plain Margaret? Though that's a denial in terms, of course. A young lady as delectable as yourself could never be just plain anybody. But you must tell me, ma'am, before I create a *faux pas*.'

She listened in a kind of daze, never having heard anyone make such outrageous statements before. She was not used to the art of flirtation, but she recognised it in a man when she heard it. . . and she recognised more than that. This particular man was definitely laughing at her!

'I would ask you not to make light of a young lady's misfortune,' she said freezingly. 'Do you think it fair sport to tease a lady left all alone in the world?'

Dear Lord, Rosalind thought, this was going from bad to worse, and she couldn't seem to stop it.

'I don't imagine you need be left alone in this world for very long. Not if the men of the county have eyes in their heads,' Captain Holden retorted. 'But since you don't take kindly to my banter, please give me directions, ma'am, and then you'll be rid of me.'

Rosalind looked at him suspiciously. There was something about him she couldn't fathom. A *knowing*, and that was the only word she could think of to describe it. She clamped her mouth together and said nothing until the welcome sight of Cranbourne Hall appeared among the rolling Downs.

'You can leave me at the gates of the big house, please,' she said then.

'Left you well provided for, did he?'

Rosalind looked at the man blankly until he prompted her.

'Your *man*, Widow Wood. The unfortunate husband. Or have you forgotten him so soon?'

'I don't own the place,' she mumbled. 'I merely said I lived there.'

'I've heard tell of the place. They say Cranbourne Hall has a dragon of an owner, with a wilful daughter who repulses any man who even looks at her. Is that true?'

Rosalind gasped. The nerve of him took her breath away. He couldn't know who she was. . .but that didn't lessen the insult.

'I've always thought Miss Cranbourne was a perfectly reasonable young lady,' she said, in the same cold voice.

The officer chuckled. 'That's not what I've heard, but you and I don't need to bother our heads over her, do we, Widow Wood? How about a wee kiss as a reward for taking you home?'

She gasped again, and then found it impossible to avoid his kiss as his arms held her captive. Short of falling off a horse for the second time that day, she had no option but to endure the contact with this man, who had suddenly assumed oafish proportions in her eyes.

'Are you satisfied now?' she snapped when the kiss ended.

Her cheeks felt slightly sore from his roughened skin, yet if she had been in a more receptive mood she knew she would have found the escapade wholly exciting. As it was, she was insulted and upset. . .as much by the thought that a gentleman and an officer could behave in this way with someone he obviously took to be a servant or a sorry young widow as by the thought that he had clearly heard rumours that Miss Rosalind Cranbourne was something of a shrew!

With sudden strength she pushed his arms away from her and slid from the horse's back. There was only a hundred yards or so to go to reach the wrought-iron gates at the front of the long drive to the house now, and she was more than prepared to walk the rest of the way. Without another word she began striding away from the man, and heard his easy laugh behind her.

'Good-day to you, Widow Wood, and I hope we meet again.'

'Not if I can avoid it,' Rosalind muttered, resisting the urge to turn around and watch his undoubted horsemanship as he galloped off. She unfastened the gates with shaking hands and marched up the driveway to the front door, where it was opened by an astonished housekeeper.

'Will you please send Margaret upstairs with some hot water at once, Mrs Barnes?' she said. She needed to remove these sticky clothes and wash her hot face and limbs, and try to regain some of her composure in a clean fresh gown. Her mother would be organising afternoon tea, and it was just what Rosalind needed to soothe her ruffled nerves.

She tried to ignore Margaret's probing questions, but in the end she couldn't resist telling her about her encounter, colouring the episode with little embellishments all the while, to the darkening face of her maid.

'You were extremely foolish, Miss Rosie,' she said severely. 'You don't know what the man might have done to you, thinking you no more than a servant.' She saw no disrespect to herself in saying such a thing.

'Ah, but he was an officer, Margaret,' Rosalind said mockingly, knowing the maid normally assumed such gentlemen to be above reproach. 'And I came to no harm, only a little bit of harm to my pride.'

She frowned, remembering Captain Holden's words. 'But tell me honestly now, Margaret, do you think I'm wilful, and ready to repulse any man who looks at me?'

The maid laughed as the ablutions were finished, and

she slid the yellow sprigged afternoon-gown over her mistress's head.

'He might have been a stranger, but it didn't take him long to get your measure, Miss Rosie,' she said, without giving a straight answer.

Rosalind tossed her head before she allowed Margaret to coil the burnished hair up into a more elaborate style on the top of her head.

'Well, if you think it's wilful to resist an insulting flirtation, and to repulse a perfect stranger, then he was probably right,' she said crossly. 'Anyway, I shall never have to see him again, for, if he's an example of the people buying commissions in the Queen's military these days, he'd do better to stay in the north of the country where I suspect he belongs!'

She felt much better after that self-righteous little outburst. And at least the excitement of the afternoon had taken her mind away from the prospect of going to London to become better acquainted with the pompous Sir George Greville. Her face in the mirror was positively glowing, and her eyes sparkled like jewels. The illogical thought rushed into her head that this must be just the way a woman looked when she was in love. Because such an unwarranted thought was inadvertently connected with Captain Holden it made her angrier than ever.

She turned away from the mirror and hurried downstairs to the drawing-room where her mother was holding court with a visitor. They hadn't been expecting company, but anyone would be a diversion from the disturbing thoughts milling around in Rosalind's head right now, and she swept into the room with her very best poise.

And then she stopped dead, as the tall figure of an officer rose from a chair to greet her. There was no hint of surprise in his eyes, only a new admiration at her changed appearance. And, to her chagrin, Rosalind knew at once that somehow or other he had known her identity all along.

'Ah, Rosalind, come and meet our guest. He arrived at the Hall while you were out, and has just returned back from a ride on the Downs like yourself. My love, this is Captain Felix Holden, who's come to escort you and Margaret to London.'

CHAPTER TWO

'It's a great pleasure to meet you, Miss Cranbourne,' the oaf said smoothly. He rose at once and moved across the room to take her limp hand in his and raise it to his lips. He looked directly into her eyes, and she could see the laughter in his darker ones.

'Smile, Widow Wood,' he breathed under cover of the small pleasantry. 'Otherwise your mother will wonder what's become of your manners!'

She smiled through gritted teeth, inclining her head towards the man and managing to shake off his courteous kiss on the hand as if he were a repellent insect.

'I'll pay you back for this,' she muttered back, finding the need for manners where he was concerned quite farcical. They had already come too far for the proprieties, except in public.

She could see how much Captain Holden was enjoying the situation, while her mother sat quietly, dispensing tea as a good hostess should, and blissfully unaware of any undercurrents between the other two people in the room.

But that was her mother's way, Rosalind thought, somewhat regretfully. She had a knack of closing her eyes to anything she didn't want to see—not that she could possibly be aware of this little charade her daughter and their visitor were playing.

A sudden recklessness took hold of her. He was obviously not about to denounce her to her mother. If it had been his intention, it was too late now. And since he obviously enjoyed a charade, two could play at that game. She moved to seat herself on a silk-covered chair, unconsciously arranging the folds of her gown as she had been taught, and accepting the dainty bone china teacup her mother offered her.

'I do believe Captain Holden and I have almost met before, Mother,' she said coolly.

She saw his eyes narrow, and read his thoughts immediately. She knew very well that if she revealed any indiscretion on his part it would put serious doubts in her father's mind about letting her go to London at all. She would achieve her wish not to go to Sir George Greville's home, and it would raise awkward questions as to why Captain Holden's mission to bring her to London had failed.

The temptation to cause him such problems was very sweet, but she disregarded it. Because, by now, it was London she wanted to see, and reading in the newspapers about the preparations for the forthcoming coronation of the Queen had aroused a natural feminine interest in the proceedings. Why should she not be there, even if it meant at the invitation of Sir George Greville's mother? She felt warmly enough towards the lady, if not her son.

In any case, all she wanted in these moments was to see this fine officer squirm a little. . .

'How can that be, Rosalind?' her mother said now.

'I was probably mistaken, but when I was out riding this afternoon, I thought I saw someone very like Captain Holden with a young widow woman from the village.'

She heard him give an easy laugh as her mother glanced at him enquiringly, a puzzled frown between her eyes.

'You're definitely mistaken, Miss Cranbourne. I'm not acquainted with any young widow women in the district. If I had been, I'm sure I would have remembered it.'

She was very sure he remembered every moment of their little encounter, just as she did.

'But you were on the Downs on horseback this afternoon?' she pursued. 'I believe my mother mentioned it——'

'Rosalind, my dear! That sounds almost as if you're doubting Captain Holden's word. Apologise at once!' her mother exclaimed.

The stranger intervened. 'There's no need, ma'am. Yes, Miss Cranbourne, I left my carriage here soon after I arrived, needing some fresh air in my lungs after the journey from London. I dare say you did catch sight of me. After all, a man in uniform is not hard to spot. But perhaps the young widow woman you thought you saw is a figment of your own imagination. Perhaps you have ghosts on your famous Downs? I'm told such a phenomenon does occur at times.'

Rosalind felt her cheeks colour angrily. He was playing with her now, just as much as she played with him, and it was time the teasing stopped before it got dangerously near to doubt on her mother's part.

'Then that must have been it, and I do apologise, Captain Holden,' she said, as sincerely as she could manage, considering the way she still seethed underneath.

'Well, if that little matter's settled, then you must hear some of the fascinating little tales Captain Holden has to tell us about the Queen's tutelage, Rosalind. You're not the only one needing to be taught certain rules, my dear.' It was the nearest thing to a rebuke Ursula Cranbourne was prepared to make in public.

The man laughed. 'Oh, well, it's understandable in the Queen's case. The poor young lass had no idea she was going to attain such a high position at the tender age of eighteen, did she?'

Rosalind gasped at this high-handed way of referring

to the Queen. Who was he, to be making so free with her name?

'Are you so familiar with royalty, Captain?' she asked.

'Her Majesty's soldiers have the fondest and highest regard for the lady,' he replied. 'It doesn't alter the fact that she was a mere child when she became Queen.'

'So what are these fascinating little tales you have to tell? Or are they tales out of school?'

Her voice implied that she didn't think much of a man who could betray such confidences. He looked at her keenly, and, although he spoke lightly enough to appease her mother's outraged gasp, Rosalind could tell that he was becoming rattled.

'They are not, Miss Cranbourne, and I'd run through the man who thought me guilty of such an indiscretion. But since it's your sweet self who asks the question, I'll forgive you.'

'Thank you, Captain Holden,' she said demurely. 'So please continue.'

His mouth tightened noticeably, and Rosalind found herself staring at it, instantly aware that it had kissed her twice. Once politely, on the back of her hand, and once. . .a kiss that had been passionate and almost wanton, she remembered with a sliver of pleasure, defining it now in a way she hadn't done before. At the time she had been so angry that she hadn't fully registered the potency of it. He had been taunting her, of course, somehow knowing who she was all along. . . but she had deluded him too, she thought guiltily. . .

'Then I'll tell you something that most ladies find charming. You'll probably not know that it's the Queen's generous habit to send a gift to important foreign personages, whenever such a gift is deemed appropriate. This is usually a little miniature of herself in the form of a brooch set in diamonds.'

Rosalind felt her mouth drop open at this revelation,

never having given any thought to the riches of a
monarch. But to be able to do such a thing as he
described so casually was certainly eye-opening.

'I certainly did not know it,' she murmured, interest
in the news momentarily replacing the hostility she felt
towards Felix Holden.

'Why should you, living so far away from the hub of
things?' he commented, which to Rosalind immediately
placed the Cranbournes in a rural setting of minor
importance in the great bustling scheme of things. 'Lord
Palmerston, the Foreign Secretary——'

'I know who he is. We read the newspapers in Sussex,
even though we're buried so deep in country matters,'
she broke in, and he gave a slight smile.

Her mother remained silent, apparently having given
up on the extraordinary way these two were conducting
themselves, and no doubt thinking that the manners of
young people left a great deal to be desired these days.

'Then it's generally known that Lord Palmerston has
been instructing the young Queen in certain formalities
to be observed. And one of the things she had to learn
was not to send a miniature of herself to any Russian
dignitary, since they're not permitted to wear the portrait of a foreign sovereign.'

'Whyever not?' Rosalind asked.

Captain Holden shrugged his elegant shoulders. 'It's
best not to question the policies of other countries, Miss
Cranbourne, just to observe them and abide by their
rules, as we expect them to observe ours.'

'That sounds like a true military man speaking,'
Rosalind's mother entered the conversation now. 'Didn't
you find the little snippet interesting, Rosalind?'

'It makes me wonder just what kind of occasion this
coronation is going to be, if the Queen can present such
costly gifts,' she said.

'The most splendid occasion of the century, naturally. Have you no conception of the cost of the preparations?'

'None at all.' Rosalind admitted she was beaten at last. This man was far more worldly than she, knew more important people than she, and somehow managed to infuriate her more than any man she had ever met. It did not bode too well for their enforced journey to London together.

'Well, parliament has voted for a sum of two hundred thousand pounds to be spent. It will be truly magnificent, with the Abbey decorated in crimson and gold, and, as well as all the various entertainments for the populace, the fair in Hyde Park, the balloon ascents and so on, there will be a state procession through the streets of London with Her Majesty in the state coach.'

By now both Rosalind and her mother were gaping. He spoke of a world they did not know, and simply couldn't imagine. The Cranbournes were not travellers, and not even for the rare chance of seeing their Queen from a distance would the older members of the family consider making the journey to London.

'If you'll pardon my liberty in saying so, Miss Cranbourne, your portrait does not do you justice,' Captain Holden said suddenly.

Rosalind was startled, then followed his glance to the oil-painting of herself above the mantel, done at her father's request on her eighteenth birthday. Her face flushed, knowing now exactly how he had known who she was, and feeling even more foolish at her own deception, and angry with him for allowing her to continue.

'It's a lovely portrait, though, Captain Holden,' Rosalind's mother commented. 'And painted by one of the county's most prominent artists.'

'Oh, yes, I see the skill in it,' the officer said, 'but

obviously Miss Cranbourne has a little more maturity in her face now, adding to her character and beauty.'

Rosalind looked at him suspiciously, sure that he didn't really mean to flatter her. The real meaning behind the words was obvious to her, if not to her mother. The Rosalind of eighteen years might have been an ingenue, with a sweet innocence of expression, while the twenty-year-old. . .

Well, she was still innocent in the full implication of the word, but she could counter anything this oaf had to say, she thought furiously.

'I thank you for the compliment, Captain, even though it's considered unworthy to refer in any way to a lady's age. Any gentleman knows that, I'm sure.'

And he could take *that* implication any way he chose, she thought triumphantly. The small gesture with which he raised his teacup to her showed her that it was noted and acknowledged.

'Rosalind has always been too outspoken for her own good, Captain, and I trust you'll be willing to overlook any slight lack of manners on her behalf,' Mrs Cranbourne said, clearly ruffled by now.

'Ma'am, I'm from a country background myself, where such things as city niceties aren't considered of the highest importance, so please don't concern yourself.'

The words were smooth and reassuring, but to Rosalind they were patronising and reeked of superiority. City dwellers, indeed. Did this man think that because the Cranbournes lived in rural England they had no idea how to behave in polite society? Had they not entertained Sir George Greville and his mother on several evenings and been most warmly thanked for their hospitality? Why else would Lady Greville invite Rosalind to her home, and possibly consider her a suitable wife for her son?

Her prickliness vanished for a second, remembering the reason Felix Holden was here at all. She hadn't even heard his full name until today, and had assumed it would be Greville, the same as Sir George's, which had contributed to the mix-up. If he'd even mentioned his Christian name when he'd 'rescued' her on the moors, she would probably have guessed his identity. . .

'How is your cousin?' she said, with more warmth towards Sir George than she actually felt. 'I trust he's well, and also his charming mother.'

'My aunt Lydia is very well, thank you. As for George, the last time I spoke with him he was in sparkling form.'

Rosalind thought it an odd term to use. 'And when was that? You speak as if you haven't seen him for some time.'

'Nor I have. My cousin and I don't have all that much opportunity for social communication.'

Rosalind got the distinct impression that not seeing George very often didn't concern the captain too much either. It was an interesting observation.

'So Lady Lydia is all alone, apart from the servants.'

'Well, not always alone. I'm not obliged to remain in quarters at all times, so I do spend a fair amount of time at the house. Then, too, we exercise our horses quite regularly on Hampstead Heath, and my aunt is usually among the onlookers.'

It sounded as if Felix Holden was as much a part of the household as George—even more so from what she heard of George's frequent travelling at home and abroad. Rosalind had a fleeting image of what life would be like as wife to an ambitious man who was rarely at home, and it wasn't the way she envisaged marriage. It would be even worse than being married to a military man, and she immediately wished the thought hadn't entered her head at all.

'I suspect that you're quite a favourite of your aunt's,'

Mrs Cranbourne said, patently glad that the conversation had mellowed somewhat. Captain Holden laughed, and Rosalind couldn't help noticing that he was even more attractive when he laughed. He had strong white teeth and a wide, handsome mouth. . .she suddenly realised she was defining her appraisal in her more familiar equestrian phrases, and she hastily hid a smile at thinking about a man in such terms.

'That's not for me to say, ma'am,' Felix was saying to her mother now. 'But since she has no other nephews, I know she has a special fondness for me, as I certainly have for her. Our mothers were twin sisters, and she always regretted the fact that when my parents married my mother necessarily moved to Yorkshire, so they rarely saw one another after that time. My mother is sadly dead now, so I'm all that's left to remind Aunt Lydia of her twin.'

He sounded almost human now, Rosalind thought, though still not wanting to think him anything but an oaf for tricking her the way he had.

'What about your father?' she asked without thinking, and then blushed. 'Forgive me. It's no business of mine——'

'On the contrary. I'm flattered that you're interested in my family,' he said blandly. 'My father and I don't always get along. He never wanted me to come south, and dislikes the thought of my being a soldier. He'd have me stay a millowner like himself with a finger in every mill pie.'

'My goodness, it sounds very grand,' Rosalind murmured, trying not to sound sarcastic.

'Not at all,' he said, with that smile widening his face again. 'Though you've probably worn some of Holden's cloth in your garments without ever knowing it.'

The thought aroused a piquant intimacy between them, thought Rosalind, without knowing why it should.

'And will you never go back, Captain Holden?' Mrs Cranbourne enquired.

He shrugged. 'One day I'll probably have no choice, but I hope that day's a long time coming. I've no wish to see ill befall my father.'

'Nor to give up the life you chose for yourself,' Rosalind commented without thinking.

'Nor that,' he agreed.

Their glances clashed, and she thought they already understood one another very well. He was as ambitious in his own way as Sir George was in his. Felix Holden wanted to pursue his military career and remain in London, no doubt under the patronage of his aunt Lydia, while George wanted to roam about the country, ostensibly in the guise of a political career, and travel abroad whenever he got the chance. She wasn't sure which of them was the less worthy—or if she had the right to decry either of them for doing what he wanted. It was the way a man was able to run his own life, a way that was denied to a woman. . .

It was decided that the journey back to London should be undertaken in two days from now. Captain Holden was pressed into staying at Cranbourne Hall during that time, and quickly acquiesced. If Rosalind expected him to flirt with her whenever he got the chance, she was mistaken, because he readily took himself off on his borrowed horse at every opportunity.

'The captain sits on that horse as if he were a part of it, Miss Rosie,' Margaret sighed, watching him ride forth from Rosalind's bedroom window the next morning. 'He's such a fine-looking man, and if I were twenty years younger——'

'Well, you're not, and if you were, what makes you think he'd look at you?' Rosalind said rudely, unaccountably piqued that, as yet, Felix hadn't suggested

they go riding together, when it would be only courteous
to have done so. She heard Margaret's crowing reply.

'Well, when he thought you were a widow woman, he
played up to you, didn't he? And it hasn't taken him
long to upset your ladyship since, has it?' She spoke
with the confident cheek of someone who had been in
the same service for a long time, and Rosalind glared at
her.

'He hasn't upset me at all! He's nothing to me, and
never likely to be. It's not Captain Holden my father
has in mind for me, ninny.'

She felt a little twist in her throat at the thought,
followed by a quickening of the senses, wondering for a
moment how different things would be if Felix were to
be her affianced and not George. . .two cousins couldn't
be more unalike, she thought in some surprise, not really
having considered it before.

Felix was lithe and strong of build, with the military-
man's upright stance; he sat his horse to perfection,
displaying good horsemanship and consideration for the
animal at all times; he was handsome and witty. . .oh,
yes, she gave him that. While Sir George. . .

It was a long while since they'd met, and understand-
ably she had a job to remember his face clearly. He was
fleshier than Felix, though not unattractively so. He was
older, thicker-set, and she remembered him saying he
hated horses, which she had thought unbelievable at the
time, though perhaps understandable, since a horse had
caused his hip injury. . .but such an aversion hadn't
bothered her then, and shouldn't bother her now.

What bothered her more was the thought that marriage to Sir George Greville would mean living permanently in London. Or sharing in his pursuit of travel,
which would seem to be one of his chief enjoyments.

She listened to her own thoughts in some amusement,
comparing the two men as if she had a choice to make.

Especially since neither of them had proposed to her—not even George, despite what her parents read into this invitation to London!

Rosalind registered the fact as if it was a startling discovery. They had all taken it so much for granted, but it was still Lady Lydia Greville who had first issued the invitation to Rosalind to come to London and her son who had written so brusquely on his mother's behalf informing them that his cousin would be sent to collect her. Could it be that George had no intention of asking her to marry him at all, and that the whole thing was merely in her father's vivid imagination? It was such a relief to think so that Rosalind let out her breath noisily.

'Well, it's an unusual thing to hear you sighing over a man,' came Margeret's mocking voice. 'But, from the way you've been staring at him for the last five minutes, anyone would be forgiven for thinking you'd taken a fancy to him, Miss Rosie.'

Rosalind started at the voice. She had indeed been staring unseeingly out of the window, lost in thought, and certainly impervious to the retreating figure of Captain Felix Holden galloping his horse out of sight and into the dipping Downs now. She turned away crossly.

'Don't be stupid, Margaret. I dare say he's gone off to find some village wench to tease, and I've got more pride than to be interested in a man like that!'

She avoided Margaret's eyes as the maid chuckled knowingly. 'It ain't always what you want as counts when it comes to affairs of the heart, miss. If Cupid aims his dart fair and square between you and the captain, you'll have no say in the matter.'

'You're being absolutely noddle-headed this morning, Margaret, and I'm not listening to any more of this! I shall go out and leave you with the final packing.'

'Goin' horse-riding, I dare say,' the maid said slyly. 'He went in the direction of the village.'

Rosalind stuck her nose in the air and changed into her riding outfit, refusing assistance. Sometimes Margaret went too far, she fumed, and sometimes her observations were just too steeped in fable to be ignored. Yes, she was going riding. It was her last chance, because tomorrow they left for London. And no, she had no intention of trying to follow Captain Felix Holden. . .

She caught up with him quite easily, reining in Hunter and trying to look quite unconcerned at the fact that he'd turned and waited for her at about the same spot where she'd fallen yesterday, just as if it were a tryst. It seemed a very long time ago now. It seemed she had been in conflict with this man for very much longer than less than twenty-four hours.

'I thought you'd come,' he said calmly.

'I can't think why on earth you should think such a thing. I always ride in the afternoons——'

'And this is still the morning, so there must be some reason for you to break a habit.'

She looked at him, dislike blazoning in her eyes. If this was the way gentlemen flirted in London nowadays, so arrogantly and boldly, she didn't care for it at all.

'Perhaps there was,' she snapped. 'Perhaps I wanted to ask if there was some other way of my travelling to London other than in your company.'

He shifted position slightly on his horse, his hands loosely on the reins, but still in full control.

'Is my company so offensive to you? If so, I apologise wholeheartedly. The last thing in the world I want to do is to offend you, Rosalind.'

The unexpected use of her name caught her unawares. He said it softly, his native accent lengthening the first syllable and softening the third. She looked at him blindly, suddenly unsure how to handle this situation, nor why she had even started it. It had been an impulse that made her blurt out the question at all, and now she had to carry it through.

She could insist that she travelled to London with just Margaret as her companion. The maid was a perfectly capable chaperon, and on her own territory a quite formidable person. But travelling to London, where neither of them had been before—nor to any other city—they would truly be two innocents abroad, and Rosalind rejected the idea even as she thought it.

She saw Felix dismount easily from his horse, and hold out his hand to her. She sat motionless for a moment, and then he gave a small smile.

'Why can we not be friends, Miss Cranbourne? I regret that we got off to such a bad start, but even the worst of enemies is usually forgiven when he truly tries to make amends. And, since you will be staying in my aunt's house, it's inevitable that we'll see something of one another during your stay in London. I know it would grieve Aunt Lydia if she thought you and I were at loggerheads.'

Rosalind gave him back the slightest smile.

'That sounds suspiciously like a kind of blackmail, Captain Holden.'

'I think you could call it that,' he laughed freely now. 'But I'd try anything to put that lovely smile back on your face again, and erase the frown.'

She capitulated, because what he said was true. If it was unavoidable that they must see one another frequently in London, then it would be embarrassing, to say the least, and discourteous to her hostess, for them to be on bad terms. She held out her hand and allowed him to help her down from her horse.

'Then for your aunt's sake I'll agree to calling a truce,' she said coolly. 'I wouldn't want to do anything to upset Lady Lydia.'

'Neither would I,' he said gravely, and before she could stop him he had raised her hand to his lips again. Above her hand she looked straight into his brown eyes, and the impetuous thought ran through her mind that they were as warm as velvet.

She snatched her hand away. 'Just remember we're tolerant of one another for your aunt's sake only,' she reminded him. 'I'll be dependent on her good nature while I'm in London, and you'll have your part to play in this charade as much as I.'

'Charade?' he said, still smiling.

'The charade that you and I can ever be truly friends,' she whipped back at him. 'I know you for what you are, Captain Holden!'

'Really, ma'am? And what is that?'

She heard the steel in his voice now, and took no notice.

'A man who feels no compunction in flirting with someone he takes to be a servant or a helpless widow——'

His hearty laugh stopped her dead.

'I hardly think you a helpless anything! I pity the man to think so, Miss Cranbourne! I'd as soon face up to an army as face your stinging tongue.'

She couldn't stop the sudden feeling of hurt that rushed through her. The temptation to give proof of that stinging tongue hardly surfaced. Her voice was oddly muffled as she stared at him.

'Is that really how I appear to you? As someone with a stinging tongue? It hardly makes me sound the most charming of young ladies, does it?'

To her consternation and rage she felt the shine of tears brimming on her lashes. She couldn't think why she felt so put out. She didn't come into contact with too many young men, and this one was just too sophisticated, despite his own country background. Presumably a military career did that to a man.

'If I didn't think it would turn your head, I'd tell you that you're the most fascinating young lady I've ever met,' Captain Holden said in a suddenly quiet voice. 'Fascinating and desirable and totally maddening, as well as being very beautiful. But you already know all that, don't you, Miss Cranbourne?'

Rosalind's cheeks flooded with colour. Whatever she might or might not know about herself, she had never had it spelled out in this way before. She had never been courted or even walked out with anyone, preferring her horses and generally spurning any young man with whom she'd come into contact. She had never been flattered in this way, because she had never given any young man the chance. But this man seemed to cut through all the formalities and say and do exactly as he chose.

A *frisson* of excitement ran through her veins, as if a new world had suddenly opened up to her, and she was only just glimpsing the possibilities inside it.

Instinctively she glanced at the man and then lowered her eyelashes, knowing it was polite to accept compliments, no matter who made them.

'You honour me, Captain, even though I deplore the fact that you find me totally maddening. I'll try not to be a trouble to you on the journey to London.'

His reply was almost angry.

'Just be yourself, and, if you'll take a tip from me, don't let others try to change you. It would be tragic for you to lose that vitality of yours and become just like every other simpering city coquette. You have a unique quality, Rosalind. Don't ever change that.'

Despite his terseness, she felt oddly choked by his words, because she'd thought he was decrying her for

what she was. Now it almost seemed as if he was praising
her for her spirit and her countrified ways. Countrified
as far as the new life on which she was about to embark,
at any rate. And that was a life she was about to
discover.

CHAPTER THREE

IT SEEMED no time at all before they were saying goodbye to her parents, the carriage stacked high with Rosalind's boxes and trunks, and the more modest effects belonging to Margaret. Rosalind had obviously needed far grander clothes than she normally wore, and to her father's credit—and because of his aspirations—he had spared no expense in fitting her out well when the invitation from Lady Lydia had arrived.

'Nobody's going to say my daughter can't be seen in the best circles,' he'd boasted, when more than a dozen new creations in watered silk and beribboned satin had been brought to the house for her approval, the cost of which must surely have stretched his bank balance. 'If there are balls and theatres to attend, then my girl will shine with the best.'

Rosalind knew her father well enough to know that behind his brash statements he truly wanted the best for her, and in his heart he thought that marriage with a successful rising politician would be the best. . .the knowledge made her hug him all the more warmly when the time for parting came.

'I shall miss you,' she gulped, facing three months away from home for the first time. 'I shall write every day——'

'You'll do no such thing,' Miles said, his voice gruffer than usual. 'You'll have a wonderful time under Lady Lydia's patronage, and you'll visit your aunt May and give her our best regards, and then you'll concentrate on enjoying yourself and making Sir George proud to escort you around London. If you've time to write once or twice a week after all that, we shall be more than content.'

'But be sure to describe everything you see, Rosalind, dear, especially any interesting titbits about Her Majesty's coronation,' her mother put in quickly. 'It will be almost like being there.'

'It's still nearly two months away, Mother! And if you're so interested in it all, why don't you come too? I'm sure Aunt May's not so infirm that she wouldn't welcome a visit,' Rosalind begged.

'We've been through all this before, love,' Ursula Cranbourne said. 'I'm perfectly content within my own four walls, and I'm already thinking we've failed in our duty in this long delay in launching you on society.'

'You make me sound like one of Father's ships!' Rosalind said, trying not to show too much emotion at this parting.

She looked at the comfortably rounded shapes of her parents and swallowed hard. Likening anyone to one of her father's ships applied to them more than her, she thought in genuine affection, wondering for a moment just how she had inherited her own neat proportions.

She gave her mother a final hug. 'You haven't failed in anything, Mother. And I *will* write often, I promise!'

'When you're ready, then, Miss Cranbourne,' Captain Holden said quietly at her side, and she almost hated him for breaking into this moment. But they had to leave, of course, and this was only prolonging the parting. She clambered inside the carriage beside Margaret, already stiffly seated and looking stoically ahead, while Captain Holden sat himself opposite them and called to the driver to take up the reins.

Rosalind leaned out of the window as long as she could see her parents in the distance, and she settled herself more comfortably. She looked directly into Captain Holden's eyes.

'Is this the first time you've been away from home, Rosalind?'

She raised her eyebrows a little at the informality. It wasn't the first time he had used her name, but it seemed to her significant that he did so now, the moment she was away from parental control. She was aware of Margaret glancing at her, clearly wondering if she should object on her mistress's behalf. But a feeling that was half devilment, half excitement was fast taking hold of her now, as the carriage swayed and rocked along the dusty road north to London.

'Is it so obvious to you—Felix?' she asked daringly, her countering use of his given name effectively silencing anything Margaret might have to say.

She saw the undiluted pleasure in his eyes at the small intimacy, and immediately regretted her impulsiveness, but it was too late to do anything about it now.

'I was merely sympathising with the way you're probably feeling right now,' he said to her surprise. 'I well remember when I left Yorkshire to come to London and join my regiment. I felt apprehension and regret as well as a natural excitement. It will be the same for you, I dare say, but at least you come to the capital in the happiest of times, and have the advantage of knowing you'll be returning home in a few months and seeing your parents again.'

Rosalind's attention was caught now. It was the first time he had referred to his background with anything less than factual information about his father's business, and the fact that presumably he would be required to take it over one day. But now there was more than a hint of bitterness in his voice, and Rosalind was undeniably curious.

'But you've seen your parents many times since that day, surely? The army gives you leave, I believe?'

He didn't answer for a few minutes, and when he did

he was looking not at her, but out of the carriage window as if he was seeing far beyond the rolling countryside through which they were passing by now.

'Oh, aye, the army gives a man leave, which is how I came to be here now. But at the time I'm speaking about, my father was incensed at my wanting to leave the family business. He became quite irrational about it, and, being a plain-speaking Yorkshireman, he made it clear that once I went away he wouldn't welcome me back. So I decided to leave things as they were for a year to let him cool off, so to speak. And by then it was too late.'

'Why was it too late? It's never too late to make amends. You said so yourself! And he must have loved you if he hadn't wanted you to go——'

He turned and looked at her, and she was startled by the pain in those fine brown eyes.

'You're very young, Rosalind. You don't understand how a man's pride can sour even the deepest love. It was pride on both sides, I admit, for neither of us was willing to make contact, and my mother always bent to my father's will and we never even wrote to one another. The next time I got any word from home, it was to say my mother had died, and my journey back to Yorkshire was the unhappiest one I could have envisaged.'

Rosalind was shocked at hearing this sad tale, and hardly knew what to say to this proud young man whose flat tones invited no sympathy from a stranger. Margaret had no such reservations, and Rosalind heard her clucking her teeth mournfully.

'You poor young sir, begging the captain's pardon. So you went home for your dear mother's funeral, and that was the chance for you and your father to patch up your differences, I dare say.'

Felix gave a faint smile. 'You dare say wrong, then, Margaret,' he said. 'No, by then my father and I had grown too far apart for us ever to find that elusive closeness fathers and sons are supposed to enjoy and we never did. In fact, I think he took a sadistic pleasure in informing me that, no matter where I roamed, in the end my real duty lay in his cloth mills, and that's where I was destined to end my days, the same as he was.'

Rosalind cleared her throat. 'And would that be so very abhorrent to you, Felix?' Somehow she found no difficulty in saying his name now.

'If you had chosen one kind of life, would you be happy at having another pushed at you and told it was your duty to accept it?' he countered.

'It's what the majority of young ladies are brought up to accept,' she commented without thinking. 'A lady doesn't have the same kind of freedom as a man. Her choices are necessarily more limited.'

'I hardly think a young lady's destiny is any less fortunate than that of a man wanting to break free of family tradition. She either chooses to remain a spinster, perhaps as governess to other people's children, thus catering for her own maternal needs in a less bothersome manner. Or she marries and comes under the protection of a man who provides for her for the rest of her days. Young ladies are not as hard-done-by as they would sometimes have us believe.'

The sheer arrogance of the statement, however mortifyingly allied to the way Rosalind had assessed her own future, simply infuriated her.

'If that's your considered opinion, I pity the young lady who comes under *your* protection, as you so patronisingly call it,' she snapped.

'Miss Rosie, I beg you not to upset yourself,' Margaret put in warningly. But by now Felix Holden was smiling broadly.

'I see that my cousin will find he has an admirable companion when he's in one of his tetchier moods,' he commented lightly. 'I deduce from your father's hints that he thinks you will be a fine match for him, Miss Cranbourne.'

Rosalind's honey-brown eyes sparkled indignantly, but she was suddenly quite calm.

'Then if that's what you believe, I'm sorry to disappoint you, Captain Holden, because I've no intention of being a match for Sir George Greville. I'm going to London at the extremely kind invitation of his mother and for no other reason. In any case, I'm quite sure a rising politician has the pick of any number of titled young ladies, and wouldn't look twice on a little nobody from Sussex whose father is in *trade*!'

As she rattled on, she was angry that he'd goaded her into unintentionally demeaning her father's occupation, of which she'd always been proud and a little in awe. She also felt certain qualms at her own observations. Why on earth *should* George Greville look twice at her?

'If your father is in trade, then so is mine. And as usual you underestimate yourself, Rosalind—or may I too call you Rosie?' Felix didn't wait for an answer, and there was a smile in his voice. 'So now we know where we stand, though I'm sure your father will need pacifying at your decision. But since you don't seem to harbour any great feelings towards George, I shall offer myself as escort during his absence. There are many rogues out and about in London at night, and, much as you belittle the need of a man's protection, it would be my pleasure to show you the city and be your evening companion whenever my duties allow.'

For a moment the temptation to crush him again was uppermost in Rosalind's mind, but mention of the nighttime rogues in the London streets quickly tempered that idea. Besides, Felix Holden wasn't an unattractive companion, and she was increasingly aware that she was almost beginning to enjoy their little spats.

It might even be fun to let him think she was falling for his charms, even though the sensible part of her told her it could be a dangerous thing to do. . .but she refused to listen to the sensible part of her, and smiled naturally at him for almost the first time since they'd met.

'I think that would be delightful, Felix, if you're sure your aunt will permit it.'

'Oh, I hardly think she'll object. But, naturally, I should be including Aunt Lydia in any of our outings,' he said. 'I wouldn't want to risk damaging that delicate reputation of yours.'

Their glances clashed, and Rosalind was the first to look away, hoping desperately that he wouldn't read her thoughts correctly at that moment. For the thought had come to her that the presence of his aunt Lydia, or Margaret, or anyone else as a chaperon coming between the two of them, was startlingly the thing she wanted least of all.

By the time they finally reached Greville Lodge in the heart of Hampstead, Margaret was nodding off to sleep and Rosalind was feeling decidedly stiff and travel-stained. They had started out at an appallingly early hour that morning, in order to do the journey in one day, and by now it seemed as if the entire world was in darkness.

Their carriage had skirted round the brighter areas of the city, and when Felix pointed out the large expanse of Hampstead Heath to her she peered out and couldn't see a thing.

'Never mind, you'll have plenty of time to find your bearings tomorrow,' he said comfortably.

In the dim light thrown back from the lanterns on the front and rear of the carriage, she could only just make out his lean and angular face. He didn't seem at all tired, she thought resentfully, while she felt as if she could sleep for a week. Country air was supposed to make one sleepy, but she was well used to country air and its blissful serenity, and was quite ready to hate the noise and bustle of the city.

They alighted awkwardly, and once more Rosalind was held close to Felix Holden's chest as he helped her down from the carriage. The darkness threw a cloak of intimacy around them, and she could almost imagine he was about to kiss her again, a thought which made her draw back at once. She knew from his voice that he had read her thoughts.

'You'll be quite safe here, Rosie,' he said softly. 'There are no rogues in this part of town.'

Then the huge front door of Greville Lodge was flung open, flooding the entrance to the house with light, and without ceremony Lady Lydia Greville was moving out to the top step of the stone flight, arms outstretched to greet her visitor.

'My dear Rosalind, how splendid it is to see you, and looking just as charming as I remember. I trust you had a comfortable journey?'

The warmth of the greeting reassured Rosalind at once. 'It was quite comfortable, Lady Lydia, but I'm very glad to be here at last.'

'I'm sure you are. I wasn't at all keen for you to be travelling in the dark, despite Felix's assurances, but, since you're here safe and sound, I'm sure he was right as usual.'

She glanced at her nephew with real affection, and as they moved inside the house Rosalind realised for the first time how alike they were. Lady Lydia was a handsome woman, with the same straight nose and firm chin as the men in her family, and the same warm brown eyes as Felix. Though for the life of her Rosalind couldn't remember Sir George's eyes having the same warmth.

'My dear, I'll instruct someone to show you and your maid to your rooms, and then you and Felix will join me in the drawing-room. We'll have a meal together later on and meanwhile your maid will be taken care of in the servants' quarters.'

Rosalind recognised at once that, even though she hadn't been here five minutes, she was already in the midst of a different way of life. She and Margaret would be separated for much of the time, and she only hoped the older woman wouldn't be too unhappy at her enforced stay in London.

She followed the uniformed Greville maid up the curving staircase and into a beautifully appointed room, with a manservant carrying the heavier baggage and Margaret puffing behind with the rest.

'My name's Lizzie, miss,' the girl said. 'If you want anything, just pull on the cord for general attention. Your maid will be sleeping on the floor right above you, and the second bell-pull will summon her for your personal needs. Is there anything else I can fetch you or tell you for now?'

'Not just now, thank you. Everything's very nice,' Rosalind said, knowing the inadequacy of such a tame word, but feeling more like a fish out of water by the minute at such grandeur. And heaven knew how Margaret must be feeling.

To her astonishment, she saw that Margaret was now looking more at ease than she did herself. She could only put that down to Margaret's relief at finding herself with people of her own class, for the young girl and the manservant were obviously true Londoners and spoke with decidedly less than cut-glass accents.

Rosalind herself was the one in the middle now, she thought. It wasn't done to be too familiar with these servants, and she was certainly not in the same social scale as Lady Lydia and her family. Not for the first time, she wondered what on earth she was doing here. . .

Presumably she wasn't meant to linger in her room for too long, and, in any case, she was too nervous to do so. The bedroom was far more splendid than anything at Cranbourne Hall, with a richly coloured deep-pile carpet on the floor, and what seemed to her like costly paintings on the walls. The bed was a very large, heavily ornate four-poster, with a pale beige damask coverlet over it, and the whole room was full of elegant furnishings.

Lining the stairs had been portraits of people she presumed to be former Grevilles, and from this small glimpse she could only guess at what the rest of the house was like. For a second she imagined the lady who would be Sir George's wife, eventually inheriting all this . . .and dismissed herself from the image entirely.

Such splendour wasn't for her. . .she decided she would counter her undoubted nervousness by mentally describing everything in a letter to her mother, and with that in mind she removed her travelling cloak and bonnet, and went out of the room and down the stairs to find the drawing-room, where Felix and his aunt awaited her. Lady Lydia turned as she entered the room.

'Come along and sit down, Rosalind. Is everything to your liking, my dear? If you require anything, you only have to ask.'

The older woman's beautifully coiffed hair, with only touches of grey in it, gleamed in the soft lamp lighting in the room, her silk gown rustling as she indicated a silver-grey armchair to her guest.

'Everything's wonderful, ma'am, and I can't thank you enough for inviting me. I can't quite believe I'm here——'

The lady gave a small laugh. 'Nor quite why I invited

you to spend a season with me when we hardly knew one another, I suspect?'

Rosalind looked startled, not having expected such frankness, although she had already suspected that the lady was more unconventional than most. She decided to match it with frankness of her own.

'I must admit such a thought did cross my mind,' she said with a smile.

'I would have been disappointed in you if it had not! One of the first things I noted about you, Rosalind, was your sharpness of mind. I'm afraid there's a tendency among we London folk to think of our country-bred friends as cabbages, but there's nothing of the cabbage mentality about your quick brain, my dear.'

To Rosalind it was a dubious compliment, since it implied that all other countryfolk were of the duller-headed variety, and she bridled at once.

'I think it's a very unfair assumption, ma'am, if you don't think it impertinent of me to say so!'

'Good Lord, no,' the older lady said agreeably. 'I hope you and I will have some very interesting discussions together, and you must feel free to speak your mind whenever you wish. I certainly shan't banish you from the house because of it, my dear. And while we're talking so freely, I wish you'd call me Lady Lydia. It's so much friendlier, and I do want us both to be great friends.'

It was all Rosalind could do not to laugh at the graciously unconscious condescension. It was clear that the lady had no idea of the way her words could be interpreted. One of Miles Cranbourne's caustic sayings swept into Rosalind's mind at that moment: when one was born to riches, one just naturally assumed that everyone else was an underling. . .

She realised Felix had been pouring pre-dinner drinks, and that he was handing her a glass of sherry. She looked into his eyes and saw the laughter dancing there, and knew he was just as aware of his aunt's snobbery as she was. It put her own father's well into the shade! It also created a small moment of rapport between herself and Felix that she couldn't deny.

He understood his aunt, and he understood just how Rosalind would be reacting to all of this. Because for all his dashing appearance in his military attire, and the way he seemed to fit into this atmosphere so well, she realised that his own family background couldn't have been as splendid as this.

She took a sip of the sherry and looked curiously at Lady Lydia now, seating herself comfortably on one of the beautiful scarlet and grey Regency-striped couches in the room.

'So just why did you invite me to London, Lady Lydia?' she asked directly.

Felix spoke first. 'You'll soon discover that my dear aunt is a lady of impulses, Rosalind, but sometimes she does have the most brilliant ideas.'

Lady Lydia laughed, not at all put out by his interruption. 'You'll learn my reasons all in good time, my dear,' she said, her eyes twinkling. 'You wouldn't want me to spoil all my surprises at once, would you?'

'I'm beginning to wonder just how many surprises you have in store for me,' Rosalind said, the sherry starting to make her feel as if none of this was real at all. At any moment now she would wake up and find herself back at Cranbourne Hall, and all of this would be a dream. . .

'Then I won't keep you in total suspense, Rosalind. After dinner this evening, if you're not too tired, I'll show you a list of the gatherings we shall attend during the next months. Do you like the theatre?'

'Oh—yes—although I must confess I've not been

very often,' she apologised, even more alarmed now at the prospect of the programme Lady Lydia had in mind.

'Well, we must certainly put that right! Every young lady should be acquainted with the works of Mr Shakespeare as well as our more contemporary playwrights.'

Rosalind took another sip of sherry, aware that she already felt hopelessly out of her depth, and not liking the feeling at all. Especially as she had the distinct feeling that Felix Holden was laughing at her now.

'Aunt Lydia, for heaven's sake give Rosalind a chance to get her breath,' he said now. 'If you bombard her with your plans, she'll take fright and wish she'd never left Sussex.'

His unintentional mockery gave her strength.

'I assure you I will not, Captain. I may be more at home in rural Sussex, but I wouldn't be so rude as to object to any of Lady Lydia's plans,' Rosalind said steadily, thinking that the pre-dinner sherry had not been a good idea at all, since her head spun alarmingly every time she turned it to left or right.

She placed the glass carefully on a little side-table without attempting to finish it.

'I'm glad to hear it, since it will be my pleasure to accompany you on so many of your outings,' he said softly.

His aunt smiled. Obviously he could do no wrong in her eyes, Rosalind thought, somewhat indignantly, since she sensed that he probably took many liberties here.

'When will Sir George be coming home, Lady Lydia? I do look forward to seeing him again, and am so sorry he's abroad at present,' she said, forcing more warmth into her voice than she actually felt towards the son of the house.

Lady Lydia gave a small sigh. 'I fear my son's plans do not always coincide with my own,' she said. 'I would have liked him to be here to greet you, Rosalind, but, as usual, he does as he wishes, and we probably cannot expect him for several weeks yet.'

Rosalind's perception told her Lady Lydia wasn't as perturbed at her son's absence as might have been expected. It seemed quite an extraordinary household to Rosalind, used as she was to the placid regime of her own home.

That the son of the house should choose to travel when a guest was invited could be interpreted as insulting. That his cousin was quite ready to step in as his agent was to Felix's credit, she supposed. But that the lady didn't really seem to mind at all was something to ponder on once Rosalind was alone in her bed that night. And, by then, she realised she knew nothing more about the three of them than she had already learned. And most of the knowledge she had gleaned was what Felix Holden had told her about himself.

'Have you seen the view from the window, Miss Rosie?'

The first thing she heard when she was awakened by the sound of curtains being drawn the following morning was Margaret's awed voice. Rosalind struggled to lift her head from the pillow, aware of its dull throbbing.

'No, I have not,' she said lethargically. 'And if you're going to tell me it's full of glittering streets paved with gold, then I'm quite ready to believe you without bothering to look. Now, can I please go back to sleep?'

She turned over, wincing as the headache reminded her not to move too quickly. She heard Margaret's practical voice again.

'Well, if you don't want to see these lovely fountains spraying over the greenest lawns I ever did see, and the little stone animals in among the flowerbeds, and the tall evergreens around the little lake that Lizzie tells me is stocked with all different kinds of ornamental fish. . .'

By now it was impossible to stop her. Rosalind sighed, but she knew she just had to get out of bed and see if this fantasy world Margaret was describing was actually real. She slid her feet into her bedroom slippers and her arms into her dressing-robe and went across to the windows that went from ceiling to floor and flooded the room with sunshine as Margaret drew back the curtains fully.

She exclaimed with uninhibited delight at what she saw.

'We might almost be back in the country! I expected smoky buildings and busy streets, but this is like a real haven, Margaret.'

'Oh, Lizzie says you'll find smoky streets in the city, all right, Miss Rosie, and dirty old cobblestones in the alleys and mews and gutters running with filth——'

'Thank you, Margaret. I must say you and Lizzie seem to be getting along very well,' she commented.

'She's a bright litle duck, and she's going to take me into the city when she goes to buy fresh meat at the market later on today. That is, if you won't be needing me for anything.'

Rosalind read the hurried words correctly.

'So you do remember you've a duty to me as well, then,' she said, but without malice, for she could hardly begrudge Margaret her eagerness in this new life. It was only for a short time, after all, so she might as well enjoy it.

'You know I'd never forget that, Miss Rosie. It's just that I'll never get this chance again, and Lizzie says she and Bertram will show me the park and everything——'

'Bertram?'

To Rosalind's astonishment, Margaret's face went a dull red.

'You met him last night, miss. He carried your trunk up to your room.'

Rosalind began to laugh at the woman's discomfiture. 'Why Margaret, I do believe you've found a beau!'

'It's not impossible, miss! I'm barely forty-one years old, only six years older than Sir George, according to Lizzie, and there's many a good tune played on an old fiddle——'

She clapped her hand to her mouth, realising the liberties she was taking with her young mistress, but Rosalind laughed good-naturedly.

'I believe I've heard the expression somewhere,' she said drily. 'But Margaret, are you really only forty-one? I always thought you were older. And now I've offended you! It's only because you've been with me so long, Margaret, dear, and you don't look anything like so old.'

She stopped abruptly, knowing she was making things worse, then to her relief Margaret began to laugh.

'I'll not take offence, Miss Rosie, because it's too fine a day, and, even though I had my doubts on my own account about coming here to London, it seems things have a habit of turning out right if you leave 'em alone, don't they?'

'I suppose they do,' Rosalind said, relieved that this little conversation hadn't turned out more awkwardly. But Margaret with a beau! It was something she had never, ever contemplated. She turned her attention to the window again before Margaret could read the incredulity in her face, and looked straight into the eyes of Felix Holden, striding back to the house from the direction of the gardens.

As he raised a hand in greeting, Rosalind drew back quickly, hot with embarrassment at being seen in her night attire, with her hair tumbling in disarray around her shoulders.

'That awful man!' she breathed. 'I swear he's probably been standing out there all night, just to catch me unawares.'

Margaret laughed again. 'You're letting yourself become too sensitive about the captain, Miss Rosie. After all the things he told you about his background yesterday, I'd have thought you'd be more sympathetic towards the poor man by now.'

Rosalind looked at her curiously. 'You like him, don't you, Margaret?'

'Better than the other one,' Margaret almost snorted. 'If you want my opinion on the two of them——'

'I don't. I shall take my bath, and then you can help me dress, and please remember that I've no wish to discuss Captain Holden again.'

She walked across the room to the adjoining door, behind which she had discovered the floral-painted bathtub, and revelled in the newly installed running hot water that Lady Lydia had instructed her to use. It was sheer bliss to feel so fresh in the morning with so little effort. Afterwards she donned her favourite yellow muslin for this first day in London, and went downstairs quite eagerly to greet the other residents.

'Felix asked me to pass on his apologies for not seeing you at breakfast this morning, my dear, and it's such a shame since you look so delightful,' Lady Lydia said at once. 'His military duties must take precedence over our wishes, I'm afraid. But we shall have the chance to see his regiment exercising their horses on the Heath this afternoon, and he's promised to be back in good time for dinner this evening.'

'It all sounds very agreeable,' Rosalind said, smiling. 'But I'm becoming embarrassed that my presence here means I may be taking up too much of Captain Holden's time.'

Lady Lydia gave an amused laugh.

'But Rosalind, dear, it's no hardship to Felix, I assure you. Haven't you guessed by now that I have very personal designs on the two of you?'

Rosalind looked at her, trying hard not to believe the gist of what she was hearing. And then she could contain herself no longer.

'The two of *us?*' she said explosively.

'Why, yes! From the moment I saw you I decided that you and Felix would make the most perfectly matched couple!'

CHAPTER FOUR

ROSALIND found Felix in the conservatory at the side of the house. She confronted him angrily amid the humid atmosphere of exotic hot-house plants. The vigorous greenery almost shut out the light beaming through the massive glass structure.

The afternoon had been spent as Lady Lydia decreed; taking a fashionable walk on Hampstead Heath and enjoying the fine spring sunshine, and then admiring the splendid display of the cavalry regiment, with Captain Felix Holden at its head, exercising their mounts. But right now it was easy for Rosalind to forget all about the fine figure he had cut, and the awe in which she had watched the drill. All she saw now was a man who had tricked her.

'Naturally, you knew all the time!' she blazed at him.

For a moment he pretended to misunderstand.

'Forgive me, but I'm not a mind-reader, Rosalind,' he said. 'Until you explain properly, I've no idea what it is I'm supposed to have known all the time.'

'Isn't it time you stopped playing these childish games?' she asked witheringly. 'Your aunt has told me everything.'

'Has she, now?' A smile began to play around the edges of his mouth. 'Then I must remember to congratulate my aunt. I always knew she was a clever woman, but to know everything makes her almost akin to God, don't you think?'

Rosalind looked at him wordlessly. He was the clever one—too clever by half. He could twist her words and make nonsense of them. And she hated to be thought a fool—one of the simpleton cabbage-heads that city folk assumed all country people to be!

'I think you're simply despicable,' she said, more calmly than she felt, turning on her heel and making for the door. But he was too quick for her. He had caught at her arm before she could open the glass door, pulling her back towards the seclusion of the huge *jardinières* overflowing with gigantic hydrangeas and sword-leaved imported palms.

'Forgive me for my clumsiness, Rosalind. You're quite right, and I am, as you say, simply despicable. And I can guess why you're upset if Aunt Lydia has informed you she thinks you and I are a perfect match. I'm afraid her tact is sometimes overtaken by her enthusiasm, but she always means well. You must believe that. I truly apologise for going along with her scheme and not telling you, and I apologise on her behalf too.'

She listened to him in silence, her feelings more bruised than she had expected. In fact, now that she'd had had time to think over Lady Lydia's preposterous statement, she was astonished at herself for taking it all so seriously. Was it so terrible, after all? Wasn't it just the fond hopes of a doting aunt who had seen a possible attachment for her nephew and acted on impulse in inviting her to London for a season?

In any case, wasn't it something Rosalind should be able to laugh off, knowing that the hopes Lady Lydia harboured were highly unlikely to be fulfilled? Felix Holden was far too arrogant and self-assured to be persuaded into marriage by anything his aunt could say. And Rosalind Cranbourne would never marry a man she didn't love. . .

'Well? Have you nothing to say to me—Widow Wood?' Felix continued quietly.

She started, remembering her own fault in pretending

to be someone she was not. An added humiliation now was that it gave him something to mock her with.

'All right, that was stupid of me,' she said through clenched teeth. 'But you allowed me to tell you I had no intention of marrying your cousin, when you knew very well it was never in his mind to ask me! No wonder he wrote such a cold little letter to me, endorsing his mother's invitation. I doubt that he even wanted a troublesome country girl here at all! Have you any idea of how foolish it all makes me feel?'

He caught hold of her hands and kept them inside his own.

'Will you believe me when I say how glad I am that George has no fond feelings towards you? And I admit that my aunt teased me about the lovely young lady she'd met while she was in Sussex, saying it was high time I married and that she'd found the perfect match for me—no, don't pull away, Rosalind! Because, just like you, I don't intend to have my life manipulated for me either.'

She stared into his handsome face, knowing her own must be flushed and upset.

'Are you saying you don't have any designs on marrying me, then?' she spoke flatly, before she had time to think, and she squirmed anew as she heard him laugh.

'Is that a proposal, Miss Cranbourne?'

'It most certainly is not!' She stamped her foot in frustration. She tugged her hands away from him and almost lost her balance against one of the *jardinières*. He reached out to steady her, and without warning she was held in his arms.

'Good. Because when the time is right I prefer to do the proposing myself, and to the girl of my own choice.' As he spoke, his mouth was far too close to her face, and she was terrified that someone would see them together.

He was outrageous to behave like this, as intimately as if this were a pre-arranged clandestine meeting.

'I wish her well of you when you find her,' she said, her voice almost inaudible, because her heart was beating much too fast and she found it dificult to breathe properly.

'I've already found her,' Felix said, and before she could stop him he was holding the back of her head so that she couldn't move, and his mouth was on hers in a passionate kiss. When it ended, he moved back just a fraction, and spoke softly. 'That was for Widow Wood. This one's for you.'

This time the kiss was more lingering, more sensual. And Rosalind, who had no idea of the feelings such a kiss could evoke until that moment, was aware of everything pleasurable she had ever dreamed about. The sensation filled her mind and body, and she swallowed dumbly as Felix finally let her go.

'I think we should call a truce, Rosalind. My aunt will be truly disappointed if you and I don't seem to have at least some small regard for one another. Would it be so objectionable to you if we pleased her for the three months you're here? After that, you're free to reject me handsomely if you wish.'

For three months only. . .no, it would probably be no hardship to pretend a regard for him. . .a *small* regard, Rosalind thought. As long as she remembered the sadness in his life and forgot the arrogance, she could probably manage it. . .

'Very well,' she murmured. 'For your aunt's sake I'll try to be civil to you, Felix.'

He gave a crooked smile. 'Only civil? That's a poor way to treat an admirer!'

She looked at him in exasperation. 'You're not going to overdo things, are you? This is only pretence, remem-

ber. I don't want to hear wedding bells in the distance
or have your aunt mentally writing invitation cards!'

He gave a rich laugh. 'I see you're already getting to
know Aunt Lydia very well, my love. But just answer
me one thing. You came here thinking George was
attracted to you, and you denied your interest in him
strongly. You're not the smallest bit disappointed about
that, are you? After all, my cousin will eventually come
into a fortune, and you would have been Lady Greville.'

The small glow she had felt from his endearment
quickly melted away. 'I won't even deign to answer such
a question. In fact, I find it quite insulting. I'm no
fortune-hunter, Felix!'

'It's just as well that I've no fortune to offer you,
then,' he said drily.

She opened her mouth to say that such material
matters didn't matter in the least to her, and then closed
it again. What was the point of arguing with him? And
why should she reassure him anyway? She had no
intention of marrying him or his cousin, and she was
determined that neither of them was going to spoil her
three months in London.

'Shall we go inside? The light's beginning to fade and
the evening promises to be chilly.'

He was gallant and charming whenever he chose to
be, and after a moment's hesitation she accepted his
arm, knowing it would be churlish to do otherwise. No
one had disturbed them, she realised, and presumably
the unconventional Lady Lydia had no objection to their
consorting together in the surroundings of Greville
Lodge. Knowing what Rosalind did now, she surmised
that the lady would even encourage it in her own
eccentric way, just to prove the success of her
matchmaking.

* * *

In the sanctuary of her bedroom she allowed Margaret to divest her of her day gown. She sat on her dressing-stool in the layers of petticoats, brushing her hair while Margaret hung up her dress, trying to decide what to wear for dinner that evening. But she was bursting to tell someone, and she hadn't had a chance to speak with Margaret all day.

'Margaret, what would you say if I tell you that Lady Lydia has me matched with Captain Holden and not Sir George?'

The maid gave her a self-conscious glance. 'I can't pretend to be surprised, Miss Rosie, although I didn't know of it until today. But when Lizzie and me went down the market earlier, she did say something of the sort——'

Rosalind spun round on the stool, her eyes wide and furious.

'Do you mean we're the subject of servants' gossip? Margaret, how could you?'

'Well, I never started it, miss! The gel merely asked if I knew you was going to be Captain Holden's intended, and I said you never was, and she said yes, you was if the mistress had anything to do with it! Lizzie reckons her ladyship was regretting asking you here with Sir George in mind now he's met some Duke's daughter. I dare say she thought Captain Holden was the next best thing for you.'

Rosalind flung her hairbrush on to the dressing-table.

'Sometimes, Margaret, you astonish me!' she snapped. 'This is nothing but tittle-tattle, and I'd have expected you to stop such rubbish immediately.'

'It's not tittle-tattle about the Duke's daughter,' Margaret defended herself. 'And his lordship's not gone abroad on business at all. He's joined his new lady-love and her parents at their holiday home in France. I bet her ladyship downstairs never told you that!'

'No, she did not,' Rosalind said slowly.

She didn't like what she was hearing. She had formed a quick and easy friendship with Lady Lydia, and hadn't thought her capable of any deviousness. But her reasons for inviting Rosalind here hadn't been as simple as Rosalind had imagined, and nor had she thought to inform her of her son's reasons for travelling abroad. Rosalind began to feel like a pawn in a game she didn't yet understand.

'Have you decided on your dress for tonight?' Margaret said helpfully. 'I suggest the blue satin. It'll help tone down the colour in your cheeks.'

'You mean I look like an apple-cheeked country girl,' Rosalind said bluntly. Even though her face seemed to be permanently flushed these days, the description was hardly apt, but at that moment it was how she felt. Out of her depth, and not liking the feeling at all.

'I mean you look as beautiful as ever, but if you're aiming to attract a certain young man then wear the blue,' Margaret said, just as bluntly.

She certainly wasn't, but she wore the blue satin defiantly, and was complimented on her appearance the moment she walked down the curving staircase. She felt more nervous this evening than when she'd arrived. She knew so much more now, and, although she had pretended not to be upset when Lady Lydia had told her the truth, she was still seething underneath.

There was also something faintly disquieting about Felix's agreeing to go along with his aunt's scheming—or, at least, not exactly opposing it. Although he'd told her honestly enough that he would only marry whom he chose—and he'd already found her, she remembered. She wondered who the lady could be. Obviously it was someone of whom his aunt Lydia had no inkling, and of whom she might disapprove. If he had any sense, he would keep it that way until he was ready to reveal her.

'Well, now, you two,' Lady Lydia said at once when they were all assembled in the drawing-room. 'Do you still think me very naughty, or am I forgiven?'

'I haven't decided yet,' Felix said candidly. 'And I know very well Rosalind hasn't.'

His aunt looked at him shrewdly. 'What would you have had me do, then, dear boy? Written to this child and told her I wished her to come to London and that I was sending a suitor to fetch her? It would have frightened her off for sure!'

'And if you hadn't put your scheming little brains to work in the first place, none of it would have been necessary!'

They spoke as if she weren't even in the room, Rosalind thought. It was time they remembered she was here, and she decided on shock tactics.

'You didn't tell me Sir George had gone to France with his new friends, Lady Lydia,' she said casually. The lady looked at her, startled for a moment, and then forced a laugh.

'Ah, I see someone has been talking, my dear. The servants, I suppose, unless Felix——'

'It wasn't Felix,' Rosalind said.

'In that case you deserve an explanation as to why I let you think he'd gone on business when you obviously thought at first that he'd be here to welcome you.'

It sounded so much as though Rosalind had been having fond hopes about the outcome of this visit that she spoke hotly.

'It really doesn't matter. It's no business of mine, and it was rude of me to mention it at all——'

'Not at all. You met my son in Sussex, and you naturally expected to see him here. But I'm afraid his decision to travel was rather sudden. He's smitten, my dear, and that's the only word I can use for it, and when the young lady's father invited him to France with his party George could think of nothing else. Please don't think he wasn't quite taken with you when he met you, Rosalind, dear, but he obviously considers this the Grand Passion.'

'So you decided to send me Felix as a kind of consolation prize.'

The minute she had spoken Rosalind was appalled at herself. Had she actually said such a thing? What on earth must Lady Lydia think of her? And Felix himself! She dared not look at him now.

'Rosalind, my dear,' there was genuine sympathy in Lady Lydia's voice now, 'I beg you not to think too harshly of my son. I confess I'm a doting mother where he's concerned, and he always got his own way even as a child. But he has a certain position to uphold if he wishes to follow his chosen career, and I must admit that Celeste is the perfect partner for him. Her mother is French and her father is very wealthy with vast estates in Norfolk and in France. It would be an ideal match in every way.'

'What my aunt is trying to say is that it's so much more advantageous for money to marry money, Rosalind,' Felix put in shortly. 'And it usually doesn't matter who gets hurt in the process.'

'Felix, that was quite uncalled-for,' his aunt reproached him quite angrily now.

Rosalind drew a deep breath. 'May I speak freely, please?'

Both of them looked at her in some relief as the atmosphere began to get prickly.

'Please do, Rosalind. You're the one caught in the middle of all this, and I did so want to make your visit a happy one.'

'Is there any reason why it shouldn't be? You seem to have got totally the wrong idea, Lady Lydia. I didn't come here with the intention of being courted by Sir

George. Indeed, the thought that it was in his mind was the one thing that worried me, if you'll forgive me for saying so. So you needn't have suggested anything to Felix at all in order to make me feel less rejected!'

Lady Lydia gave her a beaming smile. She was so transparent, Rosalind thought fleetingly. She sincerely wanted the best for everyone. In her world, where everything came so easily, nothing was impossible, and her two dear boys must clearly want for nothing. But Felix and George were no longer boys, and Lydia hadn't bargained on the strengths and weaknesses of their own characters.

'Then, if we've got all our little problems out of the way, what shall we do this weekend? I've left these first few days quite empty, Rosalind, until you feel more relaxed, but we can arrange a theatre visit for Saturday evening, and a stroll in Hyde Park on Sunday morning if you wish, and Felix will join us, of course——' She was painfully eager to please now.

The other two spoke up simultaneously.

'I would really prefer to pay a visit on my aunt in Paddington, if you don't mind. I've promised I'll go as soon as I've settled in here.'

'I'm afraid that won't be possible, Aunt. I shan't be free of duties at all for the next week, so you'll have to do without my company,' Felix said.

Rosalind wondered if this was an invented need to return to his duties, but decided it was probably not. He'd already taken time to fetch her from Sussex, and there must be a limit, even to a captain's leave.

'Well, it's no matter, and of course you must visit your aunt, Rosalind,' Lady Lydia said lightly. 'But *next* weekend we all attend Lady Marchmont's spring ball, and I insist that you let my *coiffeuse* attend you, my dear. You have such glorious Titian hair, and it would respond so wonderfully to the new styles.'

And if there was anything more guaranteed to make her feel she had hayseeds sticking out of it, Rosalind couldn't think of it! But she could see that Lady Lydia was genuinely anxious to make her feel welcome and to shower her with goodwill, and she murmured her thanks, but Felix laughed.

'Beware of letting my dear aunt try to mould you too thoroughly, Rosalind. There's nothing wrong with the way you do your hair now. It's perfect for you,' he commented.

Rosalind felt warmed by the compliment and flashed a look of gratitude towards him. But his aunt breezed on.

'So it is, but perhaps just a mite unfashionable. Such fullness at the sides and such *length* is a little—well, one hates to say it, Rosalind, but perhaps a little *rural*. It's so much more elegant to have one's hair in a smooth simple style now, and the new fashion with plaits looped up at each side of the head would suit you admirably. You're a lovely young woman, but with a little help you could be a real beauty. And I don't know anyone who would deny herself the chance of that!'

Clearly, this was to be Lady Lydia's new venture. Rosalind could see the sparkle in her eyes. It was as if she had been thrown down a gauntlet and was only too eager to pick it up. She was going to transform the *ingénue* country girl into a fashionable beauty about town. . .

'I suspect that I may be her first failure,' she managed to murmur beneath her breath to Felix as the dinner gong sounded and he gave her his arm once more. She felt the warm pressure as his arm squeezed hers in mute sympathy at the way she was being inspected and remodelled.

'I agree, not only because I think you have a delight-fully strong will of your own, but because I think you're quite ravishingly beautiful already,' he said softly, so that only she could hear.

Rosalind disentangled herself as they reached the dining-room, wondering if he was as sincere as he sounded, and suddenly discovering how much she wanted him to mean it. It might only be because she so hated the thought that he'd been sent on a mercy errand to bring her here, and might still think he had a duty to flatter her, and she hated the thought of that too.

Or it could be because she was young and impressionable, and it was the first time in her life that she had been so receptive to a young man's flattery, and it was dawning on her that she liked it. She liked *him*, far more than she had expected to, in the circumstances.

'At the risk of sounding like my aunt, Rosalind, I must say that you should wear that colour more often,' he said later across the width of the dining-table. 'It does wonderful things for your eyes.'

'Really?' She was suddenly dazzled by the candlelight, her attention taken right away from the succulent duck in cider sauce on her plate. 'I always thought blue flattered blue eyes most of all——'

'But that's something of a fallacy, my dear,' Lady Lydia put in. 'This is what I mean by getting you expert help in turning you into a swan. Of course blue flatters blue eyes, but it can also create a clash of colours in their very similarity. A gentleman hardly knows whether to look at the gown or the eyes when they're so similar. But when there's a dramatic contrast, as there is with your lovely hazel-brown eyes and that handsome dress, *then* he knows exactly where to look.'

At that moment Rosalind was very aware of where Captain Felix Holden was looking. She hadn't missed his appraisal of the *décolletée* neckline of the satin gown and the way it hugged her figure so caressingly. It was a much more daring neckline than she usually wore, and she felt her heartbeats quicken again at his look.

'It seems I do have a lot to learn after all,' she said in some confusion.

'And it will be my pleasure to teach you,' Lady Lydia said in triumph.

And mine. . . Rosalind didn't hear Felix say the words, but she knew in an instant that they were in his head. She could read them in his eyes as they met hers through the haze of candlelight. She looked down at her plate and continued eating her dinner with trembling hands, intending to turn the conversation away from herself at once.

'I want to see everything there is to see while I'm here,' she said quickly. 'My mother is so anxious for me to tell her all about the city in my letters. She never travels anywhere, and thinks it quite an adventure for me to come to London!'

She bit her tongue, wishing the foolish words hadn't run away with her. They made her sound what she was, a provincial nobody, and she forced a laugh as she continued.

'Of course, I don't feel that way! I think everyone should see something of their own country.'

'And other countries too,' Felix said. 'Have you never had an inclination to go abroad?'

'Oh, no. I'm sure I should be a very bad sailor.'

'And I'm sure that's no way for the daughter of a shipping magnate to talk!' Lady Lydia laughed.

'I'm afraid my father wouldn't describe himself in such glowing terms,' Rosalind said frankly. 'He's hardly to be compared to Mr Brunel, for instance!'

'Ah, the great Isambard Kingdom Brunel!' Felix said. 'Now there's a man of vision, and so much in the news these days.'

'Do you think steamships will be the thing of the

future?' Rosalind asked. 'My father is very interested in everything to do with Mr Brunel, having some links with Bristol himself, and he's sure the advent of steam navigation will open up the world as never before.'

'Yes, it must do,' Felix said seriously. 'The American continent is being developed so rapidly now, and Britain would be foolish and short-sighted indeed not to see the trading possibilities there. The speed of Atlantic crossings that steamships have to offer will make more things possible than was ever dreamed about.'

'And the recent trans-Atlantic race between the steamship *Sirius* and Mr Brunel's *Great Western* would seem to settle things,' she went on. 'Father and I both prayed for Mr Brunel's ship to reach New York first. It was a real blow when we heard that the *Sirius* had steamed out of Cork harbour in Ireland four days earlier than the *Great Western* left Bristol, and such a thrill when we heard the final result!'

She prattled out the information as naturally and informatively as only the daughter of a shipping man would, and then blushed to the roots of her hair at Lady Lydia's amused little laugh.

''Pon my word, Rosalind, you know more about the shipping business than any young lady I know.'

'I'm afraid you'll think it quite unfeminine to be interested in these things, ma'am, but I've been brought up to take part in frank discussions on such matters. I'm not worldly or travelled, but I do take note of what goes on in the world.'

'*Touché*, Aunt,' Felix murmured.

'Then I apologise, my dear, but I was merely full of admiration at your knowledge, and I confess it's all news to me. What is this race of which you speak?'

'Why, it was in all the newspapers, Lady Lydia,' Rosalind said serenely. 'The *Sirius* is a much smaller ship than the *Great Western*, so some thought it quite audacious for her to try and race Mr Brunel's wonderful new ship. Others even expected the *Great Western* to sink under her own weight. They both aimed to reach New York in record time, and a good many wagers were put on each of them to be first.'

'Indeed.' Lady Lydia was frankly amused now at the animation in the girl's voice. 'And did your father have a wager on his favourite?'

'I'm afraid he did,' she answered.

'Then we must congratulate him on his good sense, since I presume Mr Brunel's ship was the winner. Now, if you two young people will excuse me, I have a slight headache, and I shall take myself off to my bed. I don't require a dessert this evening and one of the maids may bring me a hot drink in bed. I'm sure I can trust my nephew to act with all decorum, Rosalind, and that you'll find many more entertaining things to discuss about steamships!'

Her tone was faintly incredulous as Felix rose from his chair while his aunt left the room. It was clear to Rosalind that the lady realised she had a far more difficult task in hand now to civilise this particular country girl! She gave Felix a rueful smile as he seated himself again and raised his hand to the maid to take the plates away and bring them their dessert.

'I've made a real mess of things now, haven't I?' she said. 'I should have realised a young lady was only supposed to be interested in hairstyles and fashion, and the way she holds her teacup in company——'

She paused as she saw Felix shake his head.

'Rosalind Cranbourne, you are truly like a breath of mountain air,' he said. 'And I find your interest in the shipping business fascinating.'

'Well, I'm a bit of a fraud there,' she said, a little shamefaced. 'It's not the shipping business as a whole that interests me, just the prospect of what Mr Brunel's achievements could bring. To think that his ship made the crossing in fifteen days is astounding, don't you think? And to arrive in New York on St George's Day must be a good omen for Britain.'

The dessert dishes were brought to the table at that moment, and they concentrated on the lemon concoctions. Lady Lydia might have gone to her bed, but there were almost always maids and chaperons about, whether one wanted them or not. . .

Rosalind felt a small thrill at the thought that she almost wished the maids away from the room. . .but this was such an interesting conversation, and it was so good to meet a man with whom one could converse so freely without having him think she must merely look decorative and have no mind of her own.

When they had finished eating, he referred to her previous comment. 'Do you believe in omens and destiny?'

She considered his question seriously.

'Perhaps. I certainly think it bad fortune that Mr Brunel himself couldn't have sailed on his great ship and stepped triumphantly on to American soil. You'll know about the accident that prevented him, of course?' she said uneasily, wondering if she was airing too much knowledge.

'Why don't you tell me about it in the drawing-room while we drink our coffee?' he invited.

Rosalind looked at him suspiciously. Was he playing with her again, wanting her to keep talking, enjoying the undoubted enthusiasm she displayed for the great engineer? Her father always said she would have been born a boy. . .but her feelings right now had nothing to do with such futile ambitions.

But they had been sitting at the dining-table long enough, and she followed him to the elegant drawing-room and nodded as he requested permission to smoke a cigar. The fragrant scent of it wafted about the room, pleasing and evocative.

'Perhaps you don't know that the *Great Western* should have sailed earlier than she did,' Rosalind said crisply, determined not to be bothered by the fact that this evening was now turning into something of a tête-à-tête after all. Once the coffee was served, the maids would retire for the night.

'I did know, yes. Also that there was a serious fire in the boiler-room, necessitating drastic repairs,' Felix said, to her surprise. 'While trying to put out the blazing decks with a hose from below, Captain Claxton was thrown to the ground by a heavy object falling through on to him. Unfortunately for him, but very fortunately for your Mr Brunel, it was the great man himself. If the captain hadn't broken his fall, Brunel might not have survived to see another day. Am I right?'

'And then he was almost drowned by the amount of water from the pumps and fire-hoses,' she added. 'It's said that his head was submerged before they lifted him out, and until then Captain Caxton wasn't even aware whom he'd saved.'

She shuddered, remembering the graphic detail in the *Shipping News* sent regularly to her father and related forcefully to his womenfolk.

'And if that wasn't luck or fate taking a hand, tell me what is,' Felix remarked more lightly, noting her pale face now. 'Just as it was pure fate that brought you to me, dear Rosalind!'

She laughed, almost grateful for this mild flirtation right now when her imagination was too stimulated by thoughts of a man half drowned with his head submerged under water. She shivered again and swiftly finished her coffee.

'Such flattery, when I thought you were truly

interested in my conversation, Captain Holden!' she
said, just as lightly.

'So I am. It's a rare treat to converse with someone so
knowledgeable and so feminine at the same time.'

She was suddenly nervous. It was foolish to be so, in
a house teeming with servants and respectability, but
still they were alone, and he was undeniably the most
handsome and interesting man she had ever met. They
hadn't known one another long, yet somehow she felt as
if she'd always known him, and she finally admitted she
was far more drawn to him than she had ever been to
his cousin. She sought for something else to say.

'No doubt the prospect of trade with America will
interest your father greatly,' she observed.

It was as if she had thrown cold water into the room.

'Oh, aye, my father will undoubtedly benefit from any
wool trade negotiations, just as he would if there was
another war,' he said shortly. She couldn't help noticing
how his northern accent had returned with the mention
of his father.

'A war! Why would anyone welcome a war?' she
exclaimed.

'Because in the wool trade, my dear, there's always a
need for cloth for uniforms. The longer a war goes on
and the more soldiers that are killed, the better the
profits for the mill owners. There's many a wool man
made rich as a result of Napoleon's battles.'

His bitterness shocked her, and only underlined the
deep hurt he still felt on his father's behalf.

'Then we must be thankful that wars are in the past,
mustn't we?' she said quietly. 'Now, if you'll excuse
me——'

He stood up as she moved to the door, and put his
hand on her arm. His voice was terse.

'I've upset you, and I'm sorry. It's the last thing I
wanted to do, believe me.'

She looked into his eyes and saw pain and vulnerability there. She had definitely triggered a nerve by mentioning his father. Without thinking, she touched the hand that was still keeping her there.

'You haven't upset me, Felix,' she said softly.

Before she could stop him he had caught her hand tight and brought it to his lips. It was a strangely emotional moment, almost without passion, but, as she turned and went swiftly up the stairs to her room, she was aware of a tugging feeling at her heart that defied explanation.

CHAPTER FIVE

THAT weekend, Rosalind visited her aunt May. The elderly Miss Cranbourne lived in a moderately fashionable part of Paddington, in an atmosphere of faded grandeur that was reflected in the way she dressed and behaved. She considered herself not rich and not poor, having neither husband nor parent to support her in her old age, but needing neither, since she had a generous annual annuity from her brother. And when Rosalind arrived with her maid in one of the Greville carriages, she welcomed her niece with genuine affection.

'My gracious, but you've gone up in the world, haven't you, miss?' her aunt exclaimed, as the driver steadied the horses and prepared to wait in the mews outside the house until the visit was over.

Rosalind laughed, kissing the papery cheek as she entered the somewhat close atmosphere of the house, glancing around her with interest at the heavy furnishings and the comfortably cluttered appearance of rooms occupied by an elderly spinster.

'Don't start teasing me already, Aunt May. My mother wrote to tell you I was coming to London, and you know very well I'm staying with the Grevilles in Hampstead.'

'Yes, I do know. Your mother evidently thinks I'm on my death-bed and couldn't look after you myself, when I've been telling her for years she should send you to town every summer instead of letting you stagnate in the country.'

Rosalind hid a smile. The country was as its loveliest and best in summer, except to someone born and bred in the stuffiness of a town, she presumed. Aunt May's shrewd old eyes looked at her niece keenly. The Cranbournes didn't travel, but Aunt May had made annual sojourns in Sussex, and Rosalind always wondered why her parents thought her almost senile! By the looks of her, she still had plenty of life in her.

'Well, come along and take off your bonnet and sit with me in my parlour. I've a woman who lives in the house and cares for me now, and she'll make us some tea. Your maid can help her if she's a mind for it.'

She waved Margaret away in the direction of the kitchen, whence Rosalind knew Margaret would be glad to escape. She was far more comfortable in kitchens and talking to servants than having to sit silently in parlours, while trying to merge in with the wallpaper.

'Now then, I suppose there's a young man involved in all this unaccustomed travel, and that I'd have heard about him in all good time?' Aunt May said at once, and Rosalind remembered her partiality to gossip.

'Do you mean to say my mother hasn't mentioned Sir George Greville and his aspirations to become a politician?' she said, teasing the old lady in return and seeing her small eyes widen with interest.

'She most certainly has not!' Aunt May said in some annoyance. 'And what of his aspirations towards you, my girl? If an engagement is to be announced, I trust you'll be considerate enough to inform me!'

Rosalind laughed. 'Oh, you needn't alarm yourself, Aunt. Sir George has gone abroad with a new lady love, but I'm not in the least interested in him, nor he in me. It was Lady Lydia Greville who generously invited me to London for the season.'

'Then if it's not this Sir George who's put the sparkle in your eyes, it's someone else. I've known you since you were a child, Rosalind, and I've been in this world too long not to know when a young woman has a romantic attachment. Does your mother know of it? Has she met the man?'

Rosalind turned in relief as a grey-haired woman brought in a tray of tea and biscuits and retired to her quarters again, where she was presumably entertaining Margaret in similar fashion.

'Really, Aunt May, I didn't expect to be bombarded with such questions! Why must you think that because I'm looking reasonably well I'm romantically interested in a young man?'

The old lady chuckled. 'And I wasn't born yesterday, my love. I recognise prevarication when I hear it, and just because these old bones of mine are beginning to creak alarmingly now it doesn't mean I don't remember how it felt to be held by a young man. Oh, yes, you may look shocked, but even your ancient auntie had her chances.'

'So why did you never marry?' Rosalind said curiously, because her aunt had never opened up like this to her before.

'The one I wanted the most went off and married somebody else,' she said simply. 'None of the rest ever came up to him. You take my advice, miss, and never settle for second-best. And since you're obviously not going to tell me anything about the one who's put those stars in your eyes, you can tell me about your new surroundings instead. Is it all terribly grand?'

'Terribly,' Rosalind murmured, sipping her tea, and wishing she'd got to know her aunt better in the past. This had been a duty call, but she was finding something very endearing about her that had never been apparent in her visits south, when she had always felt a little in awe of the city aunt.

'So who lives there? Good Lord, girl, it's like trying to get a winkle out with a pin to get information out of you!'

Rosalind laughed at the incongruous statement.

'Well, for a start, there's a houseful of servants to attend to the lady and her son—when he's there. You and she would probably get along quite well. You both have unconventional ways,' she said mildly. 'The son is Sir George, who's away in France and whom I met with his mother last year. And there's his cousin Felix, who comes and goes when his duties allow. His full title is Captain Felix Holden. . .'

'And he's the one you're enamoured with,' Aunt May finished as she paused. Rosalind felt herself redden at once.

'What a thing to say. I most certainly am not enamoured with him, or anyone else!'

'Well, from the sound of your voice you certainly don't have much time for the first one, so it must be the second,' Aunt May said calmly. 'You may not know it yourself, my dear, but your face lit up when you mentioned him, and that's a sure sign.'

'I'll have to guard against it, then, for I've no intention of giving anyone else such a preposterous idea. We're practically strangers.'

'Most people are when they first meet, or so I'm told,' Aunt May said drily.

Rosalind wouldn't be tempted to defend herself further. She declined to say anything more about Felix, remembering her aunt's canny way of assessing situations from the slightest hint. They talked of anything and everything, as long as it wasn't Captain Holden, and especially about the young Queen's coronation to be held at the end of June.

'Shall you be among the crowds to see the celebrations, Aunt May? I'm sure you'd be welcome to join the Greville party if I requested it. Even if you merely sat in a carriage and observed from a distance, it would be preferable to reading about it in the newspapers, wouldn't it?' Rosalind already knew that her aunt was an avid reader of everything that was printed.

'Oh, I'm too old for all that nonsense,' Aunt May said, with what Rosalind considered total disrespect for the monarch. 'I've lived through too many reigns already to get excited over this one. She's only a chit of a girl, even younger than yourself! Can you imagine yourself ruling the country, miss?'

'Of course not, but I wasn't born to it——'

'Neither was she, if it comes to that. If fate hadn't stepped in and taken her uncle William's children, one of them would have been crowned. And if William hadn't died so conveniently a month after Princess Victoria was eighteen years old, her mother would have continued being Regent. And who knows? William might well have sired more children if he'd been spared, and England's future might have looked very different, and not left in a mere child's hands.'

'Well, since any child of the old King wouldn't have come to the throne for another eighteen years, the Duchess of Kent might still have been Regent and poor Princess Victoria wouldn't have had a proper place in society at all——'

'It's easy to see you're dazzled by the romance of it all, Rosalind, but I dare say you wouldn't want to be in her shoes with all of them busily plotting now to find her the most suitable husband among the foreign princes. You can come back and tell me in ten years' time how it's all turning out, if I'm still here to see it, of course.'

Her aunt had the knack of waving any more logical reasoning aside whenever it suited her, and frequently reverting to her old theme of impending death. Rosalind hid a smile, recognising the ploy only too well.

'You'll probably outlive us all and well you know it. So you don't want to join the Greville party, then?'

Her aunt paused, her head on one side like a little bird.

'I don't think so, but the next time you come to see me you can bring your young man as well,' she said.

Rosalind sighed. 'I suppose you mean Captain Holden, and I suppose it's no use at all my saying he's not my young man.'

'Absolutely no use,' her aunt said with satisfaction. 'And the fact that you've so carefully avoided mentioning his name again for the last half-hour only makes me more sure of what I said. And when I meet him I shall find out for myself whether I think he's worthy of your affections.'

On the way back to Greville Lodge, Rosalind vented her feelings on Margaret, relating the gist of what had been said.

'Did you ever hear such intractable words? I know she's my aunt and I'm truly fond of her, but she does get the most ridiculous ideas in her head at times. And she dares to call *me* the romantic one!'

'So you are, Miss Rosie. You just haven't had the chance to blossom yet, that's all.'

'Now just what's that supposed to mean?' Rosalind said crossly. 'No, don't even try to explain! I've had enough enigmatic remarks for one afternoon.'

'And you've got the hair-arranging person coming to pin you up, haven't you?' Margaret remarked, knowing it would annoy her mistress even more.

Rosalind gave an impatient sigh. 'Well, if they're so intent on turning a country duckling into a swan, I may just let them get on with it. They won't change what's inside me.'

Just lately, though, she was at odds to know just what was really inside her. And for the life of her she couldn't get her aunt's words out of her head. Falling in love with Felix Holden? It was quite ridiculous. For one thing they hardly knew one another. . .yet, if she was honest, she already knew him better than any other man. She knew all about his pride and his teasing, as well as his sadness and vulnerability. And she knew the taste of his mouth on hers, and the feel of his arms around her.

Without any effort she acknowledged the thrill it gave her, and the way the warmth in his eyes could make her bones feel close to melting. . .but she still didn't know if all of that was a part of being in love. . .

Rosalind felt alternately glad and regretful at not seeing Felix during the following week. She missed seeing him, whether it was for the times that he irritated her, or surprised her with his suddenly vulnerable revelations. Each evening she hoped he would appear for dinner, but, true to his word, he was kept busy with his regiment and never appeared.

Not that she was left twiddling her thumbs. Lady Lydia saw to that. In the early part of the week Greville friends and acquaintances did their calling and were introduced to the visitor, drinking tea from dainty cups and eating wafer-thin sandwiches on porcelain plates each afternoon while they assessed this newcomer in their midst. By Wednesday Lady Lydia declared that it was time they went into the city so that Rosalind could become better acquainted with the capital.

'Danvers will take us in the carriage during the afternoon,' the lady said comfortably. 'It's unthinkable that a charming young gel like yourself should never have seen our national heritage, such as St Paul's Cathedral, or the royal mews, or Rotten Row where the gentry ride out to see and be seen after church on Sunday mornings!'

'I'm sure you don't mean to make my home life sound

so inadequate, Lady Lydia,' Rosalind said with a rueful smile, 'but it does begin to make me feel that way!'

'My dear, I mean no such thing! But a young gel like yourself should have every opportunity to meet the right people and see the right places.'

Again Rosalind resigned herself to the fact that Lady Lydia was a terrible snob. No amount of protesting that the freshness and freedom of life in the country was the best possible ambience for health and well-being was going to change her mind about what was best for Rosalind.

'Might we see Felix soon?' she found herself saying, quite without meaning to, and Lady Lydia gave a small smile.

'The dear boy sent a note to say he'll be here on Friday evening and for the entire weekend, in good time for Lady Marchmont's spring ball. You hadn't forgotten that, of course?'

'No,' murmured Rosalind. Nor the fact that the *coiffeuse* was due on Friday afternoon to restyle her hair, a performance she didn't look forward to in the least.

But that was Friday, and this was only Wednesday, and she wasn't going to spend the time fretting over it, even though she'd fumed to Margaret that she could see nothing wrong with her hair, and her maid had agreed indignantly. And the memory of Felix Holden's caressing voice, as he too had agreed in more flattering terms, had the power to send the blood singing through her veins. . .

That afternoon they did a lengthy tour of the fashionable parts of London, and Rosalind finally admitted that she was totally impressed with everything she saw. How could she fail to be, brought up in the quite sheltered atmosphere of a country house, and suddenly thrust into the pomp and glitter of a nation's capital? And a capital, moreover, that was bursting with pride and excitement on the verge of a young Queen's coronation.

St Paul's Cathedral towered over everything in the vicinity, a tribute to Sir Christopher Wren's vision.

'Of course, old St Paul's was burned in the great fire of London,' Lady Lydia informed her. 'It was after that terrible disaster that a law was passed for all new buildings to be built of brick or stone to lessen the likelihood of such a thing ever happening again.'

'I had no idea about that,' Rosalind said. There was so much she didn't know about her own capital city, and she revised her opinion of Lady Lydia as she listened to the pride and reverance with which she spoke about the national monuments that were so much a part of London. Anyone could be forgiven for thinking that everything here was of the very best.

Next they drove to the Tower of London, where so many atrocities had taken place in years gone by. Rosalind recalled her history lessons now, remembering in particular the terrible tale of the two little princes imprisoned and abandoned in the Tower. Such tales contrasted so vividly with the glory of the crown jewels that were housed there for safe keeping, and would be brought out with all due ceremony for the new Queen Victoria's crowning.

Later they went leisurely through the vast area of Hyde Park that would soon be the setting for much of the celebrations for the coronation. It was already thronged with people, on foot or in carriages, probably hoping to get a glimpse of the tiny Queen, Lady Lydia commented.

'Is she so tiny? I've heard as much before,' Rosalind said curiously.

'Well, it's true that she doesn't have too much height, but then, she is very young yet,' Lady Lydia said generously. 'And I'm sure that what she lacks in physical stature she'll make up for in dignity.'

'Where does the coronation actually take place?'

'Good gracious me, your education is sadly lacking if you know nothing of the seats of the kings and queens of England, my dear! And now I've offended you again, and I'm sorry,' she said hastily, as Rosalind flushed. 'The Queen will be crowned in Westminster Abbey, and we'll go there directly, so that you can see the magnificence of the building before the actual day.'

Rosalind stared at her. 'The actual day?' she said, somewhat huskily.

'Why, yes. They intend to erect stands all along the procession route, and London will be packed to bursting-point, with the railways bringing in people from all parts of the country, they say. But did you not realise that we shall be among the congregation? We may not have the very best seats, but we shall certainly be more privileged than those who will be lining the streets in order to see the procession pass by.'

By now Rosalind's head was spinning. She supposed she might have guessed. . . Lady Lydia was titled after all. She simply hadn't considered the possibility, despite her father's jocular suggestion that Sir George might well be formally invited and take Rosalind along with him. . .

Rosalind was stunned into silence now. It was one thing to be here, in the midst of all this excitement, and to write avidly to her parents about all she had seen today, which she must do this very night. It was quite another to know she would be present in the very Abbey when a Queen would be crowned. Although her excitement at the thought was intense, it was tempered by nervousness, and a fervent wish that she could be back at home among everything that was familiar. . .

'Are you feeling unwell, Rosalind, dear?' Lady Lydia

was asking with some concern now, and she realised she had leaned back in the carriage and momentarily closed her eyes.

'I'm quite all right,' she said opening them at once. 'Just a little scared, to be honest.'

'Don't worry. I'll be there with you, and although Felix will be doing his patriotic duty on the day, George will accompany us.'

Rosalind forced herself not to be too stunned by all this.

'You expect Sir George to be home in good time, then?' she said, for want of something to say, though his whereabouts didn't concern her at all.

'I expect him home in time for Lady Marchmont's spring ball,' the lady said, a little more grimly than usual. 'Now then, we'll take a final look at Kensington Palace, which was the Queen's old home, and then at Buckingham Palace where she's resided since July of last year as befits the monarch.'

'You know a good deal about royalty, Lady Lydia,' Rosalind commented on the lady's knowledge.

Lady Lydia laughed as the carriage lurched on its way. 'Oh, my dear, I could tell you even more, but it's wiser not to gossip. Suffice it to say that the young Queen does not get along too well with her mother. And who can wonder when that scheming Duchess has kept her so isolated and lonely all her life, so that now she finds it difficult to mingle with people and is terribly shy? Can you imagine the difficulties that entails in her position?'

'Well, not really,' Rosalind said with a smile, hardly able to imagine herself as Queen of England! 'And it's so sad to be at loggerheads with your own mother. I confess I'm already missing my own, even though you've been so kind, Lady Lydia,' she hastened to add. 'But our letters are going to sustain the parting.'

'And what about when you marry? Will you still want to be tied by your mother's apron-strings?'

The question caught Rosalind unawares, and she flushed deeply.

'I hope that wasn't how it sounded! Of course, when I marry I shall expect to live away from home, and to go wherever my husband chooses for us to live. But as that day is a long way off, I needn't concern myself over it.'

Immediately, the thought rushed into Rosalind's mind that if Lady Lydia had her way she would marry her off to her nephew, presumably as soon as possible. And she had as good as said she'd be willing to live anywhere, even here in London, although the prospect didn't appeal to her in the least. Everything she had seen was splendid and awesome, and history and tradition leapt out at her from every corner. But it wasn't home. It wasn't the glorious Sussex countryside. . .

She dutifully admired the stonework and architecture of the palaces, but by then she felt she'd had enough culture for one day. Lady Lydia was quite tireless for a lady of uncertain years, Rosalind thought. And tomorrow she was adamant that she would turn her country visitor into a city swan. . .

But that evening, before the dreaded visit of the *coiffeuse*, Felix came home.

The two ladies were sitting in the drawing-room after dinner, and Rosalind was enjoying the beauty of the sunset over the garden, and imagining that this scene at least wasn't so very different from home. It was ridiculous to feel homesick after so short a time, but sometimes the feeling just washed over her. And when the door opened with a click, and she turned to see who it was, her heart leapt with an unaccountable joy at seeing the tall figure of Captain Holden.

'Why, Felix, this is very pleasant. But we didn't expect you, and you're too late for dinner,' his aunt said.

'That's all right, Aunt. I didn't come for dinner.'

The words were serene enough, but the look he gave Rosalind was not. Her heart was beating much too fast, and helplessly she knew that Aunt May had been half right. It would be so easy to fall in love with Felix Holden, and she wasn't experienced enough to know if it was a good or a bad thing. She didn't know if he would agree to his aunt's wishes and offer for her, and, if he did, would it be merely a marriage of convenience?

For all she knew, he might stand to gain by it. Perhaps his aunt had arranged to settle a certain sum on him on his marriage, and he was ambitious enough to be unable to resist it. She didn't know any of them well enough to be sure. All she did know was that his eyes lit up when he saw her, and his mouth curved upwards in a warm smile. And she kept remembering how that mouth had kissed her. . .

'Then you'll take a cup of coffee with us and tell us why you're here,' Lady Lydia said.

'I'm here because I wanted to see my favourite aunt, and because I had a few hours to spare. I also wanted to see how Rosalind was standing up to your pace, dear Aunt,' he teased.

'Quite well, I think, but perhaps we should let Rosalind answer for herself.'

'I'm having a wonderful time,' Rosalind said sincerely. 'I've seen more impressive things this week than I ever dreamed existed, and I can't thank Lady Lydia enough——'

'Don't start thanking her yet, Rosalind, or she'll get all gloomy-eyed. But you're feeling strong enough to face Lady Marchmont's spring ball, I hope?' Felix went on. 'I must warn you, it's a taxing experience and goes

on into the small hours. Many a faint-hearted young
lady has given up long before these sprightly dowagers.'

Rosalind laughed, knowing he was teasing his aunt,
but a little alarmed all the same.

'I assure you I'm not faint-hearted,' she said defiantly.
'And, although I come from the country, I'm well
schooled in the art of dancing, so I promise not to let
you down.'

'Good. Because I plan to claim every dance, or, at
least, as many as you'll allow me.'

Rosalind realised that Lady Lydia was sitting silently
now, allowing the two of them to converse as if they
were alone in the room. And she felt suddenly reckless,
overjoyed at seeing him so unexpectedly, and not finding
the knack of a mild flirtation so difficult after all.

'Why, Captain Holden, would you really have me
refuse every other gentleman's offer of a dance?
Wouldn't that imply that you have some kind of priority
over me?'

'Of course. Why else do you think I suggested it?'

'That's a very provocative question, Captain Holden.'

'And you are a very lovely and provocative young
lady, Miss Cranbourne. And I can't think that this is
the first time anyone has told you so. If it is, all the
young men in Sussex must be blind or dumb!'

Her flirtatious inclination fled. She didn't know how
to answer that one with any decorum, and she heard
Lady Lydia give a small chuckle.

'I did well when I matched the two of you, my chicks.
And now I shall leave you to spend an hour together,
since I'm sure Felix didn't really come all the way to
Hampstead to talk to me! Goodnight to you both.'

She left the room and Rosalind felt acutely embarrassed, feeling she had driven her hostess out of her own
drawing-room.

'I wished she had stayed,' she said quickly. 'There

was no need for her to go like that. The evening's hardly
begun——'

'Then we have more of it to spend together before I
return to my barracks,' Felix said. 'There's no need to
be nervous of being alone with me, Rosalind.'

'I'm not at all nervous.'

'Then why are you twisting your hands together? It's
a sure sign, my love.'

She looked at him, releasing her linked fingers, and
hardly realising they had become so locked together.

'Why do you call me that?' she said. 'I'm not your
love.'

'But don't you know that I want you to be? Isn't it
obvious, sweet Rosie? And not just because my aunt
wishes it, but because I wish it,' he said quietly.

They were the width of the room apart. She sat
gracefully on one of the Regency-striped settees and he
was in the act of pouring himself coffee from the silver
jug on the side-table. They didn't touch, yet Rosalind
had the most extraordinary fantasy feeling at that
moment. From the surge of emotion rippling through
her body she felt as if they actually embraced and the
distance between them meant nothing at all. Her skin
felt on fire. It was as if his arms were holding her, his
mouth crushing hers in a passionate kiss. And she
wanted it to be happening so much. . .

She was suddenly frightened at the depth of her own
feelings, and the strange fantasy that had swept over
her. With a great effort she tried to talk normally.

'Please don't speak to me in that way,' she said,
hearing that her voice was higher and more strained
than usual. 'You know my feelings about the deceitful
way I was brought here. I'm sorry to say it about Lady
Lydia, who is a most generous hostess, but that's how I
see it. And I would much prefer it if you would see my
visit as being no more than a friendly gesture on your

aunt's part. I shall be here for three months, no more, and after that I doubt that we shall ever see one another again. I would rather you didn't complicate matters in the meantime. Forgive me if I speak plainly, but it's the way I was brought up to speak.'

She stopped abruptly, realising the extent of her own plain speaking. She had insulted his aunt and rejected him in no uncertain manner, and it could cause untold awkwardness between them all. And, in the midst of all that, she was probably throwing away something that could be quite wonderful. . .and if only she hadn't discovered that she had been brought here as a kind of offering for him everything might have been so different.

'I've certainly no wish to embarrass you by my attentions,' he said, more stiffly than usual. 'But I thought we'd already agreed to be *civil* to one another, wasn't it? And if my use of a harmless little endearment can trouble you so much, I begin to wonder as to the rightness of your rather cloistered existence.'

'It was not at all cloistered,' she said in some annoyance at this slight on her upbringing. 'And from all your aunt has been telling me about the poor little Queen, it was she who had the cloistered existence, not I!'

To her surprise he laughed, sitting down easily with his coffee on one of the chairs near her, his long legs stretched out in front of him in an attitude of perfect self-confidence.

'Oh, Rosie, you're already becoming indoctrinated into city ways, despite yourself.'

'What do you mean?'

'You referred to our royal lady as the poor little Queen, with all the affectionate familiarity of the true Londoner. In fact, you almost sounded like Aunt Lydia at that moment. Would you have said such a thing a few weeks ago, I wonder?'

She stared at him. It was such a little thing to make a

point about. Yet it was quite true. She had been so much in Lady Lydia's company these past days, absorbing everything she saw and heard, and some of it was undoubtedly rubbing off. She felt her face relax into a rueful smile.

'No, I would not. And I'm not sure what to make of that. I don't feel in the least like a city person. I enjoy everything I see, but it's all temporary. I could never live here. After a time I know I would feel stifled.'

He didn't reply for a moment, and she could almost read his thoughts. He had chosen to make his life here, and presumably anyone who married him would have to live here too. And since she had made her feelings perfectly clear on the matter, that would seem to be that. She felt acutely hollow inside.

'My mother was very much a city person, as you so quaintly call it,' he remarked. 'But she followed the Bible's teachings when she married my father.'

It was such a surprise to hear him mention his parents without the touch of bitterness in his voice that she answered involuntarily.

'You'll have to explain that to me, Felix.'

'I'm sure your religious education covered the famous phrase "whither though goest, I will go". I simply meant that my mother loved my father enough to leave London to go and live in the wilds of Yorkshire with him. I hope some day you'll find someone you love enough to do the same, wherever it leads you, Rosalind.'

It wasn't a young lady's place to blurt out that she had already found him. It simply wasn't done.

But right then, seeing the far-away look in his eyes and knowing that he missed his mother more than he ever said, it was the thing she longed to do most of all. To go to him and lay her head on his shoulder and tell him she would follow him to the ends of the earth, if need be.

CHAPTER SIX

THE *coiffeuse* was French. She was dressed all in black and her underskirts rustled stiffly as she walked. She had iron-grey hair that looked as if it were moulded out of metal, and a battery of crimping irons and combs with which to fashion Rosalind into a lady fit for London society. She assessed Rosalind with a determined gleam in her eyes, and Rosalind stared back at her with a mixture of dread and growing resistance.

By now she had decided she had no desire to be plaited and shaped and turned into a facsimile of every other young lady attending Lady Marchmont's spring ball. She wanted to be herself, and since Captain Felix Holden already liked her that way she saw no reason to change. And only the fact that she felt obliged to please Lady Lydia made her submit to this ordeal.

'*Mon dieu*, but we have something of a challenge here, *ma petite*,' Madame Le Nord murmured, cocking her head this way and that like a little bird.

Rosalind sat on the dressing-table stool, with Margaret hovering uneasily to do *madame's* bidding, and Lady Lydia preparing to leave Rosalind to the Frenchwoman's ministrations.

Lady Lydia spoke quickly. 'But you'll agree, *madame*, that Miss Cranbourne has a most beautiful face, and her hair is in glorious condition.'

And her fetlocks and teeth. . . Rosalind thought instantly, again almost hysterically unable to resist the comparison to a horse's attributes. The thought reminded her that she hadn't ridden since coming to London. Nor had she expected to do so, but Felix had

93

promised to take her for a ride over the Heath this very weekend.

Once the ball was over. . .but for the moment everything seemed to hinge on that, and Rosalind still wasn't sure whether or not she looked forward to it. She was as eager as any young girl to enjoy such an occasion, but it was so much more relaxing when it was on familiar ground. This time there would be so many people she didn't know. She had met some of Lady Lydia's friends by now, but, apart from those casual acquaintances, the only others she knew would be Felix and Lady Lydia herself—and Sir George if he deigned to return from France in time. So far there had been no sign of him, nor any communication, and she sensed that Lady Lydia was becoming increasingly annoyed at his absence.

'The *mademoiselle* is striking indeed,' Madame Le Nord agreed now. 'But the hair is so—as we say—untamed, far too *naturel* to be *à la mode*. It will be my pleasure to arrange it.'

'I would prefer not to be too sleek,' Rosalind ventured, recognising the true *artiste* in the way *madame* examined the tresses of hair so intently, twisting them this way and that to get the various effects of colour and texture.

'Ah, *non, non, ma petite*,' the woman admonished Rosalind lightly with a wag of a finger. 'You will put yourself in my hands, and you will not say a word until I have finished. Then you will see how elegant you can appear for the young men to admire, *non*?'

'Put yourself completely in *madame's* hands, Rosalind dear,' Lady Lydia said with a smile. 'I look forward to seeing the results a little while later.'

It would be churlish to refuse. It was also galling to have to submit to the trimming and tugging and pulling and twisting that went into the plaiting. And to watch herself being transformed from someone with admittedly rather shaggy locks to a young lady who could hold court with anyone in the land. After an hour of torture, the hair had been smoothed and plaited and wound about her head, the heart-shaped contours of the face revealed and softened by small coils of curls at the sides of the cheeks which was the only concession *madame* allowed.

'*Voilà!*' the *coiffeuse* said in triumph as she stood back and admired her own handiwork. 'Now you resemble a princess! You will be the belle of the ball tomorrow evening.'

Rosalind stared at herself. It was chic and elegant and certainly changed her appearance from that of country visitor to fashionable city lady. She looked the epitome of the young lady about town. But she didn't look anything like herself.

She caught sight of Margaret's watchful eyes in the mirror, and wondered if Margaret half expected her to throw a tantrum and say she hated the entire look, and to untangle it at once. It was a great temptation, but Rosalind remembered her manners with an effort, and nodded.

'Thank you, *madame*,' she said. 'I certainly feel like a different person.' It was the nearest she could come to complimenting the woman on her work.

'And now we will show you off to Lady Lydia,' Madame Le Nord went on, as if Rosalind was her newest creation. Which she supposed she was, Rosalind reflected. She had a mental image of legions of unkempt young women having their hair teased and smoothed and shaped by the Frenchwoman's expertise, and all emerging looking exactly the same. They would all fit the expected mould. And that was exactly what Rosalind objected to most of all.

She rose obediently and went downstairs to the drawing-room where Lady Lydia was sitting with her embroidery. She exclaimed with delight as soon as she looked up and saw Rosalind.

'What a transformation! And how wonderful you look, my dear. Are you pleased? But of course you are! How could anyone not be pleased when one is attended by such an *artiste*?'

It was all too gushing for Rosalind to cope with. She smiled politely and let the compliments wash over her. Each time she glanced into one of the huge gilt-edged mirrors on the walls it was with a little shock as she saw someone else staring out from her eyes and wearing one of her gowns. It was uncanny.

'You will sleep with a kerchief over your head tonight,' *madame* was instructing before she left. 'The arrangement will not be disturbed as long as you sleep serenely, and I am sure that a young lady of your tender years is not subject to nightmares.'

She smiled faintly at what was presumably her own wit, and Rosalind was more than glad when she left. Small and dogmatic, she was none the less a rather unnerving figure.

'Now tell me truthfully, Rosalind. You *are* pleased, are you not?' Lady Lydia said.

And how could she say that she was not, when the lady had been so kind to her, and was waiting anxiously for her to acquiesce? She compromised.

'I'm sure I shall get used to it, and I do thank you for all you're doing for me,' she said, avoiding a direct answer.

'Oh, that's not all, my dear,' Lady Lydia said gaily. 'I've decided that you must really look the part of my ward tomorrow night, so my little sewing-woman is coming this afternoon to fit you with a gown I've had specially ordered. I must confess to a guilty secret. Your maid allowed me to take one of your gowns to my woman for sizing, and the new gown will be virtually finished when she brings it today. Are you very cross with me?'

'No—I don't think so. How could I be?' Rosalind said faintly. 'I'm just overwhelmed by your generosity, Lady Lydia——'

'Oh, fiddlesticks,' she went on breezily. 'If one cannot be generous towards one's family, then who else? You know I'm already counting you as one of my own, my dear. And if that embarrasses you, let me just say that whether or not you and Felix discover a fondness for one another I begin to see you as the daughter I never had. So please remember that and indulge me in my little whims.'

Rosalind was laughing helplessly by the time she finished. The only word to describe her hostess was incorrigible. Somehow or other she always seemed to get her own way—at least for the time being.

But when the sewing-woman brought the gown she had been lovingly stitching for Rosalind's approval, she simply gasped with delight, knowing she had never had a gown like it before, and probably never would again. It was made of a deep gold-coloured silk that rippled and shone whenever she moved, and was decorated with flounces and lovers' knots of creamy lace. It was an exquisite gown that fitted perfectly without any alteration at all. There was a matching fan and gold slippers, and an ornate dance-card hanging from a gold cord attached to the pointed bodice of the gown. The card had her name stitched on it, and impulsively Rosalind threw her arms around her benefactor, her eyes shining.

'How can I ever thank you for this?' she exclaimed.

'I think you know how,' Lady Lydia said good-humouredly. 'Just be happy, and don't discard my hopeful plans for you entirely, dear girl.'

At that moment Rosalind saw herself in the long mirror as Felix would see her, and knew that she wanted to be beautiful for him. She *was* beautiful, she thought, without false modesty. She was like a beautiful peacock displaying its finest feathers. She turned away abruptly as the sewing-woman murmured that there was one bow that needed an extra stitch for safety and allowed herself to be attended.

It was such a totally different life, she pondered, the life of a lady. . .and just as instantly she wasn't sure that she could always be happy with such indolence. It was like the froth on a pudding, delicious while it lasted, but nothing like as substantial as the real ingredients beneath. She was serious-minded enough to know that life was like that. It had to be lived, not skimmed.

Felix wouldn't see the golden gown until the evening of the ball. She wondered what he would think of her, and knew that his was the only opinion that counted. He was coming home this evening for the entire week-end, and he would see the new hairstyle then, and she was unaccountably nervous.

When she was finally alone with Margaret, the new gown having been hung reverently beneath layers of tissue paper in the wall-closet, she spoke casually.

'Do you think that being in love with someone makes you apprehensive of their reactions, Margaret? I merely ask out of curiosity, as you're so much wiser than I in these matters,' she added quickly.

'It may do, or it may not. It would depend on whether or not a body's sure of the person they're supposed to be in love with,' Margaret said in annoyingly measured tones. 'Now if it was anyone special you were talking about, I might be able to give you a better answer.'

Rosalind had no intention of being trapped so neatly. 'Well, just supposing it was you and—and what was his name?'

'You mean Bertram,' Margaret said, far too swiftly, when Rosalind had time to reflect on it later.

'That's it—Bertram. Supposing you and he took a fancy to one another. Would it make you nervous of his reaction if you were to change your hairstyle, for instance, or wore a new gown he hadn't seen before?'

Immediately she had spoken she felt herself blush. Margaret ws so unlikely to do any of those things. She was plain of face and hair, and wore only serviceable clothes, and now Rosalind was embarrassing her. To her surprise, Margaret laughed, her face suddenly as pink as her mistress's.

'Me and Bertram would understand one another, Miss Rosie. We're of the same class, and wouldn't need none of the gentry's fancy trappings to fence all around the facts.'

'I see,' Rosalind said slowly. And were she and Captain Holden of the same class? She didn't think so. He would seem to have a dual background: his father's wool trade and his aristocratic relatives. And with his undoubted military success, it put him above her. For all the new hairstyle and the beautiful new gown, she was still the country *ingénue*.

She stared back at her own flushed face, and then straightened her shoulders. She'd never been lacking in spirit, and, whatever the company at Lady Marchmont's tomorrow evening, she was still capable of holding her own. She had been brought up correctly, however humble a shipping man's daughter might be compared to these self-assured city folk.

'Do you need me any more, Miss Rosie? Only I promised Lizzie I'd show her how to play a new game of patience when we had a little time free.'

Rosalind started, and then gave Margaret a quick nod.

'No, that's all right. Just help me into another dress for dinner, and then do as you wish for the rest of the evening. You seem to be getting along very well with the servants here, Margaret, and I'm glad.'

Margaret did as she was told and finally left Rosalind's room in what seemed to her like an almighty hurry. Wearing a soft peach-coloured dinner-gown and a necklace of pearls and matching ear-studs now, Rosalind looked gloomily at herself in the mirror. Gingerly, she eased the little side-curls away from her cheeks, where they seemed to be fastened down. They immediately sprang back to her face again as if attached by an invisible gum. She ran a tentative finger through the sleek smoothness on top of her head, but it too was fixed far too flat for her liking with the concoction of sugar and water mixture Madame Le Nord had used.

'Oh, well, as long as he likes it, what does it matter?'

She spoke involuntarily to her reflection, and then bit her lip. It did little for one's self-confidence to feel so dependent on another's opinion, but perhaps that was also a facet of what love did. Whatever the reason, she began to feel that her own personality was becoming swamped, and she preferred to put most of the blame on the weight of this new *coiffure*. And there seemed to be nothing she could do about that without mightily offending her hostess.

She had almost reached the bottom of the curving staircase when she heard voices coming from the drawing-room. Her heart began to beat considerably faster, and she put a hand against her chest as if to check its rapid beating, chiding herself for being so foolish. Felix had already arrived, and within seconds she would know by his face whether he approved of her new appearance or not. She walked to the door, trying not to appear too eager, and then paused outside as she heard her name mentioned.

'Rosalind will be very pleased to see you, dear boy, so you will oblige me by removing that scowl from your face,' Lady Lydia said, her voice sharper than usual despite the endearment. More than that, it was almost said with a touch of sarcasm.

Rosalind felt her spirits plummet. She knew the old adage that eavesdroppers seldom heard good of themselves, but she hadn't intentionally listened. It was impossible to avoid listening when voices were raised. And although she dreaded hearing what Felix had to say in reply, she was transfixed to the spot, and simply unable to move away. She heard a mocking laugh and froze momentarily, her mouth beginning to tremble.

'Good God, since when was it so important for me to pander to your whims, Mother? You may think it fun to bring this little chit up from the country and dangle her in front of Felix, but don't include me in your charity work!'

The mortification with which Rosalind heard the words was tempered with wild relief that it wasn't Felix's voice at all, but Sir George Greville's, apparently come home very disgruntled in time for the Marchmonts' ball. And obviously less than pleased at finding her still here. Perhaps he had expected her to take fright at the big city long before now, and go scuttling back to Sussex! Her anger cleared, suddenly realising it was the one trigger she needed to make her lift her chin high, turn the door-handle and enter the room as serenely as possible.

She walked across the room with a perfect smile on her face, ignoring the embarrassed glance that Lady Lydia threw towards her son, clearly wondering just what Rosalind might have overheard. She pretended not to notice anything but that the son of the house had returned, and in fact was at that moment gaping at her as if he had never seen her in his life before.

'Why, Sir George, how pleasant to see you again. Lady Lydia has been so hoping you would return in time for the Marchmonts' ball. I trust your business in France was conducted to your satisfaction?' she said sweetly.

Mentally, she stood outside herself, marvelling at her own composure, and betraying nothing of the way she seethed inside at this oaf's ungraciousness. Titled he might be, but he had a lot to learn in manners. And she knew very well by now what his 'business' in France had been. To court a wealthy heiress. . .and from the dullness of the colour on his neck she had a quick suspicion that perhaps the courtship hadn't gone as well as he had hoped.

'It was well enough,' he said briefly. 'But I find myself glad to be back in England after all, at least for a short time. I may well be returning to France in a few weeks.'

He paused as his mother tut-tutted, his gaze running over Rosalind as if he had never seen her before.

'But can this really be the young woman we met in Sussex? I seem to recall a mane of blazing hair to rival that of my gelding, and a comfortable house in a less than civilised part of the country. I see that my mother has seriously been to work on you, Miss Cranbourne.'

It was the kind of dubious compliment Rosalind could well do without. He was every bit as uncouth as she remembered. Some so-called gentlemen thought that a title meant they could ride roughshod over everyone else, and Sir George Greville was one of them. Rosalind compared him swiftly with Felix, and wondered how two cousins could be so different. . .

'I assure you we're very civilised in Sussex, Sir George, perhaps more so than some of the so-called gentry I find in London,' she went on, still in that innocent voice that might or might not be meant to insult. To her annoyance she saw that it suddenly interested him.

'Well said, miss,' he chuckled, and she was not sure

whether or not he realised she referred to himself. 'I like a filly with spirit who's not afraid to speak her mind.'

'Really? Then perhaps you'd oblige me by not comparing me with a horse. It's hardly flattering.'

Was she really speaking up to him in this way in his own house? It was not the done thing, and Rosalind went suddenly scarlet as she realised her *faux pas*. But then she saw that Lady Lydia was laughing at the two of them.

'Oh, Rosalind, dear, I think perhaps I made a mistake after all. Perhaps you are more suited to my own dear boy than to Felix!'

This time she held her tongue, though she dearly wished she dared answer that she most definitely was not. The sparring with Felix was spiced with excitement, while this with Sir George held an undercurrent of viciousness. Rosalind recognised the warning signs in her head. Here was a man with whom it was unwise to meddle, and the fact that he was now looking at her with renewed interest only had the effect of making her blood feel a few degrees chillier.

'But I've already told you, dear Lady Lydia, that I'm not yet ready to be attached to anyone at all,' she said, as lightly as she could.

And thankfully, before Sir George could put in another of his snide remarks, Felix arrived for the weekend. He greeted his aunt first and then shook his cousin's hand, but with that new perception she seemed to have developed of late Rosalind knew at once that there was no real affection between the two of them. They were acquainted through the ties of blood, and that was all.

Finally he moved to her side and raised her hand to his lips in greeting, and his eyes looked straight into hers.

'What have they done to you?' he said softly, as his aunt and cousin chattered in the background.

She looked at him mutely, unable to think of a single answer as he dropped her hand and moved away to accept a drink from his cousin. Rosalind remembered that Sir George had been more than partial to drinking spirits on his visit to Sussex.

But the evening passed pleasantly enough, with four for dinner instead of three, and Sir George often dominating the conversation. Rosalind felt uneasily that he looked at her far too often, as if he couldn't quite believe that this elegant creature was really the same country girl he had met on his one obligatory visit to Sussex. Perhaps she was imagining it. . .but she knew that she was not when Felix interrupted a rather questionable joke George had made by asking him a direct question in George's own abrupt manner.

'And how was Lady Celeste, George? Did you make your usual conquest there?'

George scowled at his cousin through the candlelight, his hand already quite unsteady as he raised his wine glass to his lips. Clearly this was not a question he welcomed.

'The Duke and his family decided to cut their trip short because the mother was taken ill. It was no more than a trifling cold if you ask me, but it prevented me from furthering my acquaintance with Celeste as much as I'd have liked. Still,' he said, brightening, 'it's an ill wind, as the pundits say, and our little country cousin will now have two handsome escorts to the Marchmonts' ball instead of one.'

'And you will remember that Rosalind is my guest,' his mother said mildly, 'and that Felix has already offered to be her escort and been accepted.'

It was a gentle reproof, but none the less meaningful for all that, and the other three all knew it.

'I'm sure Felix can have no objection to my marking Rosalind's dance-card,' George said, with a definite edge to his voice.

'Oh, I'm equally sure Rosalind will give her favours to whomever she pleases,' Felix answered, just as coolly.

Rosalind listened to them both in some exasperation. Again, it was as if she weren't there, a pawn in a game the two of them were playing. When, in reality, there was no contest at all. She could never respond to the one, whom she now saw as a very cold fish, while she had already given her heart to the other. . .

'And since the lady in question has the very last word, you will just have to wait and see, won't you?' she said, putting an end to the conversation.

Lady Lydia laughed, obviously enjoying this little repartee at the dinner table.

'I think you had best stick to courting your young Celeste, George. Rosalind is more than a match for you.'

Rosalind saw the glitter in his eyes, and wished his mother hadn't uttered those particular words. George Greville was not a man to resist such a challenge, and she had no wish to be caught up in an unsavoury rivalry between the two men.

She went to bed that night conscious that both of them were in the house, only doors away from her own room. There were plenty of servants in the house, and the formidable presence of Lady Lydia herself, but for Rosalind it was the presence of Felix and George that was undoubtedly disturbing her and keeping her awake long into the night when she should be getting plenty of rest in preparation for the excitement of tomorrow night.

Felix. . .and George. . .the one so handsome and everything she could want in a man. And the other one . . .she shivered, not quite sure why she disliked him so much, but certain that he would never treat a woman with the respect she deserved, and suspecting too that he was not the faithful kind. Otherwise, why should he have been so blatant in his compliments, when he was apparently enamoured of this Celeste? Especially as he had been so dismissive of Rosalind while in Sussex, treating her as the young country girl, hardly worth a second glance. Her changed appearance under the worthy Madame Le Nord's hand had apparently changed all that. . .

Rosalind remembered she was supposed to be wearing a kerchief over her head to keep the *coiffure* in place. She had no idea where to find such a thing, since Margaret had unpacked all her clothes, and liked to think she was in strict charge of them. It was very late now, and Rosalind hesitated to call her maid on such a trivial thing. But in the end she pulled the bell cord, suddenly needing the common-sense chatter of an old friend.

Margaret appeared in a fluster, and Rosalind began apologising at once. The maid waved her apologies aside and rummaged in a drawer for the silk kerchief that was to be pinned around Rosalind's head to keep the style in place. Privately, Rosalind had begun to wonder if her hair would ever become soft and natural-looking again.

'It's no matter. There's such goings-on upstairs anyway, and I was wondering if I should tell you or not,' Margaret whispered in a conspiratorial way.

'What kind of goings-on? Tell me at once!'

Margaret grinned nervously. 'All right, then, but don't you go letting on, mind. It's that Sir George, Miss Rosie, the one you met first of all. Lizzie kept mighty quiet about it all till tonight, but now she's busting with excitement, and I found out the reason why when I saw the gent come creeping into her room and heard the giggling and cavorting between 'em!'

Rosalind felt her eyes go round with disbelief. Sir George consorting with servants in his mother's house? And yet. . .oh, yes, she could believe it readily enough.

Hadn't she sensed something not quite right about him all along? Hadn't she been repelled by him without really knowing why? She felt a brief pity for the woman he would eventually marry, Celeste or whoever else it might be, immensely thankful that it wouldn't be herself. . .

'Have I shocked you, Miss Rosie?' Margaret was saying uneasily now. 'I swear it's true——'

'I'm sure it is, but you're not to tell anyone else, do you hear?'

'You know I wouldn't, miss!' she said indignantly. 'But you're not too upset by it, are you?'

She didn't really know how she felt. She wasn't at all upset on her own account, but she was certainly uncomfortable at the thought of what was happening in the rooms above her head.

'I'd rather just go back to bed and forget about it,' she prevaricated. 'And I suggest you do the same, Margaret. It wouldn't do for Sir George to know you'd seen him.'

And when she was finally alone and still willing sleep to come to her, she couldn't help wondering what it must be like to have an illicit love-affair. It was wrong and wicked to think of such things, though presumably servant girls indulged in them without too much guilt. It was still a kind of love. . .though not the pure kind of love that ended in marriage and home-making and having children — that was the only kind for her. And in her dreams the man who fulfilled all those require-ments was tall and ardent and wore a captain's uniform. She could dismiss the thought that Felix hadn't been so particular in his attentions to a certain Widow Wood, because he had known all along it was Miss Rosalind Cranbourne. . .

* * *

It was difficult to look at George Greville at breakfast
the next morning and not remember what Margaret had
told her of his night-time activities. Rosalind was perfectly sure his mother would be scandalised. She might
be unconventional in many ways, but a scandal in the
family was not to be tolerated. She might be sceptical of
the success of her son's courtship of Celeste, but since
the lady was the daughter of a Duke she was presumably
above reproach. Being the daughter of a country squire
was so much simpler, Rosalind reflected.

'A penny for those interesting thoughts, Miss
Cranbourne,' George's mocking voice reached her across
the kippers and marmalade, and she realised she had
been staring unseeingly at her plate.

'Oh, they're worth a good deal more than that, which
is why they're best kept to myself,' she said lightly, and
for a moment she saw a frown between his eyes. Is he
wondering if I know, she thought swiftly, and if my arch
remark means that I intend to blackmail him?

She was letting her imagination run away with her so
much that she began to smile at her own thoughts. And
yet perhaps she had inadvertently hit the nail right on
the head, she thought later, because to her relief Sir
George directed the rest of his remarks to his mother
that morning and virtually ignored her.

The family spent a quiet morning, reading or strolling
around the garden, and Rosalind spent some time in her
room beginning a letter to her mother, which she
intended to finish tomorrow with every detail of the
Marchmonts' ball. When Margaret appeared with some
refreshment on a tray during the morning, she avoided
any reference to their night-time conversation, and, since
the maid did the same, Rosalind surmised that she
regretted her indiscretion in mentioning it at all.

After a light lunch, Lady Lydia declared her intention
of lying down for a while to be fresh for the evening, and

suggested that Rosalind do the same. Of the two men there was no sign. But, after an hour of twiddling her thumbs and feeling bored with the etiquette of the house, during the afternoon Rosalind came to a momentous decision and summoned Margaret to her.

'I want you to wash this sticky mess out of my hair, and arrange it the way I always have it,' she said defiantly.

If she expected opposition, she didn't get it.

'Well, thank goodness for that,' Margaret said frankly. 'You look like a tailor's dummy, if you'll pardon me for saying so, and I never thought your hair suited you that stiff way at all, though it weren't my place to say so to that French *madame*!'

'But you don't mind saying so now,' Rosalind grinned. 'It's not like you to hold your tongue, Margaret.'

'Oh, I have my secrets,' the maid murmured. 'But never mind about me. Let's get your head under that soapy water before you change your mind again. Your hair takes an age to dry at the best of times, but it'll be worth it to see you looking your old self again. It's a sure bet your young officer will prefer you the way you were too, and it makes no difference what the other one thinks.'

For once, Rosalind wasn't even tempted to argue with her contemptuous tones.

CHAPTER SEVEN

ROSALIND descended the staircase that evening in some trepidation. The others were already assembled below, and she was obliged to make an entrance. She knew it would be a very different entrance from the one Lady Lydia expected. Catching sight of her appearance from time to time, she felt considerable qualms, even though Margaret had assured her she looked her very loveliest in the new golden gown. But it wasn't the gown that disturbed her. . .

Tonight was an important night in the social calendar, and a momentous occasion for Rosalind, since it was her first real launch into society. And already she had gone against her hostess's wishes. It had been a reckless, impulsive thing to do, to wash all the new hairstyle away, and she was beginning to ask herself if it had really been so important after all, to resist conforming to fashion for one night. But it was too late now, and she could only hope Lady Lydia wouldn't despair of her and send her straight back to the country.

Felix came out of the drawing-room just as she reached the bottom stair, and her heart leapt as he paused, saying nothing for a moment. She couldn't quite interpret the look in his dark eyes, but then he walked quickly towards her, catching both hands in his own and taking them to his lips.

'You take my breath away,' he said softly. 'Thank God they didn't manage to change you permanently.'

After her own indecision, the simple compliment threatened to send the weak tears to her eyes—and a

110

fine sight she would look then at Lady Marchmont's ball!

'Do you think your aunt will be very angry with me?' she said in a small voice, knowing he would follow her meaning without further explanation.

Felix touched her glossy hair with his fingers. Freed now from its harsh confines of snails' curls and plaits, it flowed effortlessly once more. Its only restraints were the onyx pins and combs to lift it from her face and allow the abundant weight of it to cascade on to her shoulders, a compromise towards the required elegance for the evening. The soft tendrils that framed her face gave an even more luminous look to her honey-brown eyes. Even more so did the narrow gold band she wore low on her forehead with its tiny pearl adornment, which was all the rage in some quarters, and which Rosalind had recklessly decided to adopt as her final fashion accessory.

'She'll probably be more than gratified that you chose to be yourself, my love, and so am I. You'll be unique among the rest of them at the ball, and no other woman will be able to hold a candle to you.'

She shivered at the intensity of his voice, wondering if he could possibly be as sincere as he sounded. Or was she being completely foolish to have her head turned so easily by a dashing young officer who might just be flattering her to please his aunt? If only she could be sure. . .but presumably Lady Celeste was as blissfully sure of George, and knowing what Rosalind knew now about Sir George's inclinations she felt that her faith in all men was being tested.

'We'd better go and face them,' Felix went on, uniting the two of them together, and for that she was grateful. He tucked her arm inside his own, escorting her into the lighted drawing-room, where Lady Lydia and her son were conversing in a congenial manner.

'May I present my beautiful companion for the evening?' Felix said. Lady Lydia turned with a smile at the formality. For a second the smile froze. She looked completely taken aback, and then George gave a guffawing laugh.

'So the little country mouse couldn't face the music with her new appearance, after all, eh? It seems that you lose this time, Mother. I only wish I'd had a wager on it!'

To Rosalind's relief, his words had the opposite effect on Lady Lydia. Seconds ago she might have felt annoyed at having all her attempts to sophisticate Rosalind thwarted, but now she threw an irritated glance towards her son, and spoke sharply.

'If you must speak in so vulgar a fashion, I think we must say that it's more a case that Rosalind wins, George.' She smiled at Rosalind completely without malice. 'You were quite right after all, my dear, in refusing to change the style of that glorious hair of yours. And now that I see you in the new gown, you truly look golden from head to toe. I compliment you on your good sense, Rosalind.'

Rosalind's relief was so great that she broke free of Felix's arm and moved swiftly across the room to her, impulsively pressing a kiss to her cheek.

'Thank you for that,' she said huskily. 'I was already wondering if I would displease you very badly. And you really aren't angry with me for undoing all Madame Le Nord's work?'

Lady Lydia laughed, her good humour quickly restored.

'Not at all. I knew you would be quite a sensation in any case. As my guest, you were already bound to be a novelty, of course, and now you'll be the undoubted unconventional beauty of the evening as well. Yes, my dear, it appeals to me greatly to present you exactly as

you are. And now we had best be on our way, or the
evening will be half over before we arrive.'

Rosalind dared to glance at George, but to her further
relief he seemed to have lost all interest in her. She had
probably only been a passing attraction on his part, she
guessed, perhaps out of boredom because he'd been
forced to cut his holiday with Lady Celeste short; or
there had been a brief interest at seeing her changed
appearance last night; or it was merely a continuance of
what she suspected might be a long-standing rivalry
with his cousin. As a rather isolated only child she knew
nothing of such things, but she had learned of them
through books and even more through her own intuition.

The carriage was waiting for them as they went out
into the balmy evening. There were rugs inside to cover
them later, but right now it was enough for herself and
Lady Lydia to have their light evening cloaks around
their shoulders and to sit snugly inside the carriage
facing the gentlemen. In case of any emergency, such as
the horses being startled and swerving, or stopping
suddenly, the gentlemen would be there to catch them.
And gentlemen always rode with their backs to the
horses.

But as Rosalind sat with her knees discreetly together
it was unavoidable for Felix's knees to touch hers in the
swaying carriage. It was a warm and exciting contact,
and every time it happened it seemed as if her eyes met
his, and caught the little smile that played about his
mouth. The shivers running through her now were more
pronounced than ever, due in no small part to knowing
she would legitimately spend at least part of the evening
in the intimacies of the dance with Felix Holden.

She was thankful now that she had been taught the
intricacies of music and dancing by her tutor, though at
the time she remembered saying airily that she'd much
rather be riding her horses. Such comments seemed to

her like those of a child now, and she realised how
eagerly she was looking forward to more adult entertainments this evening.

In due course they arrived at the spacious Mayfair
mansion where the Marchmonts lived. Lady Lydia had
previously informed Rosalind that the elderly Lord
Marchmont was little more than a figurehead in his
own household now, while the lady arranged the spring
ball and held court. It was also well known that she
was intent on having the young Queen Victoria at one
of her soirées or balls, but so far such an invitation had
not been accepted. How exciting it would have been,
Rosalind thought wistfully, if that occasion had been
this evening, and she could have reported in her letters
to her parents that she had actually come face to face
with their Queen!

The entire house and garden were ablaze with light
as they joined the long procession of carriages pulling
up outside the main door of the house. The exterior of
the estate was a delight in itself. There was coloured
water from the many spraying fountains in the grounds,
and brightly painted Japanese lanterns strung about the
tiered terraces and shrubberies. Even before they
alighted from the carriage, Rosalind could see inside the
great ballroom itself, where there were glittering chand-
eliers and wall-candelabras vying with the glittering
gowns and jewels of the ladies, and the bright uniforms
and dark evening attire of the gentlemen.

The expense of such an occasion must have been
enormous, Rosalind thought in a moment of practicality,
and then gave up thinking about such things, since they
obviously didn't concern anyone here, and shouldn't
concern herself.

The lady of the house was charming and welcoming,
and, if she and some of the other guests did indeed seem
to treat Rosalind as something of a novelty, she soon

gave up concerning herself about it and began to enjoy the experience. And, even before the dancing began, she found herself surrounded by a bevy of young men, all eager to mark her dance-card with names she didn't know and would certainly never remember until they came to claim their dance.

'Thank heaven I thought to sign up before we arrived, or I'd hardly see you again,' Felix just managed to breathe in her ear as the music began, and an eager young claimant came to whisk her away from him.

She laughed back at him, and accepted the young admirer's arm, but all the time they whirled about the room in the vigorous schottische her thoughts went winging ahead to when she and Felix would be partners in the dance. He was the only one she wanted. She would feel the warmth of his fingers even through her elbow-length gloves. She would thrill to his touch as ever, while this particular young man's touch meant nothing to her. As if to apologise for her private disregard for him, she gave him a dazzling smile and saw him go very red because of it.

'Miss Cranbourne, I wonder if you would permit me to call on you one afternoon?' he stammered, clearly seeing her smile as in invitation. 'That is, if you think your chaperon would allow it, of course. I would be very willing to approach her about it.'

She replied gently, not wanting to let him down too hard. 'I'm so sorry, Captain Bailey, but Lady Lydia has arranged a very exacting programme for me while I'm in London, and I don't think it would be possible. I'm sure you understand.'

He probably didn't, but gallantly said that he did, as did the dozen other young men who asked the same question and received the same answer. Many a young woman would be flattered and have her head turned by all the attention she was receiving, but for Rosalind there was only one man she wanted to escort her about the town, and right now that young man seemed to be paying far too much attention to a certain very young and pretty girl dressed in figured pink.

'Would you tell me the name of the young lady dancing with Captain Holden?' she asked her present partner casually.

'Oh, you mean Gabriella. That's Lord Courtney's granddaughter. She's a very sweet young thing, and I believe she and Captain Holden are old friends. I believe the Courtneys knew his mother quite well some years ago.'

At this information, Rosalind felt the most acute stab of jealousy she had ever know. It was ridiculous and unfounded, and she hardly expected Felix to dance every dance with her, or to stand about waiting for her while she was whirled about the ballroom by these eager young partners. But she was piqued all the same, and even more so at hearing that he and Gabriella were old friends. He must have known her in the cradle, she thought, with unwarranted cynicism.

Perhaps Felix himself had even seen a future connection between them, despite the girl's youth, she thought ungraciously, since her parents would seem to be vastly rich! She hated herself for the unworthy thought, but somehow it wouldn't leave her, and when Felix eventually came to claim his next dance with her she was hot and cross and her feet were beginning to hurt.

'Are you sure you can spare the time away from Miss Courtney?' she said snappily, and could have bitten her tongue out at the teasing smile in his eyes. And this was hardly the way for a young lady to behave in company. The knowledge made her even angrier with herself, with him, with everybody. She was momentarily out of sorts.

'Oh, I think I can spare you a dance or two,' he said mildly, in a tone that only infuriated her more.

'Well, I don't know that I want to dance any more right now,' she said. 'It's very hot in here——'

'Then I'll fetch you something to drink and we'll go outside on the terrace for some fresh air,' he said at once. 'I don't want you collapsing on the dance-floor. It would be very bad form.'

She knew he was still teasing her, but she was in no mood to be humoured. She didn't know what was wrong with her. She should be ecstatic, attending her very first London ball, though she had begged Lady Lydia not to make a fuss about it and to let her merge into the general company after being introduced formally to the host and hostess. But later it had been flattering indeed to have had so much male attention, and she knew she was being a complete dog in the manger to be jealous that Felix had been so attentive to the young Gabriella. The *very* young Gabriella, she amended. . .

'Are you enjoying yourself, Miss Cranbourne?'

She heard the mocking tones of Sir George Greville, and turned to face him too quickly. For a few seconds the room seemed to spin, and she put out an arm against the wall to steady herself. Immediately, George caught at it in a proprietorial way.

'I think perhaps you've taken a little too much wine, my dear——'

'I've not taken any,' Rosalind began indignantly. 'I just felt hot for a moment, and Felix is fetching me some refreshment now——' she added, before he could offer to do the same.

'Then some fresh air is what you need. My cousin will find us easily enough.'

She wanted to protest that she should wait for Felix, but somehow he was already steering her through the long open windows on to the terrace outside. There were plenty of watchful chaperons in the company that evening, but by now the mood was relaxed, and it seemed

to Rosalind that many a fond mamma might well be
welcoming a mild attachment between their daughter
and one of the well-connected gentlemen present.

The terrace outside the ballroom was as heavily
ornate with flower tubs and *jardinières* as the Grevilles'
conservatory, the waving palms and shrubs forming
discreet little nooks where couples could sit in some
privacy, but certainly not enough to risk being
compromised.

Rosalind sat down abruptly on one of the many chairs
scattered about for guests' convenience. She was not
dizzy with wine, but with the exertions of the dancing,
and the cooling evening air was like balm. She breathed
long and deeply, and glanced at George.

'Thank you. It was what I needed after all.'

He leaned towards her, dark and handsome—if a
little portly—successful and rich, and Rosalind could
see that certain women would be very attracted to him.
In fact, she supposed that the slightly ruthless way he
treated people could be an attraction in itself, certainly
to young and impressionable servant girls. . .

'Is that all the thanks I get, little Rosalind?'

She squirmed at once at the patronising phrase and
all its implications. There was a lot of noise coming from
inside the house, and, from the muted murmur of voices
nearer at hand, there must be other people outside on
the terraces and in the grounds, but none that she could
see from the little nook in which she sat. It was as bright
as day beyond the environs of the house, the mellow
night enhanced by moonlight now from the huge yellow
moon above them. It was a romantic evening, one that
was surely designed for lovers, but at the uneasy thought
her heart began to beat sickly, and the last thing in the
world she would want was for George Greville to think
of her in such a way.

'Oh, I think so,' she answered coolly. 'I'll wait here

for Felix, if you would be so good as to tell him where I am.'

She heard him give a low laugh, and then she was being pulled to her feet, and his grasp was anything but gentle. If she hadn't been wearing evening gloves, she was quite sure her arms would have shown the marks of his roughness.

'Perhaps I will—later,' he said thickly. She could smell the spirits on his breath and knew he'd already drunk more than enough that evening. 'But you'll repay me with a little kiss, my country girl who likes to play at being a lady whenever it suits. I'm not sure which version I prefer—the elegant one I saw last night, or the untamed beauty done up in her finery I see tonight. I'm beginning to wonder just which is the real Miss Cranbourne!'

She twisted away from his face as his mouth sought hers. She didn't want him kissing her, nor to know instinctively that he would never take advantage of one of the very proper young ladies dancing the night away at the Marchmonts' spring ball. It was only because of who she was—a little nobody from the country—that he tried to force her with his attentions. In his eyes, she was as much sport as Lizzie. . .and she was utterly humiliated at the thought.

'Stop it—please——' she gasped.

She knew this was an undignified struggle in the shelter of the potted palms. It would be much easier to simply give in to his kiss and be done with it. As long as it ended there. . .but how could she be sure he wouldn't take one kiss as an invitation for more. . .? The wildest thoughts flitted through her mind in those moments. She was tempted to say she knew all about him and his dalliance with servants, and would inform his mother . . .but he would naturally deny everything and it would be poor Lizzie who would be sent packing. . .

And then she realised she was being released, and George was staggering slightly as someone dragged him away from her.

'What the devil do you think you're doing?' she heard Felix say harshly, but still quietly enough not to be heard by anyone else. In any case, the noisy chatter and laughter and music coming from the ballroom covered up most attempts at conversation.

'What's it to you, Cousin?' George snarled. 'Don't tell me you haven't got your oar in there already——'

'I should break your neck for that insulting remark,' Felix said savagely. 'And you'll apologise to the lady at once.'

'I see no lady——' He suddenly yelped as Felix's hand squeezed his neck.

'I was forgetting that you weren't so used to dealing with ladies,' Felix said, quietly now, but they all stood close enough for Rosalind to hear plainly. 'Your inclinations turn more towards servants and the like, don't they, *Cousin?*'

She drew in her breath. So Felix knew what she knew, or guessed at it. Dimly, she heard George mutter something that could have been an apology or a threat, and then Felix let him go. He went blundering off around the side of the house, rubbing his neck and still muttering. Felix turned to her.

'I apologise for him, Rosalind. He can be quite despicable when he's been drinking, but tomorrow he'll have forgotten all about it, and I beg you to try and do the same.'

'You mean that by tomorrow he'll be despising me again as the unwanted interloper who's infiltrated his mother's house?' she said, tremulous now that the scene was all over, and more upset than she had expected to be.

'You're not unwanted. Haven't you learned that by now?'

She brushed away the shine of tears on her lashes. 'Don't patronise me, Felix. I've had enough of that for one evening.'

He looked at her silently, sensing the invisible wall of pride she had suddenly built around herself. The glasses of cordial he had brought from the dining-room stood untouched on a low wall, and he handed one to her now.

'Drink some of this, Rosie. It will calm you before we go back inside.'

'I can't go back in there yet! My face must be scarlet, and everyone will guess——'

'Your face is beautiful, but if you're worried about it we'll take a stroll about the grounds for a while until you've composed yourself. That is, of course, if you will trust me to accompany you. Or shall I request that my aunt comes with us?'

She heard the slight smile in his voice, and took a few sips of cordial before she answered.

'That won't be necessary, and I do trust you, Felix. I know you'll behave like a gentleman.'

'So that would seem to put paid to any designs I might have for my own courtship,' he commented, and at her sharp look he spoke quickly.

'I'm teasing, for heaven's sake. You're as tense as a spring, my love. No one's going to hurt you, I promise.'

She accepted his arm, feeling less a sense of danger than one of relief as they moved away from the brilliance of the house and the terraces, and into the shadier parts of the gardens. There was a circular lake stocked with oriental fish that was softly lit around the edges, and a pathway that went all around it with seats at intervals. It was altogether a more relaxing area, and Rosalind began to feel the tension leave her.

Felix kept talking to her as they strolled, and she

knew he was keeping her mind off the upsetting incident with his cousin. She was already feeling foolish over one kiss. . .but the thought of what might have followed could still make her feel faint and sick. . .this man was totally different, she realised. He was being thoughtful and considerate, and, whatever his motive, she was enormously grateful for his consideration.

'Have you been reading any more reports about your famous engineer?' he was asking now.

For a moment she couldn't think what he meant, and then she nodded.

'My father sent me a recent copy of the *Bristol Mirror*,' she said. 'Mr Brunel must be so proud.'

'And rightly so,' Felix agreed. 'I understand that people had such faith in the *Great Western* after her success in the race aross the Atlantic that she sailed home from New York with sixty-eight passengers on board and reached Bristol in fifteen days. But you'll know all about that, of course.'

Rosalind smiled naturally for the first time since the incident with George. She felt heartened to know that Felix took an interest in Mr Brunel's activities as well as herself. It forged an extra link between them, and she felt as warmed as if the two of them participated in Brunel's success.

'I do know. The *Bristol Mirror* reported it all in great detail, especially the excitement of the local people when the ship arrived safely. There was much bell-ringing and flag-waving and general celebrations, fit to rival anything London could offer, I dare say.'

Felix laughed at her enthusiasm, thankful he had found a topic to take her mind off his cousin.

'You're not a Bristolian by any chance, are you, Rosie?'

She smiled ruefully. 'No, I'm not, and you must forgive me if I get carried away sometimes.'

'There's nothing to forgive. It's charming and refreshing to find a young lady who can converse so intelligently. Too many of those inside the Marchmonts' house now, for instance, are completely empty-headed and think no further than the next ball or which gown they'll wear for dinner.'

'Perhaps it's more feminine to think like that,' Rosalind said uneasily.

He squeezed her arm and led her to one of the seats around the lake where they could watch the exotically hued fish, illuminated by the gentle lighting.

'You're the most feminine young woman I've ever met, so don't ever let yourself think otherwise,' he said. 'Why else would I want to marry you?'

Rosalind felt her heart leap.

'Felix, you don't have to go on with this,' she said in a low voice. 'I appreciate your bringing me here and all that you're doing in making me forget what happened on the terrace. But don't forget I know all about your aunt's wishes, and all we agreed to was being civil to one another——'

She was beginning to flounder, and she felt his hand close over hers as it lay in her lap.

'Can't we be friends? It's a far more agreeable word than civil. I'd like to think you looked on me as your friend, Rosie.'

'And so I do,' she said, suddenly choked. Because friendship was so much less than the feelings she had for him, and it seemed to her now that even he was backing away from any plans his aunt might have had for them.

'Then may I be permitted to kiss my friend?'

Rosalind felt her heartbeats quicken again. He was very close to her, and somehow his arm had slipped around her shoulders. The night air was cool but not cold, but through her shimmery gold gown the heat of his body was sending goose-bumps right through her.

Wherever their skin touched, she felt as if she was fired with a magical exciting flame. She was very aware of her situation. Alone with a handsome man who wanted to kiss her. . .it was tantamount to compromising her. . . but the temptation was so great. She had already known his kiss, and he was her friend. . .the decision was already made for her without conscious thinking, and she swayed towards him, unknowingly provocative.

'One kiss, as a friend,' she said huskily.

His arms closed around her, and she was inside the circle of them where she so wanted to be. She could feel the beat of his heart through the jacket of his uniform, as rapid and uneven as her own, and wondered briefly if this was foolishness indeed. . .and then she gave up wondering as she felt the first touch of his mouth on hers, and she all but melted into him, innocently responding with all the fervour of a young girl on the brink of love.

When they broke away, she was aware that Felix was breathing more heavily.

'Dear God, do you have any notion at all what you do to me, Rosalind?' he said, as hoarsely as if the words were forced from him.

In the lighting all around the lake, and the brilliance of the silver moonlight above them, her eyes were large and luminous as she looked into his.

'I do not,' she said tremulously. 'I only know that I feel very strange inside, and that suddenly I don't want this evening to end. I think there must be a kind of magic about this place, Felix.'

He laughed softly.

'The magic is inside you, my darling. And if that's how a kiss from a friend affects you, then you should know how it feels to accept a kiss from a lover.'

She thought she had already done that, on the various occasions he had kissed her before. Each time had been

different. . .and this time was no exception. He pulled
her close to him, and, as if in a dream, she offered no
resistance. The kiss began gently and gathered momen-
tum as she felt his mouth grow more demanding, parting her lips slightly until she could taste the tip of his
tongue against hers. It was an entirely new sensation to
Rosalind, and, far from being frightened or repelled, she
was aware of an intensely erotic pleasure.

The kiss went on and on. She was held tight in her
lover's arms, and time and place ceased to exist. Only
the approach of other people, and the soft murmur of
voices, made her break away from Felix's embrace in
hot embarrassment, knowing how freely she had given
herself to him, and how badly she wanted more of him
. . .and if she had been scarlet-faced before, how much
more so was she now!

'Why, it's young Holden, isn't it? It's good to see you
this evening, Felix. And this is Miss Cranbourne, I
believe, your aunt's delightful young guest?'

She heard the hearty male voice as a group of people
came strolling around the lake towards them. Rosalind
recognised some of the people who had been introduced
to her earlier, and she felt acutely awkward now as
several of the older ladies glanced at one another.
Whatever their reasons, she and Felix were alone by the
lake, and others might not see the situation as innocently
as they themselves did.

'It is indeed, Lord Courtney, and Miss Cranbourne is
also the young lady whom I sincerely hope will consent
to become my wife,' she heard Felix say smoothly, and
she smothered a gasp. 'Although, like most young ladies,
she believes in making a poor gentleman wait on her
decision.'

Rosalind hardly registered the fact that he was talking
to cover her own confusion and indignation. Her whole
body had tensed as he spoke, and she felt his hand

holding hers steadily once more. The small group was exclaiming with delight at having an engagement practically happening under their noses at the Marchmonts' ball, and Rosalind was not so naïve that she didn't recognise how Felix was protecting her reputation.

But she didn't want it to happen like this. Being caught together like this was as good as forcing him into offering for her, or pretending the proposal had already happened. Or had he intended this all along, taking advantage of the situation with his cousin, and bringing her here, where they would be almost sure to be discovered?

All her suspicions were back. She wouldn't be surprised if he had had a wager with Lady Lydia on whether or not he could persuade her to do as his aunt wished, and accept his proposal of marriage. The wildest thoughts spun about in her head again, even while she smiled and accepted premature congratulations from the group of people surrounding them now. Eventually she forced herself to reply to their good wishes, as whimsically as if she was in total control of her senses, which she certainly was not.

'Oh, but please do remember exactly what Captain Holden said! The lady hasn't accepted yet, and nor does she have any intention of doing so until her parents have been consulted. And until then I beg you all not to make any of this public knowledge! It would be very bad form if my parents were the last to know of it. And Lady Lydia would be so upset if the proper etiquette was not observed.'

'And rightly so, my dear young lady,' the very correct Lord Courtney said at once, just as Rosalind had hoped. 'Not that I think your parents could have the slightest objection to your marrying this handsome young fellow, what?'

And why should they, when he was a dashing captain

and so well-connected, and she was merely a shipping man's daughter?

The humiliating thought ran through Rosalind's mind again, and she was every bit as disorientated as when she had left the terrace in such relief with this man. But the slow fury was building up in her now, and when at last the party drifted off, with many promises not to divulge a single word until they saw an announcement in *The Times*, Rosalind turned on Felix explosively.

'I suppose you think that was very clever of you! And I must thank you for your quick thinking in saving my honour. But if you think I would ever consent to marry you, Captain Holden, then you're very much mistaken!'

And, almost bristling with hurt pride and shame, she twisted away from him and hurried back towards the house. She picked up her skirts to move the quicker, and the golden sheen of the costly gown in which she had revelled so much, and this whole golden evening, seemed no more than a mockery to her now.

CHAPTER EIGHT

FELIX caught up with Rosalind long before she had reached the terraces and the small groups of people beginning to mill about outside for a breath of air now that the evening was half over. He caught at her hand and spoke quietly, and no one would have guessed from his manner that she had just thrown his proposal back in his face. Not that he could possibly have expected her to take it seriously, in any case!

'Unless you want to create any further sensations, I suggest we walk casually back to the house together, Rosalind.'

'It's not I who is creating sensations,' she said stormily. 'I did not tell a blatant untruth to Lord Courtney.'

'What else would you have had me do? Let them think we had stolen away for a clandestine tête-à-tête?'

'Isn't that the truth of it?'

He said nothing in answer to that as he walked beside her and she had the grace to feel ashamed.

'I'm sorry. That was uncalled-for. I know you were doing your best to calm me down after your cousin's behaviour.'

'Poor Rosalind,' he said, in a lighter tone. 'Trying to escape the attentions of one cousin, and falling right into the clutches of the other. I suspect that by now you're wishing you'd stayed out of harm's way in the country.'

She turned to look at him, unsure whether or not he was being sarcastic. In the moonlight his profile was devastatingly handsome, and she looked away just as quickly.

'Do I seem such a mouse to you?' she asked, remembering how George had referred to her.

'If you don't know by now how you seem to me, then I've been wasting my breath all this time,' he retorted, and she had to be satisfied with that as a small group of ladies and gentlemen appeared at the long open windows. Lady Lydia was among them.

'So there you are, my dears. I was wondering what had become of you both!' she exclaimed.

'Rosalind felt a little overcome by the heat, so I took her down to the lake to show her the tropical fish, Aunt,' Felix said with accomplished ease.

'Well, it's just as well you didn't linger there for too long, as we're all going in to supper shortly, and Lady Marchmont always sets the most exquisite table you ever saw, Rosalind.'

She was swept up at once in the details of the supper table, and finally escorted into the room by Felix, her aunt, and a sullen-looking Sir George, who had clearly not forgiven either her or his cousin for their earlier behaviour. Just as if *they* had been in the wrong, Rosalind thought indignantly, and then she promptly forgot him as she entered the long supper-room, the tables sparkling with silver and crystal and generously weighted down with dishes from which the gentlemen could help the ladies, discreetly assisted by a team of maids and footmen.

There were tiny meat rolls in aspic and latticework patties containing every kind of meat or fish mixture; there were turkey plates and poultry rolls and succulent game pies; there was cold soup served in individual cups, and individual fruit desserts so that no one needed to be finicky over their eating. Every kind of etiquette was observed, including the absence of cheese, which Rosalind privately adored, though she understood that in the best circles it was considered vulgar to provide cheese at dinner parties and the like, since it could foul the breath and therefore give offence to the ladies present.

She remembered with sudden nostalgia the hearty suppers at home, and her father's delight in the huge round cheeses regularly sent up to him from Somerset. They were eaten with savoury pickled onions and fresh-baked bread spread liberally with butter, and there was none of the finesse to be found here—but nor was there here the simple pleasure of relishing such a meal in front of a roaring wood fire in the cosy parlour at home in the middle of a Sussex winter. . .

'Are you still undecided as to which titbit to choose first, Rosalind?' She heard Felix's voice beside her, and realised she had been gazing into space with the most ridiculous attack of homesickness. She had only been here for a couple of weeks, and yet already it felt like months. She forced a smile.

'I think I am. There's just so much!' she murmured, trying to appear normal, when in truth she had a great urge to be far away from here and to be enjoying simpler pleasures.

By now she knew with certainty that this definitely wasn't the life she would choose to live. Lady Lydia had already taken her to the theatre, and to several little house soirées, and made her as welcome as if she had been her own daughter. But she wasn't the Greville daughter, and, despite all the trimmings, she still didn't fit that mould.

Nor did she really care for the smoke and grime and the undoubted stink of horses that constantly pervaded the entire city—far worse than any country smells—and often caused ladies to put handkerchiefs to their noses whenever they ventured out. And if that made her the little country mouse Sir George Greville considered her to be, then rather a mouse than a lion with a roar and a bite. . .

Rosalind was glad when the evening was finally over, though by then it was well into the early hours of the following morning, and she had danced so much that her feet ached and throbbed. After the inevitable effusive thanks and congratulations to their hosts, and what seemed an interminably long wait to take their final leave as the stream of carriages slowly approached the façade of the house, they were finally seated in their own carriage, and their driver proceeded to take the weary occupants back to whence they had come.

The indefatigable Lady Lydia seemed as wide awake as ever, while George sprawled out and snored in a corner of the carriage in a most unseemly manner. Felix hardly spoke at all, and Rosalind was so tired that she hardly knew how to keep her eyes open, but she felt obliged to answer Lady Lydia, even in little more than monosyllables.

'I must say the three of you look a fine trio,' Lady Lydia said at length in some amusement.

'You forget that you took a nap yesterday afternoon, Aunt, while I suspect the rest of us followed other pursuits,' Felix said.

'Then that was your own folly, dear boy. Anyway, I'm more concerned that Rosalind enjoyed herself. Now tell me, my dear, did it all come up to expectations?'

Rosalind made a valiant effort to put some enthusiasm into her voice.

'It was all wonderful. How can I say otherwise? But I'm sure I shall be able to think more clearly about it tomorrow, when I've had some sleep!'

Lady Lydia laughed. 'You young people have no stamina. Just listen to George now! If it weren't that we're all family here, I would be most offended at that noise.'

Rosalind was too tired to comment that she wasn't 'family', and was unlikely to be. But the word prompted her to think of her own family again, and she knew the tiredness was making her weak. She simply wasn't accustomed to such energetic proceedings as tonight's. . .

'I'd like to visit my aunt again in a few days' time, Lady Lydia. Is that all right?'

'My dear girl, of course it is. You may do whatever you please while you're here.'

But no thoughts of doing whatever she liked would make her agree to Aunt May's earlier suggestion that she should bring her young man to see her the next time she came. She didn't have a young man.

In the middle of the following week she and Margaret made the journey to Paddington once more, where Aunt May greeted her as eagerly as before.

'You've not brought him, then?' she said at once, almost before Rosalind had removed her bonnet and cape.

Rosalind laughed, not pretending to misunderstand.

'There's no one to bring. And if you mean the two gentlemen of the household, then Captain Holden's gone back to his barracks, with all the preparations for the Queen's coronation taking precedence over everything at the moment. And Sir George Greville, who came home in time for the Marchmonts' spring ball, has returned to France again. It seems his lady-friend's family have resumed their holiday, so Sir George has accompanied them.'

'And am I to understand from your voice that you're not altogether sorry about that?'

Rosalind laughd again. 'You see and hear too much, Aunt May,' she said, with real affection for the older woman.

'I have a shrewd idea that you're not too taken with the son of the house, my girl.'

'Not altogether,' Rosalind admitted. 'But I didn't come here to talk about Sir George Greville!'

'Then why did you come?'

'To see you, of course. Aren't you pleased?'

She began to feel uncomfortable. Aunt May was a very direct woman, saying what she pleased and never minding who she offended along the way. And perhaps she saw this second visit as a nuisance after all. . .but the next words reassured her.

'Of course I'm pleased, love. I'm just disappointed that you didn't bring your Captain Holden along. Now tell me what you've been doing in London, and all about the spring ball you were going to attend. I suppose it was all very grand?'

'Far too grand for me,' Rosalind said honestly. 'I didn't realise I was such a home body, Aunt May. I didn't fit in with all those titled people, and when it came to eating supper I was all fingers and thumbs.'

She began to laugh at her own story, finding relief in telling it to someone not brought up to such society living, and realising it was why she had wanted so much to come here. Aunt May was a sort of stepping-stone between the old life and the new, and telling her all the anecdotes was almost as good as telling her parents.

'I miss home so much,' she said finally, looking down at her gloves and trying not to sound too pathetic.

'Well, that's a poor admission from a young and pretty girl!' Aunt May said. 'What will you do when you marry, for heaven's sake? You'll be obliged to leave home then.'

'That's different. That will be my choice, and I'll live wherever I have to because I shall love my husband, and when that happens we'll be starting a new life and family of our own.'

She stopped, knowing that in every fantasy she harboured all those requirements centred on herself and Felix, however much she tried to deny it to herself. He was the only one she wanted, the only one she could ever marry. But only if he wanted her for the right reasons. She swallowed the lump in her throat.

'By the by, Aunt May, I had a letter from my mother a few days ago. She and my father are both well and send you their best love. Mother's delighted at everything I'm telling her about the city.'

'So when is she coming to see it for herself?' her aunt said, well aware at how adroitly Rosalind had changed the conversation.

Rosalind laughed. 'You know how unlikely that is to happen! Mother doesn't like to move far from her own fireside.'

'And she's made you just as insular, hasn't she, my love? I'm thankful your Lady Lydia had the good sense to see what a waste it all was and to let you see that the world doesn't begin and end in Sussex!'

'There's nothing wrong with Sussex, Aunt!' Rosalind said indignantly.

'I never said there was, only that it's just a small part of the country. Your young man obviously realised that. Didn't you say his home is in Yorkshire?'

Rosalind gave up trying to deny that Felix was her young man, knowing it was futile to try and persuade Aunt May otherwise.

'Yes. But his career is in London, or wherever the army takes him. Right now he's very busy with rehearsals for the coronation procession, so I dare say we shan't be seeing too much of him in the next weeks.'

She realised she had managed to divert her aunt's probing questions by mention of the coronation.

'I suppose you know there's a new crown being made especially for the Queen? They say it will cost a thousand pounds. Such expense! But I dare say we can't expect a young girl to carry such a heavy object on her head for hours on end.'

'Lady Lydia was saying something about it,' Rosalind nodded. 'She told me the new crown will contain some historic jewels from earlier times, so I suppose it all needs careful designing and constructing to make it lighter for the young Queen. Felix says that, as well as diamonds and pearls taken from the old imperial crown, the new crown of state will include the Black Prince's ruby and the Stuart sapphire. He also told me a more grisly tale of another sapphire being used, one that was removed from a ring on the finger of Edward the Confessor. It was taken from his tomb, Aunt, in the fourteenth century. When you hear of such things, it seems to put our British heritage into perspective far more personally than learning from dusty history books.'

She gave a small shiver, imagining such a scene, and heard her aunt chuckle.

'My word, but we are becoming well informed, aren't we? Or should I say that your Felix is an admirable reporter?'

'I like to hear these things, if only to relate them all to Mother,' Rosalind said, a little crossly. 'Lady Lydia says that we may go to see the display of the other crown jewels and regalia in the jewel house at the Tower one afternoon. I never imagined such a thing was possible.'

'Well, isn't that just what I've been telling you, child? Your parents have let you stagnate in the country for far too long, when everything of importance happens right here in town!' Aunt May said triumphantly.

'Not everything. You can't pretend that Mr Brunel's ship had anything to do with London!'

But Miss Cranbourne was not as interested in shipping as her niece, even though she was clearly enjoying the repartee between them. It was only interrupted by the maid bringing in the tea and they sipped it companionably until Rosalind decided it was time to take her leave.

'And next time you'll be sure and bring that young man with you,' her aunt said severely. 'I've every right to inspect him, you know.'

'Perhaps,' Rosalind said with a smile. 'But I can't dictate Felix's wishes, Aunt May.'

'Nonsense. A pretty young woman with any sense at all can persuade any young man to do exactly as she wishes. And I never credited a niece of mine with anything less than horse-sense.'

And that would seem to be that. By the time Rosalind left the Paddington house with Margaret, she was in a much better humour than when she'd entered it. She was foolish to let homesickness get the better of her, and she resolved to participate eagerly in all that Lady Lydia planned over the next weeks. Discussing the new crown being made for Queen Victoria, and the reminder of actually viewing the crown jewels, had sparked off a new enthusiasm in her.

Rosalind decided it was all due to Aunt May, who was always like a breath of fresh air. She and Lady Lydia would probably get along very well, she reiterated, despite the gap in their social spheres. Lady Lydia had already suggested that Miss Cranbourne might come to tea one afternoon if she felt well enough, and perhaps Rosalind could persuade Aunt May to put her useful and mysterious ailments aside and come. And perhaps Felix would just happen to be there at the time . . .perhaps.

As soon as she went inside the Hampstead house, her heart missed a beat as she recognised Felix's cap on the hall table. She hadn't expected to see him today, and it was unusual for him to arrive during the middle of the afternoon. She hesitated at the foot of the stairs, a strange kind of premonition invading her bones. On an impulse she removed her bonnet and cape and told Margaret to take them to her bedroom, while she went straight into the drawing-room.

The moment she entered and saw the faces of the two people sitting there, she knew something was very wrong, and moreover that this was something very private and personal in which she had no part.

Form the look on Lady Lydia's ashen face, and Felix's own set expression, and the way he sat with his aunt's two hands clasped inside his own, Rosalind's first surmise was that something had happened to George. The boat taking him and his friends to France had capsized during a rough channel passage. . .there had been a riding accident, or he had been involved in a duel, on which the hot-headed French were so ghoulishly keen. . .

'Has something happened?' she said in a dry little voice, not really wanting to intrude, but hardly able to say nothing at all as the two people both looked up the moment she entered.

Her heart ached at the look of pain etched on Felix's face, and the thought went through her head that, if there had been no love between himself and his cousin, then his obvious affection and loyalty to his aunt was to be commended.

'I'm afraid we have to go to Yorkshire immediately, my dear,' Lady Lydia said, startling Rosalind by the announcement.

She looked at the two of them in some bewilderment as Felix rose politely, though such formality seemed of little importance at the moment.

'I've received word that my father has died from a seizure,' Felix said in a clipped voice. 'The funeral will take place s soon as I can conveniently get to Yorkshire. I've been given a maximum of two weeks' leave, which

is virtually stretching it to the limits in view of my
military duties at this time. Unfortunately, my cousin
cannot be contacted at present, so he'll be unable to
attend, but, as she's just indicated, my aunt is determined to accompany me.'

The abruptness of the statements almost took
Rosalind's breath away. The news was totally unexpected, but as she recovered herself she could see that it
had affected Felix badly, perhaps more badly than he
himself would have predicted. Blood was blood after all,
even though the two Holden men had parted on bad
terms. Any chance of a reconciliation now was gone forever.

Her eyes filled with sympathetic tears, and without
thinking she put a hand on Felix's arm, feeling how
rigid it was. She longed to comfort him, but it wasn't
her place, and from the way he was obviously controlling
his emotions he wanted no show of sympathy. Nevertheless, she couldn't stand there and say nothing when her
heart was overwhelmed with sadness for him.

'I'm so sorry, Felix,' she said quietly. 'So desperately
sorry——'

He turned away, his voice quite harsh now. 'Yes. It
couldn't have come at a worse time. But then, my father
always did have the most appalling sense of timing.'

He walked away from her, excusing himself to his
aunt and leaving the two women in the room. Rosalind
stared at the door as if willing him to appear again. Not
the pain-filled and almost angry Felix who had just
walked away, but the carefree, teasing man she loved. . .

'I'm afraid this news has shaken Felix rather
badly, Rosalind,' she heard Lady Lydia say gently.
'One doesn't like to speak ill of the dead, but my
brother-in-law always had a rather fiery temper, and
although he and Felix didn't always enjoy the best of
relationships——'

'I do know the circumstances, Lady Lydia,' she broke in, seeing the lady didn't really care for revealing too much family detail. 'Felix has already told me about their parting, which is why I'm rather surprised at his attitude now. I would have thought he'd take it more stoically.'

She felt her face go hot, realising she implied that Felix was reacting less like a man than he should, and no one knew better than she that he was a man of stature and pride.

'I'm sorry—I didn't mean that the way it may have sounded——' she stammered.

'It's all right, my dear, we're all thrown sideways at the moment,' Lady Lydia said. 'But I must tell you we intend to set out for Yorkshire as soon as we're ready. It will take several days of travelling to get there, and it will be necessary to stay at lodging-houses overnight. The question is, what are we going to do with you?'

'With me?' Rosalind asked stupidly. Until that moment, she hadn't thought of her own position at all. All her thoughts were with Felix, and the way he was reacting to the news of his father's death.

'You may stay here, naturally, and the servants will take every care of you, but I suggest if you do that you ask your aunt to come and stay while we're away, dear. Or you may prefer to stay with her. I don't want you to think that you must go home, Rosalind. When we return, our social visits will be curtailed a little, since we'll be officially in mourning, but Felix's father was never close to us, and I don't see the necessity of completely shutting ourselves away. Besides which, you've come to see the coronation, and so you shall. Felix will be obliged to return to his duties, anyway. There's almost a month before the great day, and we'll all be sufficiently recovered by then.'

Rosalind already knew there was no great love lost

between Lady Lydia and her deceased brother-in-law. But certain proprieties still had to be observed, at least while they were in Yorkshire. Rosalind realised the situation was admittedly made easier by the gentleman having lived so far away. Doubtless few, if any, of their London acquaintances had even heard of him.

'So the question remains, Rosalind,' Lady Lydia repeated, 'what are we going to do with you? I leave it entirely up to you, my dear.'

She didn't even have to think about it. 'Would it be very presumptuous of me to ask if I may accompany you, Lady Lydia? You've made me feel so welcome here, and I feel so much a part of your family now. If I can be of any help at all——'

'But my dear, a funeral is hardly a happy ocasion!'

'I would be even more miserable staying here alone, and thinking about you both, and I've already told you of my aunt's oddities. She wouldn't come here to stay, and my mother considers her too ailing to care for me,' she elaborated slightly. 'Besides which, I've never seen Yorkshire, and forgive me if that sounds callous, since this is hardly the best of circumstances——'

She was floundering, saying all the wrong things, when all she really wanted to say was that she couldn't bear to see Felix go away with that tight unhappy look on his face. She wanted to be near him, whatever the circumstances, and however difficult the next few weeks might be.

'Then if that is what you want, I agree most readily,' Lady Lydia said. 'Your company will relieve some of the gloom of the journey, since Felix hardly knows what mood to adopt, and I fear he will not be an easy travelling companion. We must both be prepared for that. So if that's settled, I suggest we get ready with all speed. My maid is already packing for me, so you should instruct yours to do the same. Naturally, there's no need for you to wear full mourning clothes.'

By the time Rosalind reached her room, Margaret already knew what had happened. Servants' gossip always spread very quickly.

'I'm going to Yorkshire, Margaret, and I'm sure you may come too if you wish.'

'I'd prefer to stay here unless you really need me, Miss Rosie. I don't care for funerals.'

Rosalind smiled faintly. 'I'm not fond of them myself, but I feel I must go. Very well, you can stay here. Lady Lydia will be taking her personal maid, and she can help me with anything I need. But won't you be very bored?'

Margaret said that she would not, her face already hidden as she rummaged in drawers for underclothes and gloves, trying to think of the most suitable clothes in Rosalind's wardrobe for a young lady accompanying friends in mourning. Rosalind was thankful she would not be required to wear full mourning, being not personally involved, for she was simply unprepared for such an emergency. She had a demure grey gown with matching cloak and bonnet, a deep blue and a bronze-coloured outfit. All had interchanging neck-pieces and cuffs to save on the laundering, and they must suffice. As an afterthought, she packed her riding habit and boots, in case there should be any opportunity for seeing the moors and countryside.

She kept her mind on her clothes, since it was far more comfortable than trying to judge Felix's feelings. He had seemed weighed down with a grief he couldn't express, and she guessed he'd be filled with remorse at not making his peace with his father while he had the chance. But she couldn't be sure, since each time he had previously spoken to her about his father it had always been with anger and never with love.

She wondered what would happen to the family business now. Felix had made it clear it was of no interest to him. She presumed it would be sold, leaving Felix free to follow his military career with no further heart-searching.

'How long do you expect to be away, Miss Rosie?' Margaret asked now.

'I'm not sure, but no longer than necessary, because of Captain Holden's duties. After the funeral I presume there will be the will-reading, since Captain Holden's father was a man of substance, and then I should think we'd return as soon as possible. A total of ten days to two weeks in all, I dare say.'

'That will leave barely two weeks before the coronation. Pardon me for mentioning such a thing at this time, but will it be all right for me to join the house servants for watching the processions and all? Bertram and Lizzie and some of the others are putting together to rent a hire-carriage for the day so we can go there in style. Me and Lizzie thought we might hire a couple of posh hats from a second-hand shop too, so we can look like real toffs. While you're away, we could take a bit of time finding out about it——'

'Of course it's all right,' Rosalind said vaguely, irritated by such eagerness, and unable to give her mind to such frivolity right now.

It all seemed so small, even the coronation of a Queen, compared with a man's dying. A man who had once been forceful and dominant in a family's life, and would soon be reduced to dust and ashes. She shivered.

'Have you got those boxes ready yet?' she said shortly to Margaret. 'I'm just going to write a note to my parents telling them what's happened, and another one to Aunt May. You may see that the first one is sent off as quickly as possible, and deliver the other one yourself.'

She hoped her parents wouldn't think it very odd that she should want to go off to the wilds of Yorkshire for a funeral that was no concern of hers. It was certainly a strange way to take part in a season in London. But if the unknown paternal Holden was of no concern to her, then his son certainly was, and that changed everything. If Felix grieved, then so did she. It was as simple as that. And if that wasn't love. . .

'There's really no need for you to go through this,' Felix said, as the largest of the Greville carriages began its long journey to Yorkshire late that afternoon, the horses and carriage lamps already adorned with black crape ribbons to show that the occupants were in mourning.

'But I wanted to come, and I hope you're not angry at my being here,' Rosalind answered, wondering if this strange taut man seated opposite her could really have held her in his arms and kissed her so passionately. He was as remote as the stars now, wrapped up inside himself, and clearly wanting no intrusion into his feelings. Perhaps he thought her very presence was an intrusion. All Rosalind's finer feelings at being a comfort and helpmeet were fast disappearing.

Every time she looked into Felix's once warm dark eyes, it was as if she met a granite wall of resistance. Perhaps he was regretting having ever told her so much about himself, she thought. He knew that she was aware of all his love for his mother, and his fury when his father had virtually turned him away from his heritage. It hurt a man's pride to know that so much of his inner self was exposed, and right now he would be feeling especially vulnerable. Not that anyone would have guessed it. . . Rosalind turned her gaze away from him, not wanting to see that cold, blank expression any longer.

He shrugged as if to indicate how little he cared

whether Rosalind Cranbourne was there or not. Rosalind tried not to feel snubbed, and gazed through the carriage windows, already fairly obscured by the film of dust stirred up by the horses' hoofs.

'You must excuse Felix at this time, Rosalind,' Lady Lydia said in a low voice, though Felix could perfectly well hear all that was being said. 'A person goes through all kinds of distress when someone close to him dies, and does not always say exactly what he means.'

'I understand,' Rosalind murmured, though in truth she didn't understand at all, never having faced death before. The fact suddenly struck her, frightening her with the realisation of the mortality among everyone she loved. Her parents, Aunt May, Lady Lydia, friends and acquaintances in Sussex, Felix——

'How can you possibly understand? You're only a child, with no experience of the world,' Felix's harsh voice cut across her thoughts, sending the hot colour up from her neck to the roots of her hair.

'Really, Felix, that was hardly necessary,' his aunt remonstrated, finding this a little too much to allow.

'No—Felix is quite right,' Rosalind said quickly. 'I don't have any experience of the world at all, and, the more I see of it, the more I realise the truth of that. It's patronising of me to think I can understand anyone's feelings at a time like this, because I obviously can't.'

And if she thought such a statement would bring an apology or a softening from Felix, she was mistaken. He sat stony-faced for much of the first part of the journey north, and it was left to Lady Lydia to make polite conversation and point out to Rosalind the various parts of the country they were driving through. Personally, Rosalind would rather have curled up in a corner and slept the journey away. At least then she wouldn't have had to be constantly aware of Felix's unhappy face.

CHAPTER NINE

IT WAS an interminably long way to Yorkshire. Even allowing for the frequent stops for refreshment and watering the horses, and the obligatory overnight stops, they finally emerged stiff and aching from the carriage three days later. By then, Rosalind had gleaned a little more information about the Holden household from Lady Lydia.

'My sister was as headstrong as yourself, my dear,' she had said, in the sort of regretful tone that made Rosalind unable to decide whether this was complimentary or not. 'She truly loved Felix's father, and simply refused to heed any family opposition when he took her off to live in the north of England.'

'But if she loved him so much. . .' Rosalind ventured.

'Oh, yes, it was a true love match on both sides,' Lydia said generously. 'There was never any doubt of that. But to be content to be the wife of a mill owner, when she could have had all of London at her feet, to say nothing of the pick of its handsome young men!'

Lady Lydia shook her head slightly, clearly still incredulous that her sister could have done such a thing, even after all these years.

'Did you ever visit her?'

'Several times, but not with any great joy for the surroundings, my dear. The country has a peculiar smell that I don't find altogether palatable.'

It was called fresh air, Rosalind thought with mild humour, though this wasn't the time for such jocularity. But having now spent a few weeks in London, and

145

experienced some of its rankness, she realised how she herself welcomed the chance to breathe clean air again.

There was something far healthier, too, in the knowledge that horses riding freely over moors and downs left their marks far less noticeably than in the confines of city streets, where steaming excrement lay where it dropped until it was ground into the cobbles by the next passing carriage. . .

'And what is the house like?' she said quickly now to Lady Lydia. 'It must be fairly grand, I suppose.'

'Well, certainly the mill workers would think so,' Lydia conceded ambiguously. 'It's about the size of your own father's house, my dear, run by a housekeeper and cook and several maids, who I dare say will be scuttling about by now making things comfortable for our arrival.'

Come war or famine or drought, Rosalind thought fleetingly, Lady Lydia was the kind of English noblewoman who would always expect a battery of servants to be making things comfortable for her arrival, and see nothing untoward in the fact. . .

'Felix must long to see it again,' she said softly, transferring her own thoughts of home to his. 'Even though the homecoming will be such a sad one.'

'You mustn't think he doesn't care, Rosalind,' Lydia said, in the awkward little silence.

It was difficult to know exactly how Felix did feel at present. He gave little away, except for the sense of anger.

'I know everyone has to deal with grief in thir own way,' Rosalind answered. 'One has to make allowances.'

Except that such a patronising comment was the very last thing a proud man like Felix Holden would wish to hear. It made those who wished to help the most most helpless.

The last stretch of the journey was begun early in the morning, in order to reach the house before midday.

They were already on the southern edge of Yorkshire, Felix informed them, when they peered through the windows of the carriage, well insulated with rugs on the chilly morning. It wasn't even properly light yet, and there was little to be seen except a great wave of morning fog that seemed to drift across the landscape like a ghostly blanket.

'You'll get used to this,' he commented. 'The moors are frequently hidden in fog until the sun gets up, and then the hills and dales are transformed into scenes of wild beauty, especially when they're covered in purple heather and the glorious yellow furze.'

His aunt gave a short laugh, not at all happy at being forced to travel so early in the day.

'Well, how anyone can find beauty in those barren places is beyond me! You're letting sentiment take the place of common sense, dear boy. Nothing grows on the moors, except the paltry heather of which you speak, which isn't a real plant at all, but a weed, and that dreadful furze has little but prickles to recommend it. . .'

'You see that my aunt is not enamoured of our moors,' Felix said to Rosalind with a small smile, and she realised that it was the first time he had relaxed at all on the journey, although she guessed that it wouldn't last. The real ordeal was still ahead, but the sight and scent of his birthplace was undoubtedly having its own effect on him.

'But I am,' she said softly. 'I know I can't see it properly yet, but we have morning fog on the Sussex Downs too, and if I tried very hard I could almost imagine I was at home.'

And if that was upsetting anybody, it was too late to worry about it. But the other two seemed far too lost in their own thoughts to notice it.

'Is it much further?' she ventured to say at length.

'The house and mill are near to Halifax, Rosalind,'

Felix said, 'though I don't suppose the name means much to you.'

'I'm afraid it means nothing at all,' she said apologetically, though quite unable to see what significance it was meant to have.

'It's easy to see you're not a Yorkshirewoman. The cloth trade in Halifax goes back to the fifteenth century, and there's many a moorland man who's been glad of work in the mills there.'

'I see. So you don't live right on the moors, then?' She didn't know whether to be glad or sorry. Living within sight and sound of wild moors was far preferable to a town. She surmised that it wouldn't be as exciting or as crowded and dirty as London, but a town all the same.

'Wait and see,' was all Felix would say right then. She turned to look through the window and caught her breath. In minutes, it seemed, the sun had come up with a gold and orange glory, and the fog had dispersed as if controlled by a magic hand. And all around them was green and gold, purple and bronze, as moor and scrubland was revealed in all its wild majesty.

'Oh!' she breathed. 'How beautiful it all is.'

'Then I win the wager I had with myself, Rosie. I deduced that you'd find it more agreeable than town.'

His retort was softened by the fact that he had called her Rosie once more. In the past few days it seemed he had forgotten all but the need to be hard, to remain angry, as if some invisible force inside him was decreeing it. Some demon that wouldn't let him be.

She heard Lady Lydia give a short laugh.

'I despair of the two of you. Nature's all very well, my dears, but I would be bored out of my wits if I thought I had to remain up here any longer than was absolutely necessary.'

'I promise you that won't happen, Aunt. As soon as

the formalities are over, we'll be heading straight back to London. I can't say I'll have any real wish to linger.'

Though it was't her place to say so, Rosalind was angry with Lady Lydia for breaking the spell, and even more so for reminding Felix of why they were here, and putting the remote expression back into his voice again. Not that he ever forgot, she guessed, but for a few minutes he'd been almost human again, instead of the mechanical being he'd seemed to become.

And then, after another several hours' travelling, when the moorland had given way to more fertile hills and hollows where sheep roamed, and the tracts of green were broken up by many acres of low stone walls, Felix called to the driver to stop the carriage, and he held out his hand to Rosalind.

'I want you to see this properly,' he said, and he helped her to alight. She flexed her shoulders a moment and smoothed down her skirt, and then she looked down to where he pointed.

There was a wide valley below the road along which they travelled. There was a large village community below, almost with the status of a small town, Rosalind thought. Scattered cottages and farm buildings filled one end of the valley, and groups of small cottages clustered together in higgledy-piggledy confusion at the other. There was a church and churchyard just visible, and a larger building than most with a wide yard outside that was undoubtedly an inn.

But the whole scene was dominated by a very large brick-built building, right in the centre of the valley. In one respect Rosalind thought it the ugliest building imaginable, spoiling what looked an idyllic spot. But from its many windows and chimneys it was a building of obvious importance. It undoubtedly gave employment to most of the people in the valley and perhaps beyond, evident from the white-painted message across its roof, bold enough for all who travelled this road to see.

'Holden's Cloth Mill,' Rosalind read out slowly. 'My goodness, I had no idea it would be so large.' She hardly knew what else to say. Did one praise such an ugly building that presumably gave a living to a good many people?

'Brash, wouldn't you say?' Felix said harshly. 'But then, my father was a brash man. He had the name blazoned on the roof after his own father passed on. He was nobbut a plain-speaking Yorkshireman, as they say around here, but as fair-minded an employer as you could meet. He made good cloth and he prospered because of it. He was a benefactor to the workers he employed, too, paying them a sick benefit out of his own pocket when necessary—as long as they were honestly sick. He believed in honesty in his dealings, and in the honest advertising of his mill, and if folk didn't like it——'

'Dear heaven, Felix, but you're sounding more like your father by the minute!' his aunt said, having descended from the carriage herself now, with the driver's assistance and that of her personal maid, seated ouside for the journey alongside Danvers. 'You should save your words for your eulogy, my dear.'

'I haven't decided yet on whether or not I'll speak one,' he retorted.

'I think you must,' Lydia said quietly. 'The preacher and the mill workers will expect it.'

'Will they? I should think Harry Keeley would be in a much better position to give a eulogy to my father. The two of them were always hand in glove.'

'Who is Harry Keeley?' Rosalind said, wondering at the sudden bitterness in his voice.

'The mill overseer,' he said briefly. And at his aunt's murmured protest he shrugged and went on quickly,

'Oh, I don't mean to criticise the man. He's the best in the West Riding, and we were good friends when we were lads.'

Rosalind felt as if she could read the rest of the unspoken words. It wasn't this Harry Keeley whom Felix disliked. It was the rapport between the mill overseer and Felix's father that rankled. The rapport that should have belonged between themselves. . .

'And where is your house?' she went on, searching the valley for anything that seemed remotely as large as her own, as Lydia had described it.

'We have to go a bit further yet before we reach Radley Grange,' Felix said. 'You don't have the owner's house in sight of the mill, lass. We do have a bit of class!'

He was making an effort to speak lightly now, and deliberately exaggerating his flat accent, and as they climbed back into the carriage Rosalind could feel the tension in his handclasp. And, whatever he said or did, she knew she was going to forgive him everything.

'Will you be going to the mill while you're here?' she asked curiously.

'Oh, aye, it will be expected,' he said.

'Can I come with you?'

'Now, why on earth would you want to do such a thing, Rosalind?' Lady Lydia exclaimed. 'A mill is no place for a well-bred young lady. I'm told they're hot and dirty places, so noisy with the clatter of machinery that you can't hear yourself think, and so dusty with the wool that it will give you a headache for a week!'

'Can I come with you?' Rosalind repeated to Felix, as if Lydia had never spoken.

'If you wish,' he said.

The carriage was continuing along the road above the village, and he looked fixedly into her eyes for a moment. Her heart was beating fast, and she wondered if she had reached him at last by this sudden wish to enter his world—at least, the world he had once known so well—but then he looked away, and the moment was gone.

Rosalind turned away too, with a feeling of acute despair in her soul. Of course, he could hardly be expected to think of love at a time like this, but she had come here with the half-hearted hope that her love could be of comfort to him. Instead, he was wrapped up in himself, apparently not wanting comfort from anyone at all, and least of all her.

They turned slightly away from the valley before Felix gave final directions to their driver, and the carriage began the long descent into another hollow, where an impressive house stood in its own extensive grounds on the side of the hill. Just as Lady Lydia had said, it was about the same proportions as Rosalind's own home, but this house was made of grey Yorkshire stone, weathered into an austere dark colour, and surrounded by considerably less than well-tended gardens. There were outhouses and stables visible, but the slate roofs gleaming in the sunlight seemed to Rosalind to be the only welcoming signs about it.

'Radley Grange,' Felix said abruptly. 'I regret that you won't find it as luxurious as my aunt's home——'

'I haven't come to Yorkshire in the pursuit of luxury,' she was stung into replying. 'Nor am I accustomed to it, as you very rightly know.'

'Of course, I should have remembered,' he said, 'and I apologise for my mouth overtaking my thoughts. My tongue seems to run away with me these days.'

'It doesn't matter,' she muttered, knowing that it did.

She was beginning to hate his brittleness, and the way he couldn't seem to shake himself out of it. She hadn't expected this reaction to his father's death at all, and she prayed that it wouldn't be a long-lasting one.

'Now, then, Felix, let's all try to brighten up, shall we?' Lydia said briskly.

'Yes, Aunt,' he said, as dutiful as a child, and then he gave her the glimmer of a smile. 'I'm sorry, but this is not easy for me, and I know I'm being unfair in taking things out on you.'

'My shoulders are broad enough, but I don't know if Rosalind's are,' she said.

Before he could retort that Rosalind hadn't had to come, she mumbled a reply. 'Don't worry about me. I'll survive.'

There was also a huge temptation to say that her own shoulders were also broad enough for Felix to lay his head on, if he wished it. . .but, since he clearly didn't, she could never demean herself in that way.

They were nearing the house now, and there were signs of life in it. The day was warm, but it was an overcoat cooler in Yorkshire than in London, Rosalind thought, as they finally stepped outside the carriage. And Lydia had told her the evenings could be quite cold, even in summer. But she was eager to see this house where Felix had been born, and had spent his childhood; to sleep in a room where he might once have slept, and breathe in the aura of a house that must once have known great happiness as well as sadness. . .after all, it was where his mother had come as a bride. . .

For a moment she tried to see Radley Grange as Lydia's sister must have seen it for the first time, coming from the undoubted luxury of a pampered city childhood, and a coming-out season as the daughter of a titled man. If Felix's mother could forget all that for the man she loved, then that was humbling indeed. This house wouldn't be such a shock to Rosalind herself, with no such pretentious beginnings in life. . .nor such a future of ever becoming the mistress of Radley Grange, since Felix was eager to get back to London as quickly as possible and resume the life he had chosen.

She felt a swift regret for his mother, wishing she could have known her. Somehow she was sure that the lady would have wanted Felix to return here, to continue what his father and grandfather had begun, the dynasty of Holden's Cloth Mill. . .

'Are you intending to stand dreaming all day, Rosalind, or are you coming inside?' she heard Lydia say, and from the tone of her voice she guessed it wasn't the first time of asking.

She felt herself redden. 'I'm sorry. I was just——'

'I know. It's a miserable building, isn't it?' Lydia said in a low voice, while Felix was instructing Danvers where to stable the horse and carriage and find his quarters. 'It's hard for we southerners to find anything attractive to say about these places, but it's hospitable enough inside, and the people are welcoming enough, you'll see.'

'Oh, but I wasn't meaning anything like that at all——'

It was too late to try and explain what she did mean. Lady Lydia was already mounting the steps to the front door, and Felix was hurrying back to join them.

'The servants can deal with the baggage later. We'll get inside and have a drink. My throat's parched from the road, and I'm sure you're both feeling the same.'

He inserted an enormous key into the front door, and almost immediately a stout, black-clad woman came towards him, her arms outstretched. Without a word, Felix took her in his arms, and then spoke softly as he put her aside.

'Now, then, Mrs Renton, don't start piping your eyes the minute I get inside the house. There'll be time enough for all that when we bury him.'

''Tis just that I'm right glad to see you, Master Felix.

Mr Anstey and Mr Holroyd have been organising things as best they could, but all us hands were tied until you came home!'

Rosalind heard the strange dialect and the strange way of talking with something like dismay, finding much of it hard to follow.

'Well, I'm home now, so there's nothing more to worry about——'

'Ah, but there is, lad! There's the food to prepare for the day—when we know what day 'tis going to be—and to know how many to cater for an' all, and Molly's in the kitchen fretting her cobs off, if you'll pardon the language, my lady——'

Rosalind got the gist of this, and tried hard not to smile. Despite the strangeness of the speech and idioms, the general ambience of the household was suddenly almost like home. She presumed Molly to be the cook, who would be all of a fluster right now, with guests arriving, and a funeral tea to arrange. . .

'Now calm down, Rennie,' Felix said, using what Rosalind presumed was an old affectionate name. 'Just show the ladies to their rooms and then send someone along to the villge to inform the preacher and lawyer that I'm home and that they may call on me at their earliest convenience. Then organise a nice cup of tea for us all, there's a good lass, and everything will begin to look a lot brighter.'

'It already looks that way round, now that you're here, Master Felix,' the woman said with the ghost of a smile.

Rosalind glanced at him. The assumption was clearly there that she thought he was here to stay. Even Felix himself had referred to this place as *home*, she remembered. But it was only a slip of the tongue, and she guessed there would be many more concerned faces once Felix's wishes were known. Because if the mill was sold, presumably Radley Grange and its assets would be sold as well. Felix would want the slate wiped quite clean. The thought filled Rosalind with an extraordinary sadness. This house breathed an atmosphere of continuity in the generations, and Felix was willingly choking the life out of it all.

She shook herself out of her fanciful musings as Mrs Renton herself led the way up the stairs to the homely bedrooms. There was none of London's elegance here, just good clean wholesome living, but it warmed Rosalind's heart all the same as she thanked the housekeeper.

'You'll mebbe be the one to bring him home, lass,' she said bluntly, at which Rosalind felt herself redden.

'I'm just a friend of the family, Mrs Renton,' she said, at the frank appraisal from the old eyes. 'I felt I should accompany Lady Lydia, since I was staying with her in London.'

'Aye. Well, when you've sorted yourself, come down to the parlour and have a brew. Tea will be mashing nicely by now.'

Rosalind sat down on the bed after she'd gone, trying to make sense of her words. This was the strangest homecoming for Felix, and an awkward time for visitors to be in the house. The servants would all be in mourning, and it was clear that Mrs Renton had a great fondness and loyalty to the family.

As soon as a servant brought up her boxes, she unpacked her things herself, and quickly found her way downstairs again. It was odd, but she almost felt she knew this house already. As Lady Lydia had said, it was similar in size to her own. . .but there was more to it than that. The very feel of the house was similar to Rosalind's own. She was always susceptible to atmosphere, and this was a friendly house, and not at all as cold and dour as its outward appearance. This was a house that had known a lot of love over the years, even if some of that love had grown sour and sad.

Lady Lydia had not yet come downstairs, but Felix was already in the parlour. He stood at the window, staring out, and after a few hesitant minutes, when he didn't even turn round, she moved quietly to stand beside him. She tried to see what he saw, and knew that she failed completely. How could she possibly see down the years, which was obviously where Felix was looking now?

'Has it changed very much?' she asked.

'Nothing changes here. Not the people, or the attitudes, or the air itself. The moors will be as ruthless as ever in winter, and are just as enchanting in summer.'

'And you love it just as much as ever,' she went on softly. He made an impatient gesture.

'I never said I didn't love it! Yorkshire's in my blood and always will be. That doesn't mean that old traditions must be clung to like some nursemaid's apron, does it?'

'It depends on the traditions. You say Yorkshire's in your blood and I don't doubt it, but your father's trade obviously wasn't. Personally I can't ever imagine wanting to leave this place, where the air's so fresh and clean, and there seems so much more sky than there is in London. But not everyone can be a wool man, Felix, and there's no shame in that.'

'I find no shame in anything I've done,' he said shortly, and she knew she'd chosen the wrong words again. He was so brittle at the moment, and it was so easy to offend him.

'I didn't mean that, and I'm sure you know it. I just mean that we all have to follow our hearts, wherever they may lead us. And if your destiny is in wearing the Queen's uniform, then you're right not to question it.'

'Even if it was destined that I should follow in my father's and my grandfather's footsteps?'

'But that was their choice, not yours,' Rosalind said.

She didn't quite know why she was trying so hard to underline his confidence in the the path he himself had chosen, when, if things were different, she would be proud and joyful at becoming the bride of a Yorkshire mill owner. But things were not different, and unlikely to be. The military man with such patriotic leanings would always control his own destiny, and who was she to despise him for that?

'You have a rare intelligence, Rosie, for——'

'For a young lady brought up in the depths of the country?' she finished with a half-smile as he paused.

'I was going to say for one of my aunt's protégées,' he actually manged to smile back. 'Some of them have been witless indeed, but that can never apply to you, my dear.'

'Well, thank you for that,' she said huskily, finding the strange compliment more moving than anything more flowery he might have uttered.

Mrs Renton arrived with the tea, and Lady Lydia appeared at the same time, and the mood was broken.

'One of the lads has gone to the village, and I dare say the preacher and Mr Holroyd will be here directly. They wanted to see you the minute you arrived,' she informed Felix.

'Thank you, Rennie. Show them in as soon as they get here, please.'

The three of them made small talk while they drank the tea and ate the spicy scones made with little hard currants inside them. It was hard to think of anything now but the reason they were here, and why the two gentlemen concerned were coming to see Felix.

'You'd prefer it if I left when your visitors come, I expect, Felix?' she asked.

'On the contrary. I'd much prefer it if you and Aunt Lydia would stay. I can't be doing with long faces and hints as to my filial duty. And there's nothing that's to be said that the two of you can't hear.'

'Then just you behave yourself, my love,' Lady Lydia said, to Rosalind's surprise. 'Remember the respect that's always been shown to your father in this community, and put personal values aside when you listen to the tributes paid to him.'

'I can hardly think of my father in any way other than personally,' Felix said shortly. 'Nor can I forget how he banished me from this house and the circumstances of my last visit here.'

Until that moment Rosalind had completely forgotten that it would have been when his mother died. This must be a doubly painful time for him now, with the inevitable vivid memories of that time. Her heart ached anew for him.

'Nevertheless,' Lydia went on steadily, 'the people in this valley loved and respected him, and so did your mother.'

'I know that, and, before you tell me things I already knew, I'm well aware of how much he loved her too. It's the one vindicating fact in his existence as far as I'm concerned.'

Rosalind was very thankful when the sound of hoof-beats and carriage wheels told of visitors arriving. This conversation was becoming all too highly charged, and she had the feeling that something in Felix was going to explode very soon if Lady Lydia didn't stop needling him. Maybe she did it for his own good, but in Rosalind's opinion it certainly wasn't the right way to go about things.

The two gentlemen were ushered into the room, having arrived at virtually the same moment. The Holden affairs were obviously attended to with alacrity,

Rosalind noted. The gentlemen were already acquainted with Lady Lydia, having met her on the occasion of her sister's death, and both were introduced briefly to Rosalind before turning to Felix to continue with their condolences.

'Now then, my dear sir,' William Anstey, preacher of the parish, said in a suitably mournful voice, 'you'll want to see your father, naturally, and the small chapel will be open for your convenience all this evening. I suggest that the burial takes place tomorrow afternoon. For obvious reasons, it should not be delayed for much longer.'

'Tomorrow afternoon will be quite convenient,' Felix almost snapped. 'It will give me time to go to the mill later today to give the workers the day off to attend. I presume they will want to do so.'

'Oh, most assuredly, Captain Holden.' Anstey looked shocked at the thought that they would not. It was the custom, after all, and the villagers and workers would make up most of the congregation. If it was left to relatives, the attendance would be pitifully poor, he couldn't help thinking.

The lawyer cleared his throat. More smartly dressed than the country preacher, he exuded an air of affluence and his brisk way of talking added to the illusion.

'If I may also suggest that tomorrow evening would be a convenient time for the will-reading as well, sir? I don't know what your movements will be, but I presume you'll need to get back to London to attend to various affairs before deciding on your future?'

Felix looked at him coldly, and Rosalind could see he didn't care for the man.

'My future was settled a long time ago, Mr Holroyd, but you're quite right about my wanting to return to London as soon as possible. The day after tomorrow, my aunt and Miss Cranbourne and myself will begin the return journey. You'll no doubt have heard of the sovereign's coronation, and my duties require me in London.' He positively oozed sarcasm, and Rosalind felt embarrassed on the lawyer's account at that point.

'May we not spend one more day, Felix?' she heard herself say nervously. 'It's such a beautiful part of the world.'

The other four looked at her, and she blushed deeply. What on earth had prompted her to speak up? This was not a visit for sightseeing, and she sounded as shallow and heartless as one of Lady Lydia's so-called protégées. Which was exactly what she was, she thought miserably. . .

'We must do as Felix wishes, Rosalind,' Lady Lydia said gently.

'Of course. I'm sorry.'

The preacher began talking about arrangements then, and Rosalind simply closed her ears to it all. She didn't want to hear about coffins and laying-out and headstones. Death frightened her. She'd never even thought about it before, and here she was in the middle of it. Why on earth had she come? Even as she thought it, she was ashamed of her own weakness, and had to bite her lips to stop them from trembling.

It was a great relief when the gentlemen went away at last, and she mumbled an apology to Felix for intervening as she had done. To her surprise he threw her a look that was far less hostile than of late.

'Don't apologise, Rosie. I'm the one who should be doing that for taking out my aggression on you and Aunt Lydia. And since all the business will be taken care of tomorrow, I see no reason why we shouldn't spend one more day up here. You wanted to see the mill, and I'll show you all the places I knew as a child. Why not? There are no ghosts for me to fear any more, so we'll have that one more day,.'

But, although he spoke carelessly enough, to Rosalind his speech was fraught with hidden undercurrents. No ghosts for him to fear, indeed. She sensed with a new perception that the ghosts were all in his heart, and that what he really feared was the tug of his own heritage.

CHAPTER TEN

FELIX was gone for a long time that evening. After dinner Rosalind and Lydia sat in the parlour and played every kind of card game until they tired of them all. Rosalind found it hard to concentrate, wondering just what feelings were going through Felix's mind right now. He would have gone to the chapel of rest to see his father, as the preacher had practically ordered him to do. And in doing so he would be retracing the steps of childhood and painful adolescence, and stirring up all the memories he was trying so hard to smother.

That was the thing about memories. Good or bad, you couldn't ever be rid of them. They could always catch you out. Just when you most wanted to forget, up they would come, sometimes crystal-clear, sometimes hazy as a water-colour dream, to remind you. . .

'I think we've both had enough for one evening, Rosalind,' Lydia declared at last. 'Neither of us is finding any satisfaction in the cards, and I think an early night would be a good idea. It's to be hoped these beds are more comfortable than those of the lodging-houses.'

'I'm sure they will be,' Rosalind murmured, still caught up in her thoughts of Felix, and wishing she had the power to comfort him. Instead of which, she felt so helpless. . .she felt Lady Lydia pat her hand, and realised her face must have been very transparent at that moment.

'Felix must come to terms with himself, my dear, and all the rest of us can do is be patient,' she said quietly.

'Bereavement takes its own time and won't be hurried. You'll learn that in due course.'

Rosalind wished she hadn't used that particular phrase, reminding her that she too must inevitably face the fact of losing beloved parents. She shivered, feeling the coldness seep into her very bones.

'I don't feel very much like sleeping yet,' she said. 'Would it be all right if I stayed down here awhile and wrote to my mother? She'll be anxious to know what's been happening.'

'You must do as you please, Rosalind. I'm sure Mrs Renton will fetch you some writing materials. And I'll say goodnight.'

'Goodnight, Lady Lydia,' she said vaguely, her mind already forming words and phrases to describe this new part of the country.

For despite the sadness of the occasion and her reason for being here, she was aware of an unexpected feeling of empathy with this austere landscape and its burgeoning flora, and even with the bustling industry in the valley. Yorkshire wasn't such an alien place after all, and she felt a great urge to put her feelings on paper and to try to show the beauties of the county to her mother through her own eyes.

She rang the bell for Mrs Renton and was brought the writing materials directly. She would be undisturbed in the parlour now unless Felix returned, and she intended going to bed long before that happened. She had no wish to surprise the unhappiness in his eyes again. She picked up the pen, dipped it in the ink and began to write.

. . .there's such a feeling of energy in the valley, Mother, with the curls of smoke rising from cottages and the mill, even on such a warm summer's day as this one. Father would be impressed, I know, at the way I suspect everyone in Radley has something or other to do with Holden's Cloth Mill. The whole community seems to be dependent on the mill, and Felix has a great responsibility to dispose of.

She paused in her writing, as if only just realising the truth of what she'd written. There was far more than bricks and mortar down there in the valley. There were the years of building up a family business that reached out and gave a living to countless people. If Holden's Cloth Mill was sold out, it would truly be the end of a dynasty. . .but it wasn't her decision, and she knew better than to try and influence Felix, especially in the mood he was in now.

The moors above the village are probably barren in winter, but right now they're glorious with colour. Everywhere you look, there's purple heather and yellow furze and bracken and clover. The house itself is about the same size as ours, Mother, comfortable and not too grand. I don't mean to be disparaging by saying so. But if I say that it seems to wrap itself around you like a comforting blanket, while Lady Lydia's house is more like a satin bedcover that you dare not rumple, I think you'll understand what I mean!

She smiled at her own words, knowing her mother would follow them exactly.

They have stables here too, and tomorrow evening, while the will is being read, I'm going to ask if I may take one of the horses for a ride. I certainly won't want to be present at something that's no concern of mine. Besides which, it will be so good to get some real air into my lungs again. It seems to me that London has everything but that.

Again she paused, ruefully reading between the lines of her own letter. It made her sound disenchanted with London, and she wasn't at all, and nor was she ungrateful to Lady Lydia for her patronage. But not all the pomp and glitter of a city, or the solemn ceremonial that was shortly to come, could take the place of the clean living to be found in the country. And none of it could change who and what she was. In that moment she felt thankful to be herself, knowing herself, without being beset with the problems that Felix had undoubtedly once had, and which were now thrust on him again. . .

She jumped as she heard the bang of a door, and a few minutes later he was inside the parlour. As soon as she saw him, she knew he had been drinking. It was out of character for him to display it so obviously, but circumstances could change things, she thought swiftly, and she wouldn't condemn him for it tonight.

She closed the writing folder quickly, and got to her feet, intending to finish her letter in her room.

'Not leaving already, are you, sweet little Rosie? Stay a while, for I've a great need for company.'

His words were only slightly slurred, his feet only faltering very slightly as he walked across the room and poured himself a large brandy from the decanter on the side-table.

'I think it might be better if I went to bed,' she said. 'I'm very tired, and you must be too——'

'Oh, aye, I'm tired.' He sat down heavily in a chair near to where she stood. He reached out a hand and took hold of hers in a tight grip. 'I know I'm poor company, but I need you, Rosie.'

She saw the faint film of sweat on his brow, and the way the nerves at the side of his cheeks wouldn't quite keep still. And she remembered where he had been that evening. She hesitated, and he felt her relax. Before she could think what was happening, he had pulled her on to his lap and his arms held her captive. The writing folder slipped to the floor, and she automatically held on to him to keep her balance.

'Rosie, Rosie,' he muttered thickly, his hands moving to her hair and the nape of her neck with the urgency of a man wanting a woman all too evident.

'Felix, please—for heaven's sake——' she gasped, as one hand moved around to the front of her bodice and caressed the soft warmth of her breast. His touch had the power to make every part of her tingle, and she felt weak and helpless at the look of desire in his eyes. But another, more sensible part of her was warning her that right now this meant no more to him than the need for a man to forget himself in the arms of a whore. It meant no more than his cousin George pleasuring himself with the likes of Lizzie. . .

She felt a low sob in her throat as his mouth sought and found hers, and then she couldn't resist his kiss, any more than she could stop the tide ebbing and flowing with the pull of the moon. Just as surely as that, she was pulled towards him, and knew that she could never escape the power of her own feelings.

The hand that palmed her breast caressed it sensuously now, and she knew she should stop this at once. It was wrong, it was compromising. . .and it was so excitingly wanton that she never wanted it to end at all. . .

'Do you know where I've been tonight, Rosie?'

His thickened words startled her. She had expected a declaration of love, of desire, of wanting to throw aside the mask of respectability for a moment's pleasure. . . and if that had happened, she wasn't at all sure if she would have had the strength to resist. Instead, she was aware of the brittleness in his voice. Although his hands still caressed her, and she could feel the beat of his heart close to her own, in spirit he was miles away from her, and she didn't know whether to be glad or sad or insulted.

'You went to see your father.'

'That's right. My father. My illustrious father, the acknowledged saviour of all in Radley Valley.'

She marvelled that he could say the words without stumbling, but, with the care of the very drunk, he spoke them perfectly.

'He was a well-respected man,' she ventured to say, beginning to feel slightly ridiculous sitting here on his lap while he seemed to look right through her with eyes that seemed to burn darkly with a rage he couldn't express.

'Oh, aye, he was well-loved and well-respected. I grew up on the tales of how he stood up to the accursed Luddites, barring the factory doors and windows and safeguarding his precious new machinery and promising his workers they'd not lose a single job or a penny-piece in wages at Holden's mill. I grew up knowing how we weathered that storm through my father's common sense and a good deal of my mother's dowry, and I'll not deny him the glory in that. But around Radley he was hero-worshipped from then on, and this is what they expect me to live up to.'

She couldn't follow half of this. She knew the story of the Luddites, who'd formed their own vigilante groups, breaking into factories and mills and smashing up the new machinery, believing that it would replace men and ruin families, and it had proved disastrous for many businesses at the time. But all that was years ago. . .but it seemed that Felix was ready to dredge up every bit of resentment against his father that he could muster.

'Who expects it? The workers? Have you seen some of them, then?' As she spoke, it was obvious that he had. How else would he be so glazed and aggressive. . .?

She was suddenly and rudely dumped on the floor.

Felix stood up so abruptly that there was no chance of saving herself. She'd hardly had time to cry out when he had hauled her to her feet again with exaggerated apologies.

'It doesn't matter. I'm quite all right,' she said, smoothing down her skirt with shaking hands.

It didn't matter, because she was sure he hardly knew what he was doing. He looked so strange, yet to her so vulnerable, and her heart ached for him. He had drained the first brandy and poured himself another, and she knew better than to protest. She gathered up her writing materials and edged towards the door as he sprawled out on a chair again without attempting to touch her. His voice was harsh.

'Of course I've seen the bloody workers. Some of them were at the chapel, saying farewell to "t' old lad" when I got there. They insisted I went with them to the Tar Barrel Inn, and they were all there, and after a while they began toasting my father and me just as if we were one person. It was ghoulish, if you really want to know. In some weird way I felt as if I'd *become* my father. Anyway, I drank with them until I couldn't drink any more and then I came home.'

'You mean they naturally assume that you'll be taking over Holden's Cloth Mill,' Rosalind stated.

He glared at her out of red-rimmed eyes.

'That's what they naturally assume,' he almost snarled.

'And would that be so terrible?' She had to say it, but she did so very hesitantly, knowing he could flare up at any minute, and she'd have to bear the brunt of it.

'Mebbe not, but about as unlikely and undesirable as you moving lock, stock and barrel to London, Miss Rosie Cranbourne!'

She couldn't take any more of his sarcasm. 'Look,

Felix, I'm going to bed now, and I suggest you do the same——' She stopped at his raucous laugh.

'Is that an invitation, my darling? Because if so, I'd be precious little use to you tonight. The ale plays cruel tricks on a man, building up his confidence and then refusing to let him perform at his best, if at all——'

Rosalind fled from the room, her cheeks blazing. She didn't want to hear any more of this. This wasn't the Felix she knew or wanted to know. This was a man in torment. . .in the sanctuary of her room she knew the truth of that. Tonight he hadn't been able to help himself. He'd drunk himself silly with men he'd known as children, simply because he couldn't face telling them that with his father's death it was the end of an era. And she couldn't blame him for that. He'd already rejected the past and all it stood for, and now that past had caught up with him again. In those circumstances a man could only be strong for so long. But, knowing Felix, he would be strong again.

She huddled beneath the cold bedcovers, her own mind in turmoil. A long while later she heard him come blundering upstairs, and held her breath, wondering if he would try her door-handle. She heard him pause outside, and then to her utter relief the footsteps continued on their unsteady way and the house finally became silent.

Felix was late for breakfast the next morning. Lady Lydia hadn't yet arrived downstairs either, but Rosalind was already eating porridge and toast, and declining smoked kippers, when he appeared. Apart from the pallor of his face, there was little to remind her of last night's occurrence. He had shaved and was already dressed correctly for the early-afternoon funeral, his uniform newly pressed by a servant, a wide black band dividing one scarlet sleeve of his jacket.

'Rosalind, I wish to apologise for anything untoward that might have happened between us last night,' he said at once in a low voice. 'I was not myself, and if I hurt you in any way——'

'You did not,' she said quickly. 'You were merely a little talkative, that's all, and there's nothing to apologise for. I suggest that we forget all about it.'

And if her rump was a little bruised from her undignified landing on the floor, that was between herself and her mirror. It was very clear that Felix didn't remember a single thing about what had happened between them, and she could be eternally grateful for that.

'If you're sure. . .' he said uneasily. Any further delving into what happened was stopped by Lady Lydia's appearance and that of Mrs Renton, bringing fresh tea for the new arrivals.

'Perfectly,' Rosalind said, turning to greet his aunt and to ask how she had slept.

'Very well, thank you, my dear,' Lydia replied. 'Nothing disturbs me once I put my head on the pillow.'

And if that was a tactful way of saying she had heard nothing, whether she had or not, it was a welcome relief to the other two in the room.

'Felix, I naturally intend to be out of the way this evening while your father's will is being read,' Rosalind said. 'May I be permitted to take one of the horses for a ride across the moors?'

'Of course. You'll have had a trying enough day as it is. In fact, there's really no need for you to follow the funeral procession at all——'

'But I want to, if you've no objection,' she said quickly. 'I know there will be many people there who knew your father, but your own family is so lacking in numbers, Felix. Just yourself and Lady Lydia. It's so sad——'

'Then of course you may attend if you want to feel

useful,' he said briskly, and Rosalind shot Lady Lydia a warning glance, anticipating her objection to this rudeness.

But what was the point? Rosalind thought wearily. Felix would obviously not be himself again until he returned to London, where he was far more settled than in this environment now. It was strange how a man could reject his roots so completely, but perhaps when he had strayed from them for long enough he could never truly go back.

The funeral service was to be at noon. The mill was silent for the day, so that all the workers could attend, and once the carriage had taken the three principal mourners to the chapel of rest they alighted for the short service, with the mill workers in their normal working clothes filling the grounds and walkways outside. There were other, more prosperous-looking gentlemen present, whom Rosalind surmised would be other mill owners from round about. It spoke of the prestige in which Jonas Holden had been held. The three principal participants followed the coffin in its black hearse drawn by a horse adorned with black crape, followed by the long trail of mourners, all processing to the churchyard on foot as an extra mark of respect.

Felix's jaw was held rigidly during the entire proceedings. Those who didn't know him well would say he grieved with a man's raw grief, holding it in tightly and with dignity. The eulogy he felt obliged to read was short and expressive, and there were many nodding heads as he finished, having clearly satisfied them all. Those who knew him best wondered at the churning thoughts that must be uppermost in his heart today, as his father was finally laid to rest beside his mother.

Rosalind was thankful when it was all over. Even on the periphery she couldn't be unaffected by the sorrow all around her. But to her utter surprise the sadness seemed to evaporate once the hand-shaking was done, and those who preferred not to come to Radley Grange for the 'supping', as Felix had quaintly called it, went away. There were plenty who'd accepted the unspoken invitation as their right, however, and a great number of people ate Cook's fine spread of cold meats and pickles laid out on trestle-tables on the lawn in some miraculously quick way after the party had driven away to the chapel.

And as Rosalind moved among them, more at home with them than the lawyer and preacher, who frightened her half to death with his solemnising, she kept hearing phrases like 'He were a grand lad', and, 't' young lad'll be a worthy boss like his father', and she wondered uneasily when Felix was going to tell them all that he was continuing his army career. It couldn't be put off forever, but it wasn't for her to say, and she smiled and nodded and sympathised, according to what was required of her.

'You'll be from London, then, lass,' a male voice said close to her, and she looked into the swarthy face of a man of about Felix's age.

'Oh, no. In fact I'm from Sussex, and I'm just visiting with Lady Lydia.'

'That's reet, then. It wouldn't do for Felix to take up with a townie,' the man said, a cheeky sparkle in his eyes.

She could have said that Felix hadn't 'taken up' with her at all, but she didn't particularly want to continue that line of conversation, friendly though the man seemed.

'I'm sorry, but I don't know your name,' she said.

'I dare say you don't, nor the names of many other folk here,' the man said lazily. 'I'm Harry Keeley, lass, the overseer.'

He didn't say any more, and nor did he need to.

Overseer for Holden's Cloth Mill was clearly an important job, and Rosalind had the sense not to pursue it further. She nodded, as if she knew just what a mill overseer did.

'So what have you been doing in London, then?' Harry Keeley went on, obviously enjoying having captured the attention of the prettiest girl at the wake, and, because of his privileged position among the workers, sure of not being interrupted.

Rosalind hesitated. Considering today's event, it would sound so inane to talk frivolously of balls and parties and evening soirées and visits to the theatre.

'Lady Lydia's been very generous in showing me the city,' she said instead. 'And of course it's full of excitement now with the preparations for the Queen's coronation.'

She paused. Did these people even know of it here? Yorkshire seemed so remote from London and its gaiety, and little Radley in particular. . .

'Oh, aye, we know all about that. There's to be a public holiday, so all the shops and mills will close down for the day, and there'll be flags and bunting put up in the village and parties in the street. We'll be having fireworks for the little uns in the evening too, to celebrate. Oh, aye, the twenty-eighth of June will be a day to remember, all right, even for a little place like Radley village.'

Rosalind had the grace to blush. She wasn't sure whether or not he spoke tongue-in-cheek, teasing her because of her inadvertent little show of snobbery. She hadn't meant it that way, and she was at a loss how to answer for a moment, and turned thankfully as Felix joined them.

'You've met this old reprobate, then, Rosie?' Felix said easily, just as if this were a garden party, and not a wake for his father. But she was already learning that once the burying was done the occasion was more one for rejoicing for a man's life than for mourning his dying. It was a good and healthy way to behave, she reflected.

'I take it from that remark that you two are old friends?' she countered with a smile.

'Aye, you could say that,' Harry said mildly. 'We grew up together and ran wild after the same lassies together. My father was overseer for his father, and I'm proud to know I'll be continuing as overseer for Felix.'

Class differences obviously didn't come into the affection these two had for one another, and never had. But Rosalind held her breath at Harry's words. Was this the moment for the truth to come out. . .? But Felix's smile never faltered, and he slapped his old friend on the back, and moved on as other people claimed his attention. Harry looked after him thoughtfully.

'He'll regret leaving his regiment, but he'll not flinch from it,' he commented. 'Felix always had a strong backbone.'

But how strong a backbone did a man need to have, to turn away from his chosen life, to fulfil his father's dream? For that was what it amounted to, Rosalind thought instantly, and she could find no wrong in a man fulfilling his own destiny. In the end, it made a man a man.

'He tells me you've a mind to see the mill,' she heard Harry say, and realised she too had been staring after Felix.

'Yes. Will it bother you at all?'

'Why should it? The lads and lassies will be interested to see what our new boss's intended thinks of us all,' he said with a grin.

She knew she should protest, but there was such an inevitability about this land and these people that she simply let it pass. They were honest and plain-speaking, and if what they surmised didn't happen then they

merely shrugged and made the best of what did. It was
stoical and rugged, and solid. They were what her father
would call 'salt of the earth', and neither he nor Rosalind
meant any disrespect by it. It was an admirable trait.
She smiled at Harry Keeley.

'Then I'll see you tomorrow,' she said. 'We have one
more day here before we have to return to London.'

He nodded. 'I dare say Felix will be glad when all the
coronation fuss has died down and he can get things
settled properly. He'll need a bit of time to sort things
out, but 'twill be in good hands here, never fear. He
knows that well enough.'

She was glad to escape from his confident predictions
that as soon as the coronation was over, when Felix
would be presumably freed from the most arduous and
pressing of his military duties, he would resign his
commission, and come home.

To a man like Harry Keeley, it was all so beautifully
simple. To someone more complex like Felix, it was all
so appallingly difficult.

At last the wake was over, and the village folk had
reluctantly drifted away. Awkward at first at being in
the grounds of the big house, they had gradually relaxed
and become voluble and noisy in their praise of their
'old lad', and their expectations of the 'new young un'.
And Rosalind knew just how much Radley had taken
the Holden men to its hearts. It had begun with Felix's
grandfather, and now it came down to him.

At last the house was empty save for those most
closely involved in the will-reading and those invited to
remain. These included the overseer, some of the oldest
mill employees, contemporaries of the deceased, trusted
servants and the family, and finally the lawyer was
ready to begin revealing the last wishes of Jonas Garfield
Holden.

By then, Rosalind was riding across the moors above

the village, feeling the clean early evening air lift her hair and fill her nostrils, air that was heavy and scented with summer and heavy with the drone of bees. It was not a day for sadness, she thought, and thankfully all the sadness was done with. Felix wouldn't forget his father, and no more would the people gathered for his burial today, but the memories would be muted from now on, and the man would be remembered with love. At least, as far as the majority was concerned.

She was still unsure exactly how Felix regarded his father, and she wasn't sure whether he even knew it himself. As she cantered aross the moors, its harshness softened by its carpet of bracken and heather, she thought that that was the real sadness, not knowing how to grieve.

The open moors rose quickly from the surrounding countryside, stretching as far as the eye could see, and giving Rosalind the feeling once more that there was more sky in Yorkshire than anywhere else. She knew it was merely an illusion, perhaps born out of the fact that Yorkshire was England's largest and most majestic county, but it was an illusion tht stayed with her.

She rode on, lulled by the utter quiet and peacefulness. She had wondered if it was safe to ride alone, but she had been assured by Felix and by the stable-lads that she would be perfectly safe as long as she kept in sight of the house. She looked about her now, and saw that she had come a long way from Radley Grange. Above her was a rocky outcrop, breaking the horizon, but she felt no sense of alarm, only one of calm and a sudden wish that she could stay here forever. . .

Rosalind was startled by her own thoughts. It was the first time she had thought that way, as if the strings that had tied her undeniably to her parental background were being loosened at last. And why should they not be? She had travelled a long way in these last weeks, and not just physically. She had left home for the first time, had been introduced to society, had fallen in love, known a man's caresses, and shared his pain.

She caught her breath, recognising the truth of it. The Rosalind Cranbourne who rode out that sunny early evening was far removed from the Rosalind Cranbourne who had foolishly pretended to be her own maid, and encountered Felix Holden's kiss for the first time.

She became aware that she was no longer alone, that the moors no longer belonged solely to her, and she felt her heart jolt. She was a stranger here, after all, and this was a strange place. . .she turned her head quickly, and felt as though she had stepped back in time. Felix was riding towards her, just as he had done on that first day. . .

'You shouldn't go too far from the house. The mist can come down quickly once the sun goes down.' He spoke abruptly as soon as he reached her.

'Is—is the business all finished?' she said, stammering a little and hardly knowing what to say to him. 'The business' sounded so cold and euphemistic, but she could hardly ask him if the will-reading was done to his satisfaction! That would be even colder.

He gave a short laugh. 'Aye, it's all finished.'

He dismounted, and held out his hand to her. Automatically, she put her own in his, and slid from her horse, but this wasn't an invitation to go into his arms. He took both horses' reins and motioned to the rocky outcrop just above them. He walked purposefully towards the rocks, and Rosalind was obliged to follow him.

'These rocks are known as Radley Crags,' he said, as if it was of supreme importance to her to know it. 'I used to come up here with Harry Keeley all the time when we were lads. We'd sport with the village lassies up here, and it's where I asked Annie Thwaite to marry me.'

Rosalind didn't know whether to feel hurt or bewilderment at his mood. 'Why are you telling me all this?' she asked.

He laughed that mirthless laugh again. 'Are you jealous? You needn't be. We were all of ten years old at the time, and Annie's been Harry Keeley's wife these last five years now, and has three little lads of her own.'

They had reached the outcrop of rocks now, and Rosalind looked at him squarely. He was telling her things she didn't need to know, and instinctively she knew he was avoiding telling her what was really filling his mind.

'What was in your father's will, Felix?'

For a moment she thought he wasn't going to answer. He leaned aginst one of the rocks, his eyes enigmatic, looking down that road again where she couldn't travel. She longed to go there with him so badly, but knew she never could. . .

'The usual things,' he said, his voice brisk now. 'Bequests to servants and the Church, and to Harry for good service all these years. Things like that. He even remembered Aunt Lydia, leaving her some of Mother's things that he'd never parted with until now.'

'And you?' Rosalind almost whispered.

'Oh, yes, I got the bulk of it. There was never any question of that. I was always meant to continue the family tradition, so I get the Grange and the mill and all the assets that go with it. It's all mine now to do with as I like.'

'But you expected that, surely. You knew that was what the will would contain.'

He turned stormy eyes towards her then. 'I didn't know he would add the kind of codicil that could tear into a man's heart, did I? But you'd better read it for yourself.'

He pulled the document from the inside of his jacket and Rosalind stared at the words where he pointed, right at the end. She read slowly.

> To my dearly beloved son, Felix, I also leave my forgiveness and understanding, and the hope that when we meet in heaven we can be reconciled.

Rosalind swallowed. The words were stark and spare, and yet they said so much. And Felix would have all his resolve torn from under him. She understood all that, and she could only put her arms around him and give him mute comfort, uncaring of the proprieties, even if there had been anyone around to see. But there was not. There was only the soft moorland breeze and the scent of summer, and a man's anguish.

'I could have coped with everything but him calling me his dearly beloved son,' he said in a tortured voice. 'I never even knew I meant that much to him, and now it's all too late.'

She held him close, knowing that for now she had to be the strong one. She wasn't sure if he wept or not, but if he did it didn't emasculate him in her eyes. It was part of the healing process, and, when the arms holding her became less rigid and dependent than before, she knew it had finally begun.

CHAPTER ELEVEN

IT WAS clear to Rosalind the next morning that, whatever demons had bedevilled Felix in the privacy of his room the previous night, he had wrestled with them all and won. He appeared quite calm, if paler than usual, and announced his intention of going to the mill during the morning.

'It's what Father would have expected. I want to thank everyone for their good work over the years and assure them that nothing's going to be changed. Harry Keeley's a good overseer and can carry on for the present without any assistance from me. In any case, he'll know about the orders for finished cloth and new wool, and he'll continue the way Father wanted things run.'

'For the present?' Rosalind asked.

He stared at her, and she repeated the question.

'You said that Harry can carry on being in charge for the present. Does that mean you've changed your mind about coming back here after all?'

'It does not,' he said shortly. 'It means I've no intention of starting rumours about my selling out and getting folk het up before there's any need. It can wait until they've all settled down from the shock of Father's death, and until I'm a safe distance away from it all.'

'That sounds a poor way of doing things, dear boy,' Lady Lydia put in. 'You can't shirk your responsibilities in that way, and you'll have to face them in the end.'

'I know that, Aunt. But not yet. I prefer to leave things as they are for the time being. In any case, I can't think of doing anything for the present. You know that and so does Harry. We've already spoken about it, and

he agrees that my immediate duty is to the Queen and
the regiment.'

'But I suspect you haven't spoken of your real intentions. Do you forget that you also have a duty to all
those dependent on you?' Lydia said quietly.

He said nothing for a moment and then he spoke
impatiently. 'I thought you understood. You of all
people, Aunt Lydia! You never wanted my mother to
come here, yet now you imply that it's my duty to stay.'

'Your mother was born and bred in London. She had
no Yorkshire blood in her, Felix, but you have. I just
want you to be very sure you're doing the right thing.
Once you let Holden's Cloth Mill go, it will be gone
forever. And, whatever your feelings, you can't deny
your father's blood. It's very evident in every hot-headed
remark you make,' she added.

He smiled faintly at that, and Rosalind breathed a
sigh of relief. For a while she'd thought he was going to
retreat into his private wilderness again, but he had too
much strength of character, and she sensed that Lady
Lydia was merely goading him into some positive
thinking.

'You're a wise old bird,' he said irreverently. 'But you
won't make me decide on anything on the spur of the
moment. We go back to London tomorrow, and we'll all
make the most of the pageantry the coronation has to
offer. After that will be time enough for the future to sort
itself out.'

He turned to Rosalind. 'You wanted to see the mill,
so if you haven't changed your mind about that we'll
leave in about an hour. We can go on horseback, if you
wish.'

'I'd like that,' she said, 'and I haven't changed my
mind about anything.'

Further than that, she dared not go, and she guessed
that Felix would rather not be reminded about how he'd

opened his heart to her last evening. She had said
nothing to Lady Lydia about knowing the contents of
the will or the emotional codicil at the end. It was very
private, and she felt privileged that Felix had felt able to
tell her at all. He left them together at the dining table
when he'd finished his breakfast, and Lydia spoke to her
gently.

'You know these mill people will see your visit as tantamount to announcing a betrothal, don't you, Rosalind?
They will already be viewing your presence here as
significant, especially at such a time.'

Rosalind ignored the little snobbery in referring to the
workers as 'mill people', and looked at her frankly. Even
in the warning, Lydia hadn't been able to resist the little
note of hope in her voice.

'I'm not going to bother denying that I'm very
attracted to Felix,' she said quietly. 'But I'm not thinking of marriage in any way yet, Lady Lydia, and I doubt
that it's even remotely in Felix's mind at a time like this.
I'm sure the mill workers must respect his feelings, and,
besides, they'll know by now that I'm here as your guest,
not his.' She was not unaware of the way gossip travelled
in any close community, and she suspected that Radley
was just such a place.

'Your naïveté does you credit, my dear, but they'll
only see what they want to see. And what they'll want
now is happiness for their *new lad* and a wedding to lift
their spirits, together with their *new lad* coming home to
replace the old one. You'll be on approval, my dear,
from the moment you go inside the mill.'

'I'm afraid they'll be disappointed, then,' Rosalind
retorted. 'For neither Felix nor myself are ready to fulfil
their dreams.'

'All right, but just don't throw your own away in the
mistaken belief that someone else's hopes for you can be
all wrong, Rosalind, dear. An outsider can sometimes

see things more clearly than you can see them yourself, and the moment I saw you I knew you and Felix were a match for each other. I've seen nothing yet to make me change my mind.'

'And I thought you had me destined for Sir George!' Rosalind said teasingly, because this discussion was getting all too personal, and she certainly wasn't going to admit that Lady Lydia's dreams for her matched her own exactly.

Lydia chuckled. 'It never even crossed my mind, my dear. No, Felix is the one for you, and that rascal son of mine will go his own way, no matter what his mother dictates,' she said affectionately, seeing George through what Rosalind considered were blindingly rose-coloured maternal spectacles.

'And between you and me, my dear, I suspect that his vague ambitions to enter Parliament will be enhanced by any union with this Lady Celeste of whom we've heard far too little!'

George's parliamentary ambitions seemed to Rosalind to be very haphazard altogether. By now she knew that they were spoken about, but never acted upon. Privately she thought him no more than an old roué, and as different from his cousin as chalk was from cheese.

'Will you excuse me, Lady Lydia?' she asked. 'I'd better get ready to go to the mill with Felix, and if we're riding. . .' She couldn't stop the pleasure in her voice at the thought.

'Oh, you and your horses! The more I see of you both, my love, the more I know how the two of you would fit in here in this wild country!'

Rosalind left the room quickly, wishing Lydia wouldn't go on so. Knowing only too well that she herself had found an empathy here at Radley Grange and its environs that she hadn't expected was pertinent enough. To have the fact pushed at her so blatantly from Lady Lydia, when Rosalind knew it could all come to nothing, was almost cruel.

They rode out together in a blazingly beautiful morning. The sun was already high in the sky, and the moors were bathed in its glory, a wild expanse of colour, timeless and enduring. Crowns could fall, empires could crumble, but some things always remained the same. And this was how it could always be, Rosalind thought suddenly, if only, if only. . .

'Dare I offer a penny for your thoughts?' Felix said.

'Oh, they're worth far more than that,' she said, her breath catching.

'And you've no intention of revealing them to me,' he said jocularly, and not pressing her.

'I think not. There are some things a lady prefers to keep private,' she answered lightly, glad that somehow they seemed to have regained the old banter between them.

Somehow, in the long silent hours of the night, it was as if Felix had exorcised the ghost of his father, and she was becoming wise enough not to question how or why.

They reached the village in good humour, and Felix began to acquaint her with more of the territory that was so familiar to him. Rosalind already knew the whereabouts of the church and the burial ground where they had laid Jonas Holden to rest so recently.

But now Felix pointed out the inn where he and Harry Keeley had once tried to obtain ale when they were well under the permitted age, and received the wrath of their fathers because of it, as well as a few stripes with a leather strap.

'A swift punishment where it hurt the most was always my father's maxim,' he said with a smile at the memory. 'We never went inside the inn again until we were older.'

'And what of the sport with the village lassies up at

Radley Crags? Did you get striped for that too?' she
teased him.

She prayed that the memory of the place and his
revelations to her last evening wouldn't bring the black-
ness back to his face again, but felt that this was a good
time to bring the name to the fore again. She saw him
grin.

'As you yourself said, some things are best kept
private, Rosie. Harry and I were canny lads, and if our
fathers ever suspected where we went of an evening they
never let on, and probably allowed that lads would be
lads.'

There were times when his very *Yorkshireness* wouldn't
be denied, however hard he tried, Rosalind thought.
And, amazingly, she could feel a swift envy for the girls
he'd taken to Radley Crags all those years ago, and a
poignancy for all the years she hadn't known him.

'I bet you and Harry were real Jack-the-lads in those
days,' she ventured to say.

He laughed naturally for what seemed like the first
time in a very long while.

'We were that,' he grinned, lost in memory. 'But I
wish you'd been around then, my darling. I'd have had
you hog-tied long before now.'

'Had me *what?*' she said, laughing back at the incon-
gruity of his words.

They were clattering over the cobbles in the mill yard
now, and he was already dismounting and coming to lift
her down from her horse. She looked directly into his
eyes, thankful that the life had come back into them
again after the bleakness of these last sad days. And she
couldn't deny the beating of her heart that always
quickened so much when she was in close proximity to
him.

'I'd have wed you long ago and given you a parcel of
children by now,' he said softly. 'If I'd known you years

ago, there was no way I'd ever have let you go, any
more than I intend to let you go now.'

He spoke so quietly that she wondered if she'd really
heard him say the words. They were seductive and
outrageous and wonderful. . .but before Rosalind could
gather her senses, and try to think of some suitable
reply, Harry Keeley was striding out of the building, his
arms outstretched in welcome, his rugged face showing
great pleasure in seeing his old friend. Being owner and
employee obviously created no barriers between them.

'It's good to see you, Felix, and looking a mite less
fraught than the last time we met. The workers will be
relieved to see it, and to make the acquaintance of your
lass too.'

Rosalind knew it would have been quite pointless and
snobbish to say that she wasn't his lass. Lady Lydia's
words came into her mind. 'They'll only see what they
want to see. . .and what they'll want now is happiness
for their new lad. . .'

She realised Felix was tucking her arm in his, and
that the two men were already talking enthusiastically
together, and she gave up worrying about anything.

The moment she stepped inside Holden's Cloth Mill
she wondered how anyone could ever hear themselves
think in the cloying, wool-dusty atmosphere, let alone
speak. Or how anyone escaped permanent deafness from
the thunder of machines. This must be what was called
a hive of industry, she observed in amazement, watching
the young girls in their serviceable brown dresses and
with workmanlike caps over their heads speaking in a
kind of sign language to one another as they went
cheerfully about their work on the heavy looms. She was
also enveloped in the mixture of smells emanating from
every corner—wool fibres, oils and chemicals, to say
nothing of the sweat of honest labour. . .

Together with Felix and Harry, she walked slowly

among the workers, trying to follow what Harry was shouting about wefts and warps and the strength and suppleness of the cloth that was so prized hereabouts. She was hardly able to make sense of any of it, even if she could have heard it properly, which she certainly could not. But, by the intentness of Felix's face, it obviously all made sense to him.

She was acutely aware of the intricate sign language from the busy fingers of the young girls. It meant nothing at all to her, but, from their flashing smiles as the girls glanced towards her and then back at each other, she had no doubt that she was the subject of much of this strange, silent discussion.

After they had been through the main weaving shed, they went into the carding-shed, then the dye shed and the drying sheds, where samples of newly dyed cloth were hanging up to dry to check on fastness and depth of colour before going into full production on any new patterns.

They went into the quieter design room, where the new patterns for cloth were constantly being considered, and into the busy office where Harry's secretary quickly outlined the mass of orders that were obviously going to keep Holden's Cloth Mill prosperous for the foreseeable future.

There was far more to a cloth mill than Rosalind had ever dreamed about, and it dawned on her that Felix was keenly interested in all that Harry and everyone else had to report to him. And, more than that, that he was familiar with every aspect of operation in the mill. She queried him on that when they finally left the building.

'My grandfather initiated me into the workings of the mill many years ago, even before we had the machinery installed,' he said. 'He insisted that no boss could take over anything successfully without knowing how everything worked from floor level. I was shown how to spin wool and work a handloom when I was no more than a wee lad, and could probably do it now if I had to.' He spoke with unconscious pride, and Rosalind wondered anew if he could ever really reject his roots. To sell out would be to sell something far more precious than mere bricks and metal. It would be selling out part of himself.

The temptation was there to say as much to him, but she knew better than to blurt out the words. The next minute she knew she had been right.

'But it's just as well I don't have to. The mill can almost run itself now, and with Harry at the helm it'll come to no harm. I'll make damn sure it's written into the contract that any new owner keeps on every one of my workers too.'

He spoke almost grimly, and again Rosalind could see the fierce pride in his family's achievements and the affection with which he held these employees. The marvel was that he couldn't seem to see it for himself. But, wisely, she decided it was no business of hers to intervene and ask whether he was totally sure. . .he'd been totally sure all those years ago when he'd made his decision to move south and taken up his chosen career.

'Have you seen enough?' he enquired. 'We can take one last ride up to Radley Crags if you like, and, if you're desperate to see town life again, we could take a drive into Halifax this afternoon.'

They had reached the horses again now, and Felix gave her a helping hand into the saddle. She waited while he mounted with the ease of an expert horseman, feeling resentment rather than pleasure wash over her at his words.

'I'm not in the least anxious to see Halifax or town life again! I don't know why you think I would be.'

He shrugged. 'I just think all this must be a terrible anticlimax for you, Rosie. You came to visit my aunt to have a good time and be launched into society, and what did you end up with? A miserably long ride to Yorkshire for the funeral of a man you never knew. It's hardly fair to you, is it?'

'Life's not always fair,' she commented, 'and if you really think I enjoy being *launched* on society, as you put it, as if I'm one of Father's ships, then you don't know me at all.'

She dug her heels into the horse's side and the animal cantered off at once. She knew she was being foolish, but suddenly all her pleasure in this day was slipping away, just because Felix's words implied that she was the shallow kind of female who'd be openly bored with the country life and spending the morning looking around a cloth mill.

It implied that she was more empty-headed than those village girls who communicated so cleverly with their hands and were able to fashion good cloth for the gentry to wear from the most basic raw materials. It made her feel less than adequate, and she didn't like the feeling.

He'd always said how much he enjoyed their intelligent conversations, and she knew she was being irrational and foolish for taking offence over nothing, but she couldn't seem to help it. It was all bound up with the feeling that Felix was throwing away his birthright and would one day live to regret it. And it was not her place to tell him so. She'd somehow been relegated to the position of demure little wife who went along with all her husband's plans while saying nothing—and she wasn't even anybody's wife. . .

'Rosalind, what the devil's the matter with you?' Felix's voice came from behind as she leaned lower over the horse's neck and suddenly urged him into a gallop through the village and up to the wide expanse of moors beyond. 'You'll have the nag crazed if you don't slow down.'

She knew that, but she was horsewoman enough to be able to control the animal. She felt a wild need to get away from him, from everyone. She had to feel capable of *something*, even if her life had been useless so far. She wasn't normally given to such pessimistic thoughts, and the very fact that she was thinking them now was throwing her off-balance even more.

She could still hear Felix's angry voice behind her, and finally she smothered a sob in her throat, soothing her heaving horse with soft words as she drew him to a standstill. They hadn't come as far as Radley Crags yet. The rocks stood like gaunt sentinels some distance away, and the moors all around them were as silent as ever except for the whispering bracken. The clattering world of Holden's Cloth Mill seemed very far away, but the sights and sounds of it were vividly imprinted in Rosalind's mind.

'What the devil's got into you?' Felix said, leaping down and grabbing her reins before she could charge off again. He pulled her none too gently from the horse and glowered at her.

'I'm not an idiot child, to be pampered by excursions into the town, and taken here, there and everywhere because you think I expect it,' she raged. 'I came to Yorkshire because I thought maybe I could soften the blow of your father's death by my presence, but that was obviously quite unnecessary, because you didn't really care about him or what he stood for at all. Then today I was genuinely interested in how the mill operated, and you insult me by telling me I was bored by it all, and treating me like one of Lady Lydia's—*protégées*, wasn't it? Are you some kind of clairvoyant, to tell me how I even *think* now?'

The glimmer of laughter in his eyes as she went into her tirade had died by the time she finished. His grip on her wrists had tightened and although she winced with pain she was determined not to cry out.

'And do you dare to tell me how *I* think?' he said harshly. 'What do you know about caring, or the way a man feels when he's faced with something he can't change? Do you think I'd have wanted my father dead before I had the chance to put things right between us? You know nothing of the world, Rosalind, and that's the truth of it. But I suggest you look at what's inside yourself before you try to interfere in anyone else's life.'

'And what's that supposed to mean?' she snapped, hating him for his analysis of her.

'It means you haven't yet learned how to love, or how many different kinds of love there are,' he said, some of his anger lessening. 'Do you really think I don't love all of this?'

He let go of her arm and embraced the entire countryside around him with one sweeping gesture.

'Then why leave it? Why not stay?' she blurted out.

He looked at her steadily. 'Because if a man's got any sense at all he doesn't let emotions rule his head. It's well known that after a bereavement a person can't think rationally for a while, and may be led into things he doesn't really want to do. It's far better to wait a while and assess situations coolly and calmly.'

'But you've already assessed your situation, haven't you?' she said.

He said nothing for a moment, and then she realised he was no longer gripping her wrists, but held her hands gently inside his own.

'Rosie, if a Queen is obliged to wait a year after her accession for her coronation, why should we lesser mortals be rushed into anything? Mourning doesn't take a day or a week. It's a slow process, to give time for the mind as well as the heart to heal. And anyway, I'm not discarding the mill completely. None of the people you met today is anything other than content that things will go on exactly as before.'

'Until you sell out. But they know nothing of that, do they?'

'Even then, nothing will change for them, except that there'll be a new name on the roof-top.'

And if he couldn't see how symbolic that was, then Rosalind knew it was time to give up the argument.

'It's no business of mine anyway,' she muttered. 'And I'm sorry I upset you unnecessarily, Felix.'

He drew her hands to his lips and looked at her over the tops of them.

'Everything I do is your business. When are you going to realise that?'

She pulled her hands away. She didn't want to have any declaration of love from him now, false or not. Hadn't he just told her that a person's thinking was coloured after a bereavement? She didn't want to be drawn into a hasty betrothal because Felix was perhaps suddenly conscious of his own mortality and needed to feel the continuity of existence that a wife and children brought. . .

He was wrong about something else too. She might not have the worldly experience of a townswoman, or the knowledge of these capable village girls, but she knew how it felt to love. And right now she was discovering that love could hurt.

'I realise that you and I should be getting back to the house,' she said quietly. 'It's been a very interesting morning, Felix, and I want to begin a letter to my mother before I forget some of the details. I want to surprise her with how much I've learned in so short a time.'

'Do you think you could spin a bobbin of wool now, then?' he said, catching her mood.

'Why not?' she said. 'Not that I'd like to try using one

of those noisy machines of yours. But I think we have an old spinning-wheel in the attic at home. I mean to try my hand at it as soon as I return to Sussex, just to prove I can do it.'

Felix was smiling now. He gave her an approving nod.

'And I've a shrewd suspicion that, when Rosalind Cranbourne wants to do something, she does it.'

But not always, Rosalind thought. She wanted to say that she loved him, and that she desperately wanted to take his one-time marriage proposal seriously. . .but unless she could be absolutely sure that he loved her in return they were words that were destined to remain unsaid.

Rosalind and Lady Lydia spent the rest of the day enjoying the summer sunshine in the garden, relaxing before the start of the journey back to London the following day. It was decided that they would start out early, and it was clear that Felix was becoming restless now, and anxious not to be away from his duties any longer than necessary. He'd gone off on his own that afternoon, and Rosalind wondered if he was revisiting the graveside of his father, the way mourners did.

Lydia was clearly bored with the Yorkshire surroundings, now that the sombre business of the burial was over, and wanted to return to her own domain. Only Rosalind, it seemed, would have been content to stay forever. She realised uneasily that in this atmosphere she and Lydia were beginning to run out of things to say to one another, and she was thankful when Felix rejoined them in the garden, bringing the scent of the moors with him.

'I know this is hardly a time for social chit-chat, Aunt, but I've invited Harry Keeley and his wife for dinner this evening. I trust you won't object to a bit of company,' Felix said.

'Not at all! One can't be steeped in gloom forever, and life has to go on,' Lydia said glibly.

Rosalind avoided Felix's eyes, feeling she could read Lady Lydia's mind so clearly. The lady hadn't been at all steeped in gloom over the death of her brother-in-law, only because of the fact of having to make the tedious journey here. And even making conversation with these mill folk would be a bit livelier than the three of them merely spinning out the time until they could be on their way again from these dull surroundings.

But she realised Felix must have been to the mill again, since she was quite sure he hadn't invited Harry Keeley and his wife to dinner while they had been at the mill that morning.

Unless Felix had called on Harry's wife out of courtesy that afternoon—she remembered immediately that first time they had been up to Radley Crags, and his eyes had grown soft as he recalled how he had proposed to Annie Thwaite. They had been all of ten years old at the time, and there was simply no accounting for the stab of jealousy that ran through her now. It was more than just jealousy of the unknown Annie, though, who had now been married to Harry Keeley for five years and had three little lads. It was more a regretful envy for all the years of childhood when she and Felix hadn't known each other. . .

'Do you have any objection to our having company this evening, Rosalind?' he was asking her now.

'Of course not. This is your home, Felix, and it will be a pleasure to meet Harry again, and I look forward to meeting his wife too—Annie, isn't it?'

She met his eyes steadily and saw him nod. She was being quite foolish in begrudging him his memories, she told herself in some bewilderment later. By then she had begun her lengthy letter to her mother, outlining all the things she had seen at the mill, and becoming quite enthusiastic over the fascination of seeing the lumps of rough, oily wool finally emerge as beautiful soft woollen cloth fit to grace the most noble gentleman's back. It must say something about herself that she could identify more easily with those industrious mill workers than with someone living the life of an idle lady, she thought ruefully.

But she found she was quite nervous of meeting Annie Thwaite Keeley. Since Annie had produced three little boys in five years, Rosalind almost expected to see a rotund little woman, but Annie was bright and pretty and without an ounce of spare flesh on her. Felix kissed her at once, perfectly at ease with old friends, and introduced her quickly to his guests. There was no false humility on the part of the overseer and his wife at being in the company of a military captain and his autocratic aunt. These were old friends, and class barriers simply didn't exist here. Against her own expectations, Rosalind warmed to Annie Keeley at once.

'I hope we'll be seeing more of you, Rosalind,' Annie said eventually, when they had exhausted every topic of conversation and dinner was well behind them. By then Lady Lydia had retired to her bed, leaving the 'young things', as she called them, to their own pleasure.

'Unfortunately, I hardly think it's likely, unless you ever make a visit to Sussex. If so, you'd be very welcome at my parents' house.'

'And *that's* not very likely, with three lively lads to care for,' she laughed. 'But surely if you and Felix—oh, now my tongue's running away with me, and I'm embarrassing you.'

'Not at all. Felix and I are good friends,' Rosalind said steadily. 'But unless his aunt takes pity on me and invites me to stay with her once more, I don't suppose our paths will cross again.'

She felt an enormous pang at the thought, and she

didn't miss the glance the married couple threw at one another. It was obvious they had assumed she was Felix's intended bride, and to cover the embarrassment they launched into more childhood memories with Felix, so that for a while she was shut out.

It didn't matter. She needed these moments to recover herself, but, as the talk went on, she realised how much she had missed. They spoke of times she didn't know and places she couldn't enter. They shared a past, while she wasn't even sure how much more of the future she was going to share with Felix.

And the complacency of this old friendship could be ruined in a moment if they even remotely suspected that Felix had no intention of ever coming back here to live. . .it was the one topic that had been carefully avoided by herself and Felix all evening, she realised.

'Do you remember asking me to marry you on Radley Crags?' Annie suddenly said, with memory brightening her eyes.

Rosalind kept her eyes lowered. This had been one of the memories Felix had allowed her to share. It had seemed a sweet and innocent secret, and now it seemed it was common knowledge. She felt idiotically betrayed, and wondered if she was going slightly mad. Was this what love did to a person?

'And you said you weren't going to marry a mill owner's son, because he'd be too uppity,' Felix added.

'So you ended up with an overseer, who's just as uppity and twice as bossy,' Harry put in with a grin.

Felix laughed. 'If I remember correctly, Annie had no trouble getting her own way with either of us, uppity or not.'

Harry's eyes were warm as he looked at his wife. 'Aye, but she's a good lass for all that, and I'd not change her.'

'You'll have me blushing next,' Annie said, 'and if

you're fishing for compliments, Harry Keeley, you'd best wait until we're alone for that.'

Rosalind listened to the little interchange, recognising the teasing undercurrents between a married couple for whom all the compliments—and the loving—could wait until later. They had all the time in the world for it. At that moment she envied them so much, and felt almost embarrassed at witnessing such unashamed affection between two people.

As if aware of the small silence between the other two, Harry glanced at the grandfather clock in the corner of the room and decided he and Annie must be on their way.

'You're having an early start, I understand,' he said to Rosalind. 'So we'll say goodbye now, but I sincerely hope it's not goodbye forever.'

'So do I,' was all she could say to that, without bursting into tears. For it probably would be. She couldn't ever see herself coming this way again.

She waved goodbye to Harry and Annie, feeling that she was losing dear friends. It was the weirdest feeling, since she had known them for so short a time. But friendship, like love, could spring into life just when you least expected it, and be all the richer for it.

And she had drunk too much wine, and was in danger of becoming maudlin. . .

'Goodnight, Felix,' she said, once the door had closed behind the guests. 'I'm very tired, and we have to be up early in the morning——'

'And I want to kiss you so badly,' he said softly. 'Would it be so very wrong to give my friend a goodnight kiss?'

For a fraction of time she resisted his passion. Mutely at first she allowed herself to be held in his arms, and felt his hungry mouth on hers. And then she gave up resisting and allowed her own nature to dictate her needs, giving him back kiss for kiss, as starved as he.

CHAPTER TWELVE

WHEN they left Radley the next day, the village was enveloped in an early-morning pall of smoke from mill and cottage chimneys and the lingering valley mist. It was hard to make out buildings clearly, and Rosalind felt a little cheated that this last sight of the village should be so nearly obscured. But not so Lady Lydia, who couldn't wait to get away from what she called this miserable area, and was anxious to be back in London with all speed.

'I'd love to have had a last look at the village, though,' Rosalind said. 'It's so pretty in sunlight.'

Lydia gave an unladylike sniff, tucking the travelling rug more firmly about her person. 'There's nothing pretty about that hideously common sign on the mill, my dear. If I were Felix's father, I'd have had that removed long ago.'

'It's tradition, Aunt,' he said mildly. 'You can't fight tradition, and it's good advertising.'

The word seemed to scandalise his aunt even more, which Rosalind realised was the object of his word. He could tease her quite unmercifully at times, and she didn't even notice it.

'I know what Felix means, Lady Lydia,' she said hastily. 'In business you do have to advertise——'

'My dear girl, I know nothing about such things, and I'd have thought it quite unnecessary for you to know about them too. There are more important things in life than advertising!'

The way she said it made it sound almost akin to

raping and pillaging, Rosalind thought with a secret smile.

'I'd still have liked to see the village in sunlight before I left, advertising or not,' she said in her own defence.

'I'll tell you an old Yorkshire saying, Rosie,' Felix said. 'When you visit somewhere you especially like, you should always leave something to see another time, so then you'll be sure of returning.'

'I think you've just invented your old Yorkshire saying,' she said lightly, but, whether he had or not, the words gave her a little lift. In all likelihood she would never come back here, but she still liked to think that some day she might.

After their return to London, Felix reported back to his barracks immediately, and Lydia told Rosalind that of necessity they would spend a quiet few days, but that she saw no need for the two of them to be gloomy.

'It's not as if Jonas Holden meant anything to me, my dear,' she said. 'And frankly, Felix didn't seem unduly upset, so I don't want you thinking you have to go about with a long face. We'll resume our plans for going to the ballet just as soon as you like.'

'Would you think it terribly rude of me if I say you don't have to put yourself out too much on my account, Lady Lydia?' Rosalind ventured to say. 'I have to confess that I'm not enthralled about going to the ballet——'

'Then why haven't you said so before, dear girl? Of course we needn't go if you don't want to. I'd far rather my intimates spoke their minds and didn't hide their misery behind so-called good manners. And I do class you among my intimates now, Rosalind. You're a sweet girl, and I'm wondering if you've given any more thought to my hopes for you and Felix, now that you've got to know him a little better?'

Rosalind looked down at her hands. 'I haven't changed my mind about anything,' she said, which was no more than the truth.

Lydia spoke briskly. 'Well, for goodness' sake, don't look so downcast, Rosalind! I'm not going to banish you from the house just because you're honest enough not to pretend a fondness where one doesn't exist.'

'I didn't say I wasn't *fond* of him——' she said, and then stopped, because if she went any further she might very well blurt out the truth: that she loved Felix Holden to distraction, and that with her own far more intimate knowledge of the man she knew he was still in some kind of torment over his father and the legacy he didn't want. He hid it very well, but Rosalind knew how he hated the thought of going back to Yorkshire and telling his friends and mill workers that he intended to sell up. And, knowing him as she did, she was aware that he would want to face them to tell them personally. He wouldn't shirk that duty, just as he didn't shirk any other.

She heard Lydia give an indulgent laugh.

'You don't have to soften the blow, my dear. Fondness is a poor substitute for love, and I wouldn't want to see a young and healthy girl like yourself lose that youthful bloom because she married the wrong man. You'll find the right one some day, I'm sure of it.'

In the meantime she was growing older. . .at twenty years old, a young lady was already beginning to attract speculation as to her marital prospects. It was quite ridiculous, but Rosalind knew how true it was in fashionable circles. Guiltily, she thought with some relief that she didn't have to move in fashionable circles forever. When this visit was over, she could return to the country and be herself again, instead of acting the part Lady Lydia had mapped out for her. She knew how ungrateful she was being in even thinking that way, and she pushed the thought out of her mind immediately.

'I think we're both in the grip of an anticlimax at the moment,' Lydia went on. 'Despite the reason for travelling to Yorkshire, the days have been busy, and now there's nothing to do. We must scan the newspapers and see what events have been happening recently, and what we can do to amuse ourselves and rouse us out of our lethargy.'

Rosalind thought with amusement that it was rare for Lady Lydia to be afflicted by lethargy for too long. She was determinedly bright and cheerful and full of energy for a lady of her years. It was herself who felt limp and suddenly out of sorts.

'While you do that, I'd like to speak with Margaret, Lady Lydia, and finish my letter to my mother to let her know of our safe return. Will you excuse me?'

'Of course, my dear. And give your mother my best regards,' she said vaguely, already ensconced in the social events and tittle-tattle of *The Times* and other newspapers. She suddenly sat upright.

'Bless my soul, just listen to this, Rosalind, before you rush off.'

Rosalind reluctantly came back into the room, having felt a great need to be alone. She hadn't been alone for days, she thought, and she was a person who needed and appreciated solitude occasionally, while Lydia obviously did not.

'There's a report here about a letter from Mr Swift, the keeper of the jewel house at the Tower. You remember I told you before that the poor man has a large family to support and relies for his income on the shillings that visitors pay to see the crown jewels?'

'I remember,' Rosalind murmured, wondering what could have happened to the man, and, more importantly, to the large family of children.

'Well, it seems that since the crown has been made for the Queen the jewellers responsible have put it on display in their shop on Ludgate Hill.'

Rosalind looked more interested now. 'How wonderful. Then we could perhaps go and view it too?' Such a prospect was far more to her liking than sitting in a theatre, she realised. She was undoubtedly a country mouse. . .

Lady Lydia looked at her severely. 'We may, if you've a wish to do so. But cannot you see the distress this event has brought to Mr Swift? He complains that with the crowds of people viewing the new crown at Rundle, Bridge and Rundle's none of them will visit the jewel house at the Tower, and his loss will be enormous.'

'I'm sorry for the man, but I suppose if the crown is on display, it's not wrong to go and see it? It's obviously of great public interest.' She couldn't quite see what all the fuss was about.

'The keeper of the jewel house receives no proper salary, Rosalind, and depends for his livelihood on the shillings from visitors. Now do you see what a disaster this must be for him?'

She did, and felt distressed that she had seemed so heartless and unfeeling minutes before.

'Then we won't view it either,' she declared.

Lady Lydia gave her the glimmer of a smile. 'Yes, we will, dear, since it would be a shame for you to miss the opportunity. But we'll also make a point of going to the Tower after the event as well, and supporting poor Mr Swift. I shall see to it that my friends all do the same.'

She was quite a lady, Rosalind thought with sudden affection. Snobbish to the core, and yet full of indignation about the loss of earnings to this poor Mr Swift. But Lydia was already intent on reading more gossip, and Rosalind made her escape to her bedroom and rang the bell for Margaret.

'I'm that glad to see you back, Miss Rosie!' she was greeted at once. 'Was it a terrible tedious journey, and is Yorkshire an awful miserable place?'

'Not at all!' Rosalind laughed. 'It was quite beautiful, in fact, and apart from the sad circumstances of our visit I found it very enjoyable.'

'Lordy, yes, I was forgetting. How is the poor captain?'

'The poor captain is very well,' Rosalind said evenly. 'I doubt that we shall be seeing much of him until after the coronation now, and his duties will no doubt help to take his mind off his bereavement.'

To say nothing of the problems facing him when he returned to Yorkshire, she thought. She guessed he'd want to return there at the earliest opportunity after the coronation. He wouldn't want to postpone his speech to his mill workers. She wondered if even the lawyer was aware of it all yet, and decided that he was probably not. Felix would want it all kept very close to his chest until he was ready to speak out. The unheavals would be great—the sale of the house as well as the mill—and many people were going to be distressed because of it. She defended Felix in her mind. It was his life, and no one else's.

'I was asking if you're going to see the crown, Miss Rosie. You seem mighty distracted, if I might say so.'

'Oh—yes. Lady Lydia was just telling me about it.'

'Me and Lizzie and Bertram went up Ludgate Hill two days ago. You could hardly get near the shop for the crowds and carriages, with policemen keeping 'em in order,' Margaret went on excitedly. 'They won't let nobody inside the shop without a free ticket, but Bertram got 'em for us. We was all pushed and shoved, regardless, but it was all worth it to see the crown, and Bertram took good care of us.'

'Bertram's name seems to pop up in your talk quite a

lot, Margaret!' Rosalind said with amusement, and saw her maid blush.

Why, she was quite pretty today, Rosalind thought in some astonishment, and her hair looked softer than usual too. Perhaps it was just the shine in her eyes that was making her look younger than usual. Or perhaps it was something else altogether. . .

'Me and Bertram get along real well, Miss Rosie. There's no harm in that, is there?'

'None at all. Only don't get too fond of him, will you? Remember we have to go back to Sussex in a few weeks' time, and I doubt that you'll see him again.'

Margaret looked uncomfortable.

'I didn't want to talk to you about that too soon, Miss Rosalind.' The fact that she'd used her full name alerted Rosalind even more that something was in the wind.

'I think you'd better talk to me about it right now,' she said quietly.

'Well, what would you say if me and Bertram wanted to take up new positions here in London? He knows of a footman and senior housemaid's position for a married couple in one of the swanky large houses, and he thinks we could swing it. We ain't had no real experience of the jobs, but we've seen plenty of others do it, and we know we could manage it——'

Rosalind ignored everything else but the one fact.

'A married couple? Are you telling me you're thinking of marrying him? Margaret, you hardly know the man!'

Margaret looked resentful. 'I've known him nearly as long as you've known Captain Holden, miss. And probably got to know him far better, since servants ain't so pompous in their doings as the gentry, begging your pardon for saying so. And don't go telling me you ain't falling for the captain, because I've known you too long, and I know I shouldn't speak so plainly——'

'No, you shouldn't.'

But there was no reason on this earth why Margaret and Bertram shouldn't have fallen in love, just as swiftly and completely as she herself had fallen in love with Felix.

'So what would you say to it? Losing me, I mean? Would it upset you? I swear I don't really want to leave you, Miss Rosie, but I've me own life to consider as well.'

'Of course you have, and if you're sure then I wouldn't begrudge you your happiness, Margaret. Oh, come here!'

She went to the stiff-necked maid and hugged her close. They'd been friends as well as mistress and servant for too long for Rosalind not to feel a pang at this news, but Margaret's marriage to a man she loved was infinitely preferable to being dependent on the whims of Miss Rosalind Cranbourne for the rest of her life.

'Don't say nothing yet, though, Miss Rosie,' Margaret said, her eyes suspiciously brighter now. 'Bertram's still got to get the new positions sorted out.'

'And if he doesn't? You'd want to stay on in Lady Lydia's household when I go home, I suppose, and you'd still be intent on marrying him. Is that the rest of it?'

It obviously was, and, amid all the assurances that Margaret had to do what her heart dictated, Rosalind began to feel more restless than ever. Her own maid had found happiness so unexpectedly, while she. . .

Oh, why hadn't she and Felix met in other circumstances? she thought wanly. Why have this so-called match thrust upon them, so that Rosalind had been so ready to resent him? Lady Lydia's meddling, however well-meaning, had backfired so miserably. And, right now, Felix was in no mood to even think about marriage. All his thoughts and energies would be directed towards his military duties for now, and once the great day was over his thoughts would turn to Yorkshire. There simply seemed no place for her in his thinking for the present. The irony of it was, the more she knew she was being inevitably pushed away from him, the more she longed for him.

'We'll go up to Ludgate Hill very soon, Rosalind,' Lady Lydia announced when she came downstairs for dinner that evening. 'I've persuaded a gallant escort to take us to see the new crown, so we needn't be afraid of the crowds.'

Rosalind's heart had already leapt at her words. Felix was coming home, or was already here. . .she turned eagerly as she heard footsteps entering the room, and then her heart plummeted with disappointment.

'G-good evening, Sir George,' she stammered. 'It's good to see you again.'

'And you, Miss Cranbourne,' he said, with the little touch of mockery in his voice she disliked so much. 'I trust the dreary wilds of Yorkshire weren't too boring for you?'

She flushed. His words implied that, since she'd come here to see the bright lights of London, she must have found it galling to find herself involved in a family funeral instead.

'Not at all. I loved everything about it,' she retorted. 'And you seem to forget that Felix's reason for going to Yorkshire was a sad one.'

'Good God, I see he has a little champion here!' He stared at her as if she was something peculiar. 'Well, naturally I'm sorry Felix had to curtail his business to go chasing up there, though I doubt he'd be too sorry over losing his father. They had little in common, and he'll be damned glad to be rid of the responsibility of the place.'

'I think you're wrong about Felix,' Rosalind found herself continuing the argument. 'I think he had very deep feelings about his father, despite their differences. One does not always have to agree totally with someone else to think highly of them.'

She was both seething at his high-handed dismissal of Felix's feelings, and appalled at herself for being so rude in George's own house. But Lady Lydia seemed amused by the whole episode.

'You won't get the better of Rosalind, George. She has a mind of her own, and isn't afraid to speak it.'

'So I see. You did well to match the two of them, Mother. Felix always did enjoy setting the sparks flying in an argument. He'll get plenty with this one.'

Rosalind held her tongue, refusing to be goaded into any further retort about whether or not she was going to marry his cousin. That had already been decided.

'So you're going to escort us to see the Queen's new crown, are you, Sir George?' she asked coolly, when they were all seated at the dinner table.

'I'm taking Celeste and her young cousins, so you and Mother may accompany us,' he said, with what Rosalind considered gross ungraciousness. But her attention was caught now by his reference to his lady-friend.

'So we shall meet Celeste at last. I confess I began to wonder if she really existed,' she said with a teasing smile.

But George Greville was not a man to be teased. He looked at her coldly.

'Of course she exists. In fact, I wanted to ask you something, Mother,' he turned away from Rosalind. 'Celeste's staying in town until after the coronation with her cousins' family. Her parents won't be attending the ceremony, and I was wondering if Celeste may accompany us to the Abbey.'

'But my dear boy, you know that won't be possible. We have our seats, and that's that.'

Rosalind spoke quickly. 'Please don't think me entirely ungrateful, Lady Lydia, but you may give my seat to Celeste. I would much rather be among the crowds watching the procession, and I'm sure I can persuade Aunt May to come with me.'

Lady Lydia shook her head. 'I can't let you do this, my dear. An occasion like this will probably never occur again in your lifetime, and it will be something to tell your children.'

'I'd rather tell them of the crowds and the excitement, and of seeing Felix riding escort to the Queen,' Rosalind said, hardly realising what she was saying until the words were said. As if to say that Felix would be the father of her children. . .but it was too late to retract the words now, and, since the other two obviously thought she would be quite mad to give up the chance of marrying an officer and a gentleman, she was thankful they let it pass.

'I don't know what to say to you, Rosalind,' Lady Lydia said dubiously. 'I'd be lacking in my duty if I let you roam the streets of London alone——'

'Hardly alone, Lady Lydia! And I know Aunt May will agree to coming with me——'

'But you say yourself she's a frail old lady, my dear.'

'Well, that's what my mother says, but I know that Aunt May's made of sterner stuff. May I ask her to call on you?' she said, beginning to feel desperate, and only just realising what an ordeal the coronation in Westminster Abbey was going to be. For the young Queen, and for a young girl from Sussex, who'd much prefer to be out of doors, no matter how hot the day, than in the confines of a church with hundreds of others. . .

'Let Rosalind have her way, Mother. It will suit everyone,' George put in. 'And have this aunt of hers to tea if it will ease your mind. You can send a couple of grooms along to accompany them, can't you?'

He was so gross in his dismissal of her, Rosalind thought angrily. Allying her with servants. . .she was ashamed of herself for the snobbery, but he had the knack of making her feel that way. She pitied the unknown Celeste, if she intended marrying him, and hoped she was a strong-minded woman. She'd need to be, to live with Sir George Greville.

'Very well. We shall both call on your aunt, Rosalind, so that I may see the lady's condition for myself, and whether she wishes to view the procession with you. Then we'll decide. I hope she'll overlook the informality of my not sending a calling-card in advance.'

Rosalind hid a smile, saying she was sure Aunt May wouldn't be offended. Calling-cards didn't figure largely in Aunt May's social scene. The real hurdle would be to persuade the lady to come out of the house on coronation day, and that might not be easy. If only Felix were here to help persuade her. He could charm the birds from the trees, Rosalind thought, with undisguised longing. It was days since she had seen him, and then, just as if she had conjured him up out of her wishes, he arrived at the house before the midday meal the very next day.

He looked better than when they had left Radley, and Rosalind guessed that he'd come to terms with himself. Back in his familiar army routine, he could view things from a distance and know he'd made the right choice. The outward mourning would be over, except for the grief he hid inside himself, and life had to go on.

'I have the rest of the day free,' he said to his aunt. 'Though it was a devil's job to get here. The city's bursting with people, arriving every hour it seems, from every part of the country. Even the ports are busy with foreigners curious to see our new Queen crowned, and the day not even here yet.'

'Then if you've time on your hands, may I suggest you accompany us to Rosalind's aunt's house as soon as we've eaten?' Lydia said at once. 'I wish to speak with the lady myself on a certain matter.'

'Of course,' Felix said, puzzled, and then Rosalind hastily told him her reasons. It would kill two birds with one stone, she thought irreverently, showing Felix off to her aunt, and proving to Lady Lydia that Aunt May was only as ill as her wily needs dictated.

Felix spoke to Rosalind for the first time.

'You'd really prefer to watch the procession than be in the Abbey?'

'I would. Is that so very strange?'

'Not to me.' He gave a slight smile. 'I'd probably feel the same in your shoes.'

'That's the difference between you and me, Cousin,' George drawled, coming back into the room at that moment. 'By the by, I was sorry to hear your news. Naturally I would have accompanied you and the ladies to Yorkshire for the funeral if I'd been in England at the time.'

'Naturally,' Felix said, stony-faced.

'Then if that's settled, let's have our meal, and make the most of the afternoon,' Lady Lydia said briskly, seeing the beginnings of antagonism between the two men.

But she forgot all about George as the three of them went to Paddington that afternoon, and Rosalind was very aware of the crowds in the city. The sheer volume of people made it more cloying than ever, and Felix repeated his aunt's anxiety about Rosalind watching the procession with the hordes.

'I shall insist on two grooms accompanying them, as George suggested,' his aunt said. 'He does have the occasional good idea, Felix. But under no circumstances would I allow Rosalind and her aunt to be out and about without proper escorts.'

'I wish I could be with them,' Felix said. 'But of course it's impossible. However, I have two days' leave immediately following the coronation, so it will be my pleasure then to escort you both around Hyde Park and the festivities.'

Rosalind felt overjoyed at the words. The two-day fair in Hyde Park sounded so exciting, and to share it with Felix would be even more so, even though his aunt would be there with them. As if she could read her thoughts, Lady Lydia laughed.

'I doubt that I shall want any more excitement after the coronation, dear boy. I dare say I shall leave all of that to you younger ones.'

And Rosalind found herself praying that she wouldn't go back on her word.

They arrived at Aunt May's house, and Rosalind rang the bell in some embarrassment. It was one thing to come here with Margaret and to dispatch her maid to the kitchen for gossip. It was quite another to be driven expertly by Felix himself and to bring him and his autocratic aunt unannounced. Thankfully, Aunt May rose to the occasion beautifully.

'I've been telling this girl of mine that I should meet your nephew,' she said to Lady Lydia, immediately treating her like a second conspirator intent on the same result as herself. 'And now that I have I thoroughly approve.'

'Aunt May, please don't embarrass me,' Rosalind said swiftly, knowing her colour was heightened.

'Nonsense, girl, there's no need for embarrassment when an old lady likes the look of a young man,' she chuckled. 'There's no cause for jealousy, I promise you.'

She had the audacity to wink at Felix, and Rosalind squirmed. But to her relief Lady Lydia seemed to find the whole episode highly amusing, and settled herself easily on one of the comfortably worn armchairs as the inevitable tea and biscuits were brought in.

'You'd best explain to your aunt why we've come, my dear,' she said eventually.

Rosalind took a deep breath and explained all the circumstances.

'I know you said you couldn't be doing with all the fuss, Aunt May, but couldn't you make an exception just this once?' she wheedled. 'It would mean so much to me, and you'd have the chance of seeing Felix as one of the Queen's mounted escorts.'

Quite blatantly, she pushed the advantage of her aunt's undoubted admiration of the handsome captain. If she'd been thirty years younger, Rosalind hazarded, she'd have flirted outrageously with him herself.

'And there will be two of my best grooms to accompany you both at all times,' Lady Lydia added. 'I will insist on that, dear Miss Cranbourne. In fact, I think I shall invite you to spend the previous night with us, so that you and Rosalind may start out as soon as you're ready the next day. After the coronation is over, I hope you will join us for dinner that evening.'

'Shall the captain be there for dinner too?' Aunt May said, her roguish old eyes twinkling.

Felix laughed. 'I shall make a point of it, and of personally escorting you back home again.'

'Then how can I refuse? All right, Rosalind, I shall come with you to be crushed in the crowds, though I know your mother will think you quite mad for not wanting to be inside the Abbey. But no matter. I've no doubt that we shall hear every detail from Lady Lydia, whom I thank most sincerely for her hospitality, and gratefully accept.'

So it was all arranged, and Rosalind came away from Aunt May's house in something of a daze. She'd hardly expected her aunt to be swayed out of her original decision without something of a struggle, but it had only taken a little persuasion from Felix to make her change the habits of a long lifetime. So much for the charismatic power of a handsome military man, Rosalind thought with a wry smile. But she turned to him with thanks as they went homewards to Hampstead.

'I liked her very much,' he said in answer. 'She has a mind of her own and isn't afraid to say what she thinks. I see where you get some of it from, Rosalind. It's a pity everyone can't always be as frank with one another.'

'Ah, but you must agree that some things are best left unsaid, Felix,' his aunt put in, obviously well pleased with the afternoon and not averse to a little light discussion now.

And some things were far better brought out into the open, Rosalind was thinking, as her hostess prattled on. Such as just why she was being so hesitant in admitting her own feelings, even to herself, She loved this man sitting beside her in the open carriage, loved him more than she had ever thought herself capable of loving anyone.

She looked at his hands, strong and capable on the reins, and felt an overwhelming longing to have those same hands holding her. She glanced at his profile, elegant as the head on a golden coin, and wanted him so much. . .

If only there was some way to tell him without breaking the strict code of etiquette that decreed that a lady never revealed her feelings to a gentleman until he had declared them first. And he had never actually said he loved her, she remembered. He'd taunted and teased her about marrying her, but whether that was merely to pander to his aunt's wishes, or because of any real desire of his own, she wasn't even sure.

She still didn't know the heart and soul of him. She didn't know whether or not he stood to gain anything if he married his aunt's choice, unworthy though that sounded. That he was dashing, amusing, tender and ardent as a lover should be when the need arose she certainly had no reason to doubt.

But somewhere deep inside her she knew that the man she wanted him to be would be rejecting everything that was here in this exciting, enervating, dirty and boisterous city. The man she wanted would be returning to his roots, to continue with dignity and pride what his father and grandfather had begun, and he would have no hesitation in taking her with him, knowing in his bones that the glitter of the high life wasn't for either of them, but that together they could begin a new and wonderful chapter in the Holden story. And the likelihood of that happening seemed as remote to Rosalind as wishing for the stars.

CHAPTER THIRTEEN

ONCE Lady Lydia discovered that most of her contemporaries had been to view the Queen's new crown, she wasted no more time in declaring that they must all go at once to the shop of Messrs Rundell, Bridge and Rundell on Ludgate Hill.

'I knew this would be a foolish expedition, Mother,' Sir George roared at them as he attempted to keep the horses under control among the throngs of people and vehicles.

The fourth person in the party looked at him impatiently. The young cousins had not been allowed to accompany Lady Celeste Pattinson on the excursion after all, but the lady herself had been a complete surprise to Rosalind. She was handsome rather than pretty, and nearer to thirty years old than twenty, and anyone with uncharitable thoughts would say that put her well back on the shelf. She was a forthright woman, and Rosalind had discovered that she was more than a verbal match for George, but presumably her dowry and connections were enough to make her an entirely suitable marriage prospect.

'Now, George, don't upset your mother,' Celeste said. 'We all want to see the new crown of state. It's an important piece of social history, and we're hardly ever likely to see it again so closely, so please try to keep your temper in check.'

Rosalind all but gasped, waiting to see how George reacted to this admonition, and how Lady Lydia appreciated this high-handed manner. Astonishingly, the lady seemed quite amused, and George was momentarily calmed by his friend's words.

'I think I approve of Celeste,' Lady Lydia said beneath her breath to Rosalind, when they finally alighted at the shop amid much jostling and pushing and organising by the constables.

Rosalind was bound to agree with Lady Lydia, especially as she thought privately that if these two were to wed she was sure Celeste would keep an eagle eye on her husband. There would be no more dallying in servants' quarters.

And then she forgot all about such things as she was steered inside the shop along with all the other eager viewers, gaping with awe at the sight awaiting them. The crown was simply dazzling, and so beautiful that it almost brought tears to the eyes. Rosalind tried to imagine how a young girl must feel on the day she wore it as the symbol of a nation's fealty, and her imagination simply wouldn't stretch that far.

There was little time to linger over the viewing, for the crowds behind were pressing to enter the premises, and reluctantly they had to leave the viewing to others and struggle back to their waiting carriage. George's impatience was almost tangible, but, to give credit to Celeste's influence, he managed not to complain too bitterly over what he considered this waste of a day.

They drove back through the city and Rosalind realised that what Felix had said was true. London was full to bursting with people, and there could hardly be a hotel or a lodging-house that wasn't doing wonderful business in these days leading up to the coronation. The noise and confusion from every quarter was indescribable, and adding to the general excitement there were stands being erected along the whole route of the procession, so that workmen jostled with the raucous crowds who hampered their progress even more.

'Shall we take a detour through the park?' Lady Lydia said. 'I swear I have a such a headache coming on with all this hammering and knocking that it feels as though the hammers are inside my own head.'

'Poor Lady Lydia,' Celeste said swiftly as Sir George began a low muttering. 'I'm sure it will be no hardship for George to take us through the park. It will be a relief to get away from these congested streets and see some of the preparations there too.'

And, to Rosalind's amazement, George simply did as he was told. He responded to a strong woman, she thought, and Celeste was obviously the one for him. She caught Lady Lydia's amused glance, and knew that their thoughts were the same.

But Hyde Park was no less noisy and congested than the jammed streets and pavements. Tents had been erected for every kind of stall and fairground amusement, and banners waved from every pole. The costermongers were already selling their wares to curious out-of-town visitors; the hot-food vendors were filling the air with their delicious aromas; the organ-grinders turned their wheels ferociously, while little bright-eyed monkeys dressed in frilled pierrot costumes danced to whatever tune emerged and begged for pennies. The official two-day fair wasn't due to start until the day after the coronation, but there was no stopping any of these impromptu performances now.

To add to the entertainment a parade of mounted soldiers drew sudden applause and cheers from the milling crowds, their helmets glinting in the sunlight, their spurs and harnesses clattering, the sight of them charming every lady in the vicinity.

'Oh, there's Felix,' Lady Lydia said, her voice full of pleasure at seeing her other darling boy so elegant and proud at the head of the column.

Rosalind's heart seemed to leap out of her chest at

seeing him so unexpectedly like this. Red and black and silver dazzled in front of her eyes, and when he caught sight of them he gave a smart salute before cantering on ahead of the several dozen soldiers following on behind.

'Your cousin sits a horse very well, George,' Celeste said admiringly.

'So he should, considering the hours he spends in the saddle,' George commented. 'It's the way he chooses to spend his life, and I must say it's preferable to the alternative.'

'You mean taking over his father's mill? You think such an idea is quite impossible, then?' Rosalind couldn't help asking the question, even though she knew the answer only too well.

George gave her a pitying look. 'My dear girl, when one's lived in town and enjoyed the life of a captain in the Queen's military, one can hardly compare the two styles of living. You must have seen that for yourself on your sojourn to Yorkshire.'

'You're quite right,' Rosalind said evenly. 'You can't compare the two styles of living at all.'

But that didn't mean that one was any better or more satisfying than the other. But she heard the confident way George spoke, and knew that Felix too must have weighed everything up in this way a long time ago. He had known then what he wanted, and there was no reason now to think he was going to change his mind. She felt unutterably depressed at the thought as the horses drawing their carriage began their slow progress again.

'Miss Cranbourne, I don't believe I've thanked you properly yet for giving up your seat to me at the Abbey,' Celeste said, covering the awkward little silence. 'You're quite sure about this, aren't you?'

'Quite sure. My aunt is looking forward to

accompanying me now, and I wouldn't deprive her of the excitement.'

'But I'm not sure I'd be as happy, with so many people about,' Celeste went on dubiously. 'There are sure to be rogues and pickpockets——'

'They'll be quite all right with the grooms to look after them,' George said shortly. 'Mother's sending the largest and strongest, so they'll come to no harm.'

And if it began to sound to Rosalind as if he implied that it was as much as a country girl could expect to be looked after by trusted servants, she ignored it and concentrated on searching through the crowds for a last glimpse of Felix.

They escorted Celeste to the imposing house where she was staying with her cousins until after the coronation. Once George had escorted her to the door, he returned, looking well pleased with himself. It had been an unconventional way of introducing the young lady to his mother, but the family was a fairly unconventional one, and no one seemed concerned.

'Well, Mother? What do you think of her?' he said, with almost boyish eagerness.

'I think she'll do very well for you,' Lady Lydia responded. 'Have you approached her father yet? You realise you'll be expected to observe a timely courtship if you're mixing in those circles, George.'

'I think the Duke knows my intentions are honourable, but nothing's been said as yet. Celeste's still concerned about her mother's recurring bouts of bad health, and wishes to wait until she's quite well again before any decisions are made. Neither of us is in the first flush, so we're not desperate for the marriage stakes.'

It was hardly gallant to include Celeste in such a statement, Rosalind thought, but then, she had never found anything about Sir George Greville very gallant.

'Shall we invite her to dinner on the night of the coronation, Mother? We'll be having Rosalind's aunt there as well as Felix and the rest of us, so we may as well make a party of it. Do you agree, Mother?'

'It sounds an admirable idea,' Lady Lydia said, and Rosalind breathed a sigh of relief, because if Celeste was there to occupy George she wouldn't always have the feeling that he was sneering at her, and, even more so, at the homely Aunt May.

The following evening Felix arrived at the house just as Rosalind and Lydia were finishing dinner. George had an engagement elsewhere, so the two ladies had dined alone. As always, Rosalind's heart missed a beat when Felix came into the room.

'Good evening to you both. This is horribly short notice, but I've got some tickets for a new play at the Alhambra in Paddington this evening. A fellow officer was taking his sisters, but they've come down with the chicken-pox so he's passed the tickets on to me. I know it's not the done thing to be out on the town so soon after my father's death, Aunt Lydia, but since the play's a tragedy I'm sure I can be suitably mournful. Is it too late for you to agree to come?'

'Far too late for me, because I have the beginnings of a migraine. I know you mean no disrespect to your father, and since none of our acquaintances is aware of your recent bereavement it's between yourself and your conscience. But you must ask Rosalind if she wishes to go with you.'

'You'd allow her to come with me unchaperoned, then?' he asked, with a slight smile.

'I've every faith in you, my dear, and I should think Rosalind knows whether or not she can trust you by now. But the decision is hers, of course.'

Felix looked at her, his eyes pleading with her to

accompany him. And, all other considerations aside, she had caught the brittleness in his voice and guessed that he needed this diversion. He might not be mourning his father in the accepted manner, but she knew he mourned him deep down all the same. And what good did it do anyone to hide away from the world? It didn't change the sorrowing or the regrets. . .

'I'd love to come,' she said swiftly, thankful that they normally dined early at Greville Lodge, and that the theatres started late. 'Should I change?'

'Definitely not. You look exactly right as you are,' Felix said quietly. She was already dressed in a fresh gown for dinner, a soft blue silk that nipped in her waist over the restricting corsets and petticoats and then flared out into a rich full skirt adorned with bows. Worn with her grey velvet evening cloak and bonnet it would be a perfect ensemble for the theatre.

She felt a surge of excitement. Since coming back from Yorkshire, Lady Lydia's plans for entertaining had waned a little. Guiltily, Rosalind had already become somewhat tired of sitting in the elegant houses of her contemporaries, drinking tea and coffee and making polite conversation, or listening to the daughter of whichever house she was in playing the pianoforte or reciting. The theatre would be a welcome change.

'Whenever you can be ready, then, Rosie,' Felix said now, his voice noticeably warmer. 'I presume we may take the gig, Aunt Lydia?'

'Of course,' the lady said, so adroitly that Rosalind thought suspiciously that her supposed migraine had come on very unexpectedly indeed. But, recklessly, Rosalind knew she didn't even care if it had been a white lie. She would be spending the evening with Felix in the darkened intimacy of the theatre, and the knowledge was enough to make her joyous.

Fifteen minutes later they were stepping outside into

the cool evening air, and Felix was helping her into the gig and sitting beside her. In the small, two-wheeled vehicle, she could feel the warmth of his thigh against hers, and made no attempt to move further away. In any case, there was nowhere to go.

'I'm glad of this time alone with you,' Felix said, as they clattered through the cobbled streets. 'I need to know that you don't entirely condemn me for continuing with my career.'

'Is my opinion so important to you?'

'You know that it is.' For a second he took his hand off the reins and put it over her gloved ones, held tightly in her lap. She shivered as the warmth of his skin penetrated through the silk of her gown, and he removed his hand at once.

'Well, then,' she said, choosing her words carefully, 'I do understand how you feel, Felix. You've made your choice, and it's a noble and patriotic one, and no one has the right to condemn a man for that.'

'But?' he said, knowing there was more.

'But what I don't understand is how you can be so blind in not seeing how rewarding the alternative can be. Especially now you've been back to the mill and spoken with the workers, and seen how loyal they were to your father, and how they have every intention of being just as loyal to you!'

'And that's it, is it?'

'Well, you did ask me, although you couldn't really have been in any doubt of my answer! I've already made my feelings plain, even though it has nothing at all to do with me.'

He glanced at her as they jogged along the streets. They had already skirted the large area of Hampstead Heath, with its frosting of early evening mist, and the streets were already becoming noisier and more populated the nearer they got to the more brightly lit areas.

'Everything I do and say and think has something to do with you, Rosalind. I value your opinions highly.'

She gave a rueful smile. 'Thank you for that, even though I doubt that anything I say could influence you one scrap. You're obviously dedicated to your career, and I respect that.'

'So you think I should stick by my decision?'

She was helpless to know what answer he really wanted. Whatever she said, he objected to it, or countered it, or became angry about it. She hadn't forgotten how she had tried to influence him before they left Yorkshire, and she had no wish to encounter his wrath again. Particularly on this evening, which was such an unexpected outing. Without thinking she put her hand on his arm, and felt how rigid with tension it was.

'Could we not just enjoy this evening, Felix?' she pleaded. 'I can't make up your mind for you, and nor would I presume to try. Particularly when you know very well you've already made it up. Nothing's going to come between you and your military career, so why pretend otherwise? I'd really prefer not to be brought into it, if you don't mind.'

She looked down at her lap, clasping her two hands together again.

'Besides, in a few weeks from now our paths are hardly likely to cross again since I shall be returning to Sussex. I'm very grateful to Lady Lydia for giving me this wonderful time in London, but I confess that I'm looking forward to seeing my family again and leading a rather less eventful life.'

Felix's voice was short. 'That sounds remarkably like the voice of someone who's afraid of life in its broadest terms. I never thought I'd be suggesting such a thing to you, Rosie. I always considered you a young woman of singular spirit.'

'I'm not afraid of life,' she said indignantly. 'But I

know what's the best kind of life for me, and it's not here in London. I'm sorry if that sounds ungrateful, and I beg you not to pass on the remark to Lady Lydia. The last thing I'd want to do is distress her.'

'Naturally I wouldn't repeat your remark. But it would seem to divide you and me as well. Is that what you want?'

She felt acute misery wash over her. No matter what she said now, they were destined to be far apart in the very near future.

'We were never close enough to be divided, Felix,' she said quietly. 'I tried to tell you that, but you would never listen. But true friends will always be friends, no matter what their differences or in what directions their lives lead them, and I do count you as my friend.'

She heard him give a low oath and pretended not to notice. She was well aware that this was a time of anxiety for him, both in his career and his personal life, and although she longed to give him comfort it seemed she simply didn't know how. She felt inadequate and lost, loving him as she did, and being unable to tell him so.

She sought to find something else to say.

'I gather you haven't met your cousin's intended yet, Felix. She's to join us for dinner after the coronation. You'll like her, I'm sure.'

'If she's anything like as pompous as George, I'm sure I shall not,' he said perversely.

'Not quite, I think,' Rosalind said. 'She's very lively, and about the same age as Margaret Wood. That's another thing—Margaret has become attached to one of Lady Lydia's manservants and——' She almost said they intended looking for a post together, and stopped herself in time.

'And what?' Felix said.

'Well, I think it's probable that she'll want to remain

here instead of coming back to Sussex to what she thinks
is the dull old country life,' she said lamely.

'It seems that everyone is finding a new life for his or
herself except you, then. Doesn't that tell you something
about yourself?'

She looked at him steadily. 'Yes. It tells me that my
feet are firmly on the ground and that I'm perfectly
content to be who I am,' she told him. 'How many
people can say that?'

'Only those too complacent to see what's around the
next corner,' he retorted. 'And you dare to call me the
blind one.'

'I hardly think we're talking about the same thing,'
she said. They rarely were of late. Their ways seemed to
be drawing them even further apart, and Lady Lydia's
audacious plan to bring them together seemed nothing
short of a hollow mockery to Rosalind now.

They were nearing the theatre, a small select building
in a normally quiet Paddington street, though it was
anything but quiet now. Carriages and pedestrians
thronged the narrow street, and Felix waited impatiently
until he could catch the attention of a man to look after
the horse and gig for a few coppers. Once it was settled,
they alighted from the gig and entered the theatre itself.

Rosalind had never been to this one before. There was
a small auditorium, above which was a balcony and
side-boxes, and when Felix had given up the tickets they
were shown to one of the side-boxes overlooking the
stage itself.

'What wonderful seats,' she said, well aware that they
were in an intimate little world of their own.

'We were lucky to get them.' He spoke quite coolly, as
if the fact of being anywhere with Rosalind Cranbourne
was of little importance at all.

She tried not to feel she was being slighted, and
concentrated instead on watching the theatre-goers fill-

ing the rows of seats below them, and alongside in the balcony. The ladies were bright and glittering in their evening gowns, their escorts just as resplendent. There was a fair sprinkling of officers' uniforms as well as the dark, elegant attire of the civilian gentlemen. Rosalind picked up the little opera glasses to peer at the crowds still filling the auditorium and filing into the other boxes, and became suddenly aware that someone in the opposite box was waving towards them.

'Is that someone you know, Felix?' she murmured.

'Well, you know them, too. Don't you recognise Lord and Lady Marchmont and the Courtneys' granddaughter?'

She had a swift recollection of a young girl smiling adoringly up into Felix's eyes as he whisked her around the ballroom floor at Lady Marchmont's spring ball, and felt the same sliver of jealousy she had felt then. She blinked the feeling away quickly, and gave a small nod back.

'Of course. How silly of me. I just never expect to see anyone that I know in London.'

'So I understand. You should realise that the world's far wider than the area comprising Sussex, my love.'

'I do know that. I'm not a complete idiot.'

She bit her lip. He hadn't been trying to pick a quarrel with her, and had spoken quite mildly. It was she who was so out of sorts, so on edge, that she couldn't seem to take anything he said light-heartedly any more. She was always looking for the hidden meanings beneath his words.

'I didn't expect to see such important people in a small theatre like this,' she began, trying to make amends.

'They're patrons of various small theatres. I happen to know they're doing their best to initiate young Gabriella into the pleasures of the theatre, as she's turning out something of a tomboy. She was bemoaning the fact to me at the ball.'

Rosalind felt oddly in sympathy, then, with the young girl who would be rebelling against all that other people had planned for her, however well-meaning.

'It's a shame to feel so obliged to be moulded into what other people want for you,' she said.

'Isn't that just what I've been telling you?' Felix said, as the lights were dimmed and the velvet curtain went up to deafening applause. And, too late, she realised what she'd said, which seemed to epitomise all the differences between them, and the unlikelihood of their ever agreeing.

But she wasn't going to brood all evening over something that couldn't be changed, and she gave all her attention to the play. The theatre was small and the actors no more than provincial players, but they played their parts excellently, and the tragedy that unfolded was one of accidental deaths and unrequited love, and there were many audible sniffs and a few outright sobs among the audience long before the final curtain.

'Good Lord, and we came here to be entertained,' Felix said beneath his breath, under cover of thunderous applause and shouts for more curtain calls.

'I was entertained, and very moved,' Rosalind told him with a catch in her voice. 'It was so sad, but so very believable.'

'I'm glad you enjoyed it, though on reflection I'd rather we'd seen a comedy,' he said. A tragedy obviously had done nothing to improve his gloomy mood, and Rosalind didn't quite know how to answer him. She was saved the necessity by a brief knock on the door of their box, followed by the appearance of the Marchmont party. Lady Marchmont's eyes took in every bit of their appearance at the Alhambra.

'Felix, my dear boy, we thought it was you, and Miss Cranbourne too. How very nice to see you both again.'

'Good evening, Lady Marchmont—Lord March-mont—Gabriella. My aunt will be sorry not to have seen you. She was to have accompanied us here this evening, and insisted that Miss Cranbourne should not miss the performance because of her indisposition.'

'Oh, how sad for your aunt,' Lady Marchmont said, no doubt seeing the reason for his explanation at once. The two of them did indeed look so cosy in the theatre box, and Rosalind was glad the flickering lights in the auditorium were still low enough to hide her fiery cheeks.

'Shall you come backstage with us, Felix?' Gabriella was saying eagerly. 'We're invited to the supper, because of Grandmama's patronage.'

'I hardly think the invitation would extend to inter-lopers,' Felix smiled, but Lady Marchmont waved his objections aside.

'Nonsense. You are both my guests, and I'm sure Miss Cranbourne would enjoy meeting a few theatrical people?'

'Very much,' she said, not sure whether this meant she might be more at home with working-class people, however colourful, or if the remark was genuinely friendly. But there was no point in fretting over it, since the group was already leaving the box, and she had no option but to be swept along with them.

'Don't be alarmed,' Felix murmured in her ear. 'Lady Marchmont has a habit of gathering up everyone around her like a mother hen with her chicks.'

It sounded such an incongruous statement for the aristocratic lady that Rosalind was forced to laugh. This evening wasn't ending at all as it had begun, and she was still sure Lady Marchmont viewed her unchaperoned appearance with Felix as somewhat surprising.

But she was immediately drawn into the noisy and bohemian atmosphere backstage, where the cast was exuberant after the first-night reception of the play. Rosalind found it highly comical to see the actors still in their stage costumes and cosmetics, who minutes before had been performing a tragedy of huge proportions, waving bottles of champagne about now, and passing around plates of titbits. Supper was obviously a very informal affair.

She was amused to see mounds of cheese among the offerings, and obviously there was no thought of stuffy etiquette here. She didn't know whether or not Lady Marchmont ate any, but Rosalind certainly did, and was glad to see that Felix indulged as well. She saw him chatting with Gabriella, but was cornered by the bulkiest of the gentleman actors, and had no chance to move away from him.

'We're honoured by your presence, ma'am,' he boomed, in his strong Thespian voice. "So tell me how you enjoyed the play.'

'I thought it was excellent,' she said honestly.

'And your husband? I swear that if he weren't a military man I'd try and persuade him to join our company. He has the looks and the presence for the stage. He'd hold an audience captive, especially the ladies!'

'Captain Holden is not my husband,' Rosalind managed to break in, aware of how the man's voice carried, and that Felix was glancing their way.

The actor chuckled, and dropped his voice a fraction. 'Then I'd keep an eye on him, little lady. You don't want to let that pretty little baggage gain all his attention. But since you ain't married, I shall claim your arm and offer you some of this delicious champagne.'

Lady Marchmont was hovering near by, and smiled graciously at the two of them.

'Now then, Barnwell, don't go turning this young lady's head with your nonsense. And since I doubt that you've bothered with proper introductions, may I inform you that this is Miss Cranbourne, who's staying for the season with Lady Lydia Greville, Captain Holden's aunt? And this, of course, is the star actor in the company, Mr Barnwell Fitzallen.'

The man gave a flamboyant theatrical bow, not in the least put out by her words.

'Thank you, me lady, for putting me straight,' he said. 'And where does Miss Cranbourne normally reside, may I ask?'

He steered her to the side of the room, to the amusement of Lady Marchmont, who had obviously seen all his ploys before. And whether Rosalind wanted to or not, she was obliged to talk with the man for the next half-hour, while he kept her glass filled and called for anyone handy to bring them titbits from the food table. It was the oddest evening Rosalind had ever spent, and by the end of it the cosmetics were beginning to run down the actor's face and turning it into a grotesque caricature. The room was hot, but she was told it was considered bad luck in the company to remove any bit of stage make-up until the last visitor backstage had gone. It would ruin the illusion the actors had spent all evening creating.

'Normally, of course, this just means the admirers who come to congratulate us on the performance,' Barnwell said without false modesty. 'But first nights are always special, and it's a delight to meet you, my dear Miss Cranbourne.'

'Thank you. It's a pleasure for me too,' Rosalind murmured, beginning to wish Felix would come and claim her and that they could get out of this cloying atmosphere. The room was a crush of people, and, exciting though it had been to meet and converse with real stage actors, she longed for her bed. But they could hardly leave until Lady Marchmont decided the evening had come to an end.

When she finally did so, Rosalind turned to Barnwell Fitzallen with a feeling of relief. By then they had been joined by several other actors, and also the large lady who had played the leading tragedienne's role in the play.

'It was so nice to meet you all, and thank you so much for allowing me to join the party,' she said sincerely. Felix came to echo her words, and Barnwell Fitzallen gave him an exaggerated wink.

'You take my advice, Captain, and tie the knot with this little lady before somebody else comes along and steals her away,' he said.

'Oh, I've tried, man, but she won't have me,' Felix replied in the same light-hearted fashion amid the general noisy chatter. 'But I don't give up easily.'

Barnwell slapped him heartily on the back. A lesser man would have winced, but Felix stood his ground.

'That's the ticket. Here's to you both, then.'

He raised yet another glass of champagne to his lips with a none too steady hand, and drank noisily. And as the other actors closed around them to say goodbye they made their escape into the cool night air. Felix called to the dozing man standing guard over their gig, and turned to thank the Marchmonts for the entertaining end to their evening.

'Please tell your aunt I trust her migraine does not linger, dear boy, and that I shall call on her quite soon.'

As they drove away into the night, Felix finished her unspoken words.

'In other words, Aunt Lydia will undoubtedly receive a small reprimand for allowing the two of us to attend the theatre unaccompanied. For all her association with actors and the like, Lady Marchmont is a stickler for etiquette.'

'Even Mr Fitzallen assumed we were married until I assured him we were not,' she reflected.

'And the thought of marrying me is such an impossibility to you, isn't it, Rosalind?' he stated rather than asked.

She caught her breath, unable to answer for a moment. The sweetness of being married to Felix, of living with him intimately until the end of their days, was suddenly too poignant. But still the question took her unawares. He had been so wrapped up in his own affairs recently: the duty to his regiment, and the deeper duty to his father that was still so unresolved. She couldn't even tell if this was a serious question, or how she was meant to take it. All her instincts urged her on to saying how desperately she wanted to marry him, loving him as she did. . .but she knew he didn't love her, and she had never thought herself a woman to settle for less than love. And she was silent too long.

'Don't bother answering the question,' he said bitterly. 'It was facetious and embarrassing, and you'll think it in very bad taste, considering I'm officially in mourning. I'll try not to bother you again, Rosalind.'

And at his uncompromising words all she could do was to stare unseeingly ahead of them as the gig clattered through the night towards Greville Lodge, and agonise over whether she had just thrown away everything that she loved the most.

CHAPTER FOURTEEN

It was the day all England had been waiting for. Shops and factories were closed, street parties were organised, firework displays arranged for the evening, bunting appeared in every street and window and flags were clutched in every urchin's hand.

On the twenty-eighth of June, 1838, the young Alexandrina Victoria would be crowned Queen Victoria in Westminster Abbey, in the ancient ceremony of coronation. No one could be unconscious of the tradition and pageantry of the occasion, and excitement in the city was running feverishly high.

Rosalind awoke to the sound of her curtains being drawn back, and winced at the burst of sunlight filling the room.

'It's a lovely day for it, Miss Rosie, and your aunt's already up and about,' Margaret was saying excitedly.

Miss May Cranbourne had arrived at Greville Lodge the previous evening. She had been urged to stay for several nights, and had readily accepted Lady Lydia's invitation. It was remarkable how the two of them had found kindred spirits in one another, Rosalind thought as she sprang out of bed to view the day from her window.

'It's perfect,' she agreed with Margaret. 'I suppose you'll be wanting to get off as early as possible?'

'When you're ready, miss. Me and Lizzie have hired our posh hats, and Bertram's arranged for a vehicle to take us all and bring us back. Bertram says folk have camped out all night along the route. If we don't get there early, we'll get trampled on and that will be that.'

'Good heavens!' Rosalind stared at her. 'Then we should get ready early too. You needn't fuss yourself about me this morning, Margaret. As long as there's hot water for myself and Aunt May, I can manage.'

'Well, if you're sure——'

'Go along now, Margaret, and don't keep Bertram waiting.'

Aunt May knocked on her door a few minutes later. She was already dressed.

'There's such activity in the house, I couldn't sleep any longer, and I certainly expected you to be ready by now, Rosalind. We'll want to have a good view of your captain in the procession.'

'I thought we were going to see the Queen in the state coach!'

'So we are, but we'll be looking out for Captain Holden as well, won't we?'

Rosalind gave up. Aunt May, supposedly so frail and infirm, had suddenly come to life. And, in doing so, she had adapted to the role of matchmaker with Lady Lydia far too easily.

'What time is it now?'

'Just after six o'clock,' she was told.

'That's practically the middle of the night,' Rosalind groaned. 'And was it my imagination, or was there thunder a few hours ago?'

'It wasn't thunder. At four o'clock this morning they fired off guns in the park, and the bands started playing soon after. I doubt that many people slept after that.' She looked almost accusing that Rosalind had apparently done so. 'Don't forget the procession begins at ten o'clock. Have the grooms decided on the best point for us to watch?'

Rosalind grinned good-humouredly. 'For someone who wasn't in the least interested in this day, Aunt May, you've completely turned turtle. I spoke with

Thomas and Kenton, and they say we should make for Piccadilly. The procession goes up Constitution Hill and along Piccadilly, then down St James's Street and across Trafalgar Square to Westminster Abbey.'

'Well, just as long as we get a good view, and our two strong young men to protect us, I don't care where we sit.'

Rosalind looked at her uneasily. 'Don't count on getting a seat at all. Margaret says people have been camping out all night to get the best views.'

'Nonsense. When they see a frail old lady about to expire I'm sure I'll be given a seat, and my niece will need to be with me at all times.'

'You're not a frail old lady. You're a wily old fox!' Rosalind said.

They were on their way before eight o'clock. Lady Lydia had no need to leave so early, being assured of a place in the Abbey, and Sir George couldn't resist several disparaging remarks to Rosalind on preferring to be in the crush of *hoi polloi* rather than in the majesty of the Abbey.

'But then you wouldn't have had my seat to offer to Lady Celeste,' she replied smartly. 'It's an ill wind, as they so rightly say.'

And she was thankful for whatever wind had blown her well away from the odious Sir George Greville.

'George, please don't be objectionable,' his mother put in. 'Rosalind, dear, the grooms are awaiting you and your aunt whenever you're ready, and we shall see you both this evening, when we'll tell you *everything* about the ceremony.'

She was glad to get away from George's superior looks, wondering again how two cousins could be so different. . .she pushed the thought aside, preparing to leave the house to find the two brawny grooms already awaiting them in the carriage.

Thomas spoke up. 'I've arranged to leave the carriage in a nearby mews, miss. A friend who works there will see to feeding and watering our horses, and the carriage will be safe. It'll only be a short step to Piccadilly.'

'That will be fine, thank you,' Rosalind said at once. 'I suppose this extra duty is agreeable to yourself and Kenton?'

Whether or not it was the done thing to enquire after the grooms' plans in this way, it seemed courteous to do so, and Thomas nodded.

'It's a pleasure to be of service to you, miss. We'd have tried to see something of the little lady's great day, in any case.'

Rosalind avoided Aunt May's eyes. Little lady indeed! It was a fine way to speak about their sovereign, but from the size of these two men every other person they met must be little. They were men of some stature, and the Cranbourne ladies were fervently glad of the fact when they neared the city and saw the thousands of people who had poured into London for this event.

'The day will be a very long one, ladies,' Kenton added. 'We've brought refreshments for the waiting time. That is, if you intend to wait until the procession returns from the Abbey.'

'Of course! We want to see the Queen wearing her crown,' Aunt May put in. 'No matter how long the day, if she has the stamina for it, then so do we.'

They heard the crowds in the city long before they saw them. The noise was deafening, and if Rosalind began to feel qualms at their going among so many she was constantly reassured by the height and broad backs of their escorts.

It was a long and wearisome experience to inch their way through the streets to find the mews behind Piccadilly. The main processional route was banned to carriages and pedestrians, and everyone who wasn't on foot was trying to edge his vehicle through the side-roads for the nearest point to the route.

'It would be quicker if we got out and walked the rest of the way,' Aunt May said.

'Not without escorts, ma'am,' Thomas replied. 'You'd be crushed in a moment, so just leave everything to us.'

By the time the carriage was safely housed in the mews, together with the picnic basket one of the grooms would fetch later, it was nearing ten o'clock. The procession would take an hour and a half to reach the Abbey, and as they approached Piccadilly on foot every inch of space seemed to be taken up. Aunt May saw the futility of pretending to faint in these crowds, but they had reckoned without the ingenuity of the two grooms as they reached a gap in the stands.

'Make room for police escorts to pass through, if you please,' Thomas and Kenton roared out in tones to rival that of Mr Branwell Fitzallen at his theatrical best, and they began elbowing their way among the crowds, with Rosalind and her aunt between them.

Incredibly, the crowds seemed to melt away and then close around them again with much grumbling and cat-calling, but allowing them to pass. Few would argue with two such authoritative men, and none questioned their identities. Those at the front of the stands simply shuffled along to make room for the newcomers, and they found themselves with an undisturbed view of the entire proceedings.

'Have you done this sort of thing before?' Rosalind whispered to Thomas.

'We've had our uses, miss,' he said drily.

But everything else was soon forgotten as the shouts from the crowds beyond them heralded the approach of the start of the coronation procession, and Rosalind felt her heart begin to beat more rapidly. The chance to see their Queen was almost here, and the excitement of it all was finally taking her breath away.

The lengthy procession of coaches, bands and cavalry provided a dazzling array, every bit of it cheered and clapped along its length. They applauded the most at the sight of the slight figure inside the state coach with her attendants. With the Londoners' superior knowledge of their city, word was quickly passed around to all the strangers that these were the mistress of the robes and the master of the horse. Names were abandoned in favour of titles, in order to impress. Anyone who could intended to claim some special knowledge of today's proceedings.

As the young Queen constantly raised her hand in pleasure at the reception, each began declaring that the wave was especially for them. Rosalind joined in the cheering just as loudly as the rest, enchanted by the sight of the young woman, a year younger than herself, who was taking on such an awesome responsibility. Nevertheless, slender and proud, wearing a red velvet kirtle over what looked like a simple white satin gown, and with a circlet of gold, glinting with diamonds, on her head, she looked every inch a Queen. Watching her pass, Rosalind felt a great sense of history and loyalty surging through her, and a sudden enormous thrill at the moment when Victoria seemed to look straight into her eyes and smile.

'Did you see that?' She turned to her aunt, as uninhibited as a child. 'She looked straight at me then!'

'If you don't stop clutching me so excitedly, you'll miss your young man,' her aunt said drily, and Rosalind turned at once. In those moments she had almost forgotten Felix, but now she heard the clatter of more horses' hoofs striking sparks on the cobbles and saw the escorting cavalry regiment following on behind the state coach, with Felix almost alongside her on their side of the road.

Her eyes almost blurred with pride. How could anyone be less than proud to be a royal escort on such a day? How could she ever expect him to give up this life, when it was what he had chosen for himself, and every moment must have been leading up to this? Without even realising that she did so, she did as every other young woman in the crowd was doing to the handsome soldiers, and blew him a kiss.

He smiled slightly, and acknowledged the gesture with a salute especially for her, and she blushed with embarrassment.

'Well, you've certainly shown yourself in the likes of a housemaid now,' Aunt May murmured. 'We're supposed to be under privileged police escort, my girl, so behave like a lady, or the crowds will wonder who they've given their seats to.'

There were so many waving and hand-kissing young women that Rosalind doubted that anyone noticed, though she hadn't seen anyone else getting a salute in return.

'Anyone who saw it would probably assume that the captain's my husband,' she said defiantly. 'It's permissible to blow your husband a kiss, even for a lady.'

She felt an overwhelming longing for the fantasy to be real. To know that Felix would be coming home to her that night, filled with his own stories of the coronation day, and that they would sleep in one another's arms. . . Shocked, she realised just how wanton her thoughts had been at that moment, and she turned away from her aunt to cheer and wave more of the procession, just as if she was afraid the lady could read everything that was in her mind.

Once the procession had passed, there was little else to do for the rest of that interminable day. Some of the crowds drifted away, but the majority clung rigidly to their little portion of London, loath to abandon it, since the crowds would undoubtedly swell again by late afternoon when the long ceremony would be over and the triumphant Queen would begin the return journey to Buckingham Palace.

The crowds were enjoying the sunshine of the day, many relating anecdotes or unwrapping their picnic baskets for an outdoor feast. The air was filled with the sounds of festivity and goodwill, with only the occasional outbreak of fighting, quickly controlled by police.

Uneasily, Rosalind hoped none of it would occur near them and cause the crowds to call on Thomas and Kenton for assistance. Happily, it didn't, and by early afternoon Kenton had brought their own repast to the front of the stand, and they munched their pies and drank their cordial in warm and harmonious surroundings, taking a little exercise afterwards. All the time Rosalind wondered what was happening in the Abbey, and just how Felix was faring in full ceremonial uniform in the heat of this long day. That any man was so willing to endure it was further testimonial to his loyalty.

But at last the afternoon shadows began to lengthen, and the procession was returning along its route to fanfares and cheers. The Queen was now attired in purple velvet, the dazzling crown on her head, and carrying the sceptre in her right hand and the orb in her left. This prevented her from waving to the crowds, but in any case Rosalind observed that she looked far paler than earlier in the day, and could only guess at the ordeal the ancient and lengthy ceremony must have been.

Felix was now on the far side of the street, looking neither to left nor right. And somehow, in the pageantry of this day, Rosalind felt she had lost any hope of ever appealing to him to change his mind over his inherit-

ance. This day, so splendid for all of London and the
nation, seemed to epitomise the fact that this was Felix
Holden's life, and no one had the right to question it.

'Wasn't it all simply wonderful?' Aunt May was
enthusing long after the last of the procession had
passed, and people reluctantly began to disperse. 'I
can't thank you enough, Rosalind, for insisting that I
get back into society. I wouldn't have missed it for
anything.'

'I'm glad,' Rosalind murmured, making an effort to
sound just as enthusiastic, though in truth she felt a
huge anticlimax, and the sting of tears behind her eyes.

Everyone else around her was still caught up in the
magic of the day, but Rosalind Cranbourne was exam-
ining her own position more clearly. And how foolish it
all seemed now—all Lady Lydia's ideas of matchmaking, and her own indignant resistance. All so much a
waste of time, when it was as clear as daylight that Felix
and the army were made for one another.

That was his real destiny. Not herself, not Holden's
Cloth Mill, perhaps not even marriage at all. A man
could be married to his career, and a military career was
a more demanding mistress than most. She swallowed
the lump in her throat and was thankful for the chatter-
ing going on all around her as Thomas and Kenton
escorted herself and her aunt somewhat more easily
through the crowds now to the mews where their
carriage awaited them.

Rosalind was calmer by the time the guests at Greville
Lodge met for a very late dinner that evening, both to
give everyone time to recover, and for Cook and the
servants time to prepare and serve the meal.

By then she had faced the fact that she had been no
more than an amusement for Felix, and perhaps a bit of
a challenge too. He might even have married her if she'd
accepted the bait, and, since a wife would be no more

than an added accoutrement, then someone reasonably attractive and towards whom he could undoubtedly feel some passion would presumably have been enough. If Rosalind attributed him with less than worthy reasons for matrimony, it helped to keep up her spirits to think that way.

They were a lively party of six at dinner that evening, and if Miss Rosalind Cranbourne was the least lively no one seemed to notice. Lady Lydia sat at the head of the table, with Sir George at the foot. Next to George sat Lady Celeste, with the older Miss Cranbourne opposite her. Felix sat between the two aunts, with Rosalind opposite him. And naturally all the talk was of the coronation.

'It was such a pity you missed the ceremony, my dear,' Lady Lydia said to Rosalind. 'It was very moving indeed, and so colourful too.'

Sir George sniggered. 'A bit too moving for that old buffoon Lord Rolle, Mother, wouldn't you say?'

'Shush, George, and please don't be disrespectful,' his mother admonished him, and turned to Rosalind and her aunt. 'What George refers to is when the old gentleman went to pay his homage to the Queen and overbalanced, falling back down the steps. The poor man is all of eighty-two years old, but when he attempted to walk up the steps again the Queen very kindly stepped down to meet him so that the incident wouldn't occur again.'

'It would have made the proceedings even longer if he'd gone back and forth all afternoon,' George said mirthfully, and according such little reverence to the day that Rosalind disliked him even more.

'But there were several awkward moments,' Celeste added, clearly as practical and unaffected by all the pomp as George. 'The Archbishop handed her the orb far too soon, and rammed the coronation ring on to the wrong finger. We heard that the poor girl almost screamed in pain at the incident, and later she had to soak her hand in cold water to remove the ring.'

'That may be, but there were some truly beautiful moments as well,' Lady Lydia said, clearly disapproving of the pair of them, but too well-bred to say so in company. 'The music itself was simply wonderful, and the singing was like that of angels. After the enthroning and the homage, the Queen left the throne, removed her crown and her robe of cloth of gold and all the other regalia, so that she remained in a simple white gown to receive the sacrament. And at this point a shaft of sunlight seemed to come through the windows to light up her bare head. It was truly magical, and more than one person was moved to tears.'

'Mother, you'll be saying next that it was a divine moment,' George said. 'It was a pure accident, that's all.'

'Perhaps so, but an accident that happened at a most providential moment, my dear,' Lady Lydia said.

'What of the unfortunate incident of the Bishop of Bath and Wells, Aunt Lydia?' Felix put in, seeing how tension was rising in the room. 'The tale went around the barracks very quickly that the ceremony was in danger of ending too soon, when he turned over two pages of the order of service at once. Did that really occur?'

Lady Lydia sighed. 'You all seem intent on making a mockery out of this wonderful day, and I wash my hands of you all,' she said, and then her mouth twitched. 'Well, yes, I suppose that could be said to be one of the farcical moments of this most eventful occasion,' she finally admitted. 'The Queen was told that the service was concluded and was escorted into the Confessor's Chapel. After some argument, it was revealed that the service was *not* yet over, so she was brought back for the final moments. We at the back of the Abbey were only dimly aware of all this, but obviously it created a less than stately image.'

'It sounds more like a total disaster,' Rosalind couldn't help saying. 'I'm sorry I missed it all, but Aunt May and I had a marvellous day viewing the processions and listening to all the gossip in the crowds, and we had a good view of the Queen.'

'Rosalind was convinced the Queen waved especially to her. And when Felix saluted her the crowds around us were very impressed, sure there was some nobility in their midst.'

Rosalind wished Aunt May hadn't revealed all that, bringing to her mind the moment she had blown a kiss to Felix. Nor did she like the superior look George threw at her down the table, as if to say no one in their right minds could possibly have mistaken Miss Rosalind Cranbourne for nobility!

Later, they watched the fireworks on Hampstead Heath from an upstairs window, and when it was finally time for bed Rosalind realised how crushingly tired she was. She simply didn't know how Aunt May had stood up to it all, but she seemed quite undaunted, and by now both she and Lady Lydia had changed their minds about going to Hyde Park tomorrow, and Felix would be taking the three ladies there for the festivities.

There had been no opportunity at all for Rosalind to snatch one private word with Felix. She wasn't even sure that she wanted to, or what she would say if they were alone. But her heart ached to realise how far apart they seemed to have drifted, and how effortlessly.

Although she was so tired, she couldn't sleep, and eventually she donned a dressing-gown and crept downstairs to fetch some milk from the kitchen. As always, the oil-lamps in the house were turned down low for the

night, but she could see quite well, and besides that
there was a full moon outside.

Rosalind knew how Cook hated anyone invading her
domain, but this was necessity. Then, as she reached
into the cold cupboard for the jug covered with its lacy
beaded cloth, she almost dropped it at hearing a noise
behind her.

'Don't be alarmed,' Felix's lazy voice said. 'It seems
we're here on the same mission.'

Except that he held a glass of spirits in his hand, and
looked as if he'd had more than enough already.

'You scared me half to death,' she breathed. 'I have a
headache, and thought some milk might help. I'll leave
you to your drinking in a moment.'

She had intended warming her milk, but now she
poured some quickly into a glass and replaced the jug.
Her fingers felt all thumbs, but she knew that the quicker
she got out of here the better. If there was ever a
compromising situation, this was it. As if she expected
the entire household to appear from every cupboard and
denounce them, she turned to leave the room.

'Are you so afraid to be alone with me?' Felix said
evenly.

'No. But I hardly think your aunt would approve.'

'I wanted to talk to you before you rushed upstairs
with your aunt after dinner,' he said, suddenly very
serious. 'I've got something to tell you, Rosalind.'

She felt the start of tears in her eyes. He was about to
tell her what she already knew, that he had found his
true forte today, and that nothing was going to deter
him from it. And she couldn't bear to listen to it,
knowing it was the end of all her hopes, all her dreams.

'Tell me tomorrow, when you don't have a glass in
your hand,' she stammered, and turned and fled from
the room, uncaring whether she spilled the milk or not.

She knew he wasn't anywhere near being drunk. He

wasn't in the habit of drinking to excess except on rare occasions, and nor was he a man who would need Dutch courage for anything. Unless it was to break a silly young girl's heart, she thought bitterly. And that was simply too much for her to bear. She reached her room, drank the milk and felt as if its chill crawled around every part of her. Then she slipped between the cold bedcovers, buried her head beneath them and cried her heart out.

The following day she had to pinch her cheeks to try to make herself look less maggoty, as Margaret called it. Margaret was full of yesterday's proceedings, and Rosalind simply let all the chatter wash over her. She had slept late, as had everyone else in the house, and the pretended headache of last night was now a reality. It served her right, she thought wanly. Nothing good ever came out of lies. She would dearly have loved to cry off going to Hyde Park today, but, since both Aunt May and Lady Lydia had now decided they wanted to see everything, she knew she couldn't spoil their day.

'It's to be hoped the crowds will have lessened a little by this afternoon,' Lady Lydia remarked over the late but hearty meal that she was calling breakfast and lunch combined.

'There's no chance of that, Aunt,' Felix said shortly. 'Visitors to the city will be making a holiday out of it, and no one can blame them for that.'

And the streets would be even more stinking with so many horses trampling their excrement into the cobbles, Rosalind thought, but knew better than to observe such a thing at the dining table. It was a relief that neither George nor Celeste was there, having gone out earlier.

'I'd just like to jot down some notes about yesterday to include in a letter home, if you don't mind,' she

murmured. 'We won't be leaving for an hour or so, will
we?'

'Whenever you ladies are ready,' Felix said, still in
that remote voice.

'Do as you please, Rosalind, dear, although the newspapers will be so full of the proceedings that all you'll
need to do is cut out the pieces and send them to your
parents.'

'It won't be quite the same, though, and I always like
to give Mother my own impressions,' she said.

And about the only thing she'd carefully avoided all
these weeks was giving her mother her real impression
of Captain Felix Holden. Never once had she said what
was really in her heart, and now she was glad. A broken
heart was far better kept private, especially from those
who loved her most and would want to offer comfort
when there could be none.

But she knew she couldn't stay in her room indefi-
nitely. The others would be impatient to see London
still *en fête*, with the atmosphere of a gigantic party still
lingering. She went downstairs to find the older ladies
talking animatedly. She was struck again at how well
they seemed to get on together. She surmised that when
she returned to Sussex Aunt May might well have found
a new friend.

With Felix driving them, they eventually reached
Hyde Park amid more huge crowds. They strolled
among the throngs of people, all intent on enjoying
themselves now that the pomp and circumstance of
yesterday was behind them. They watched the hurdy-
gurdy man for a while and moved on past the children's
entertainments—the Punch and Judys, the mime shows,
the merry-go-rounds.

They reached the scene that was attracting the biggest
and most curious crowds, where a gigantic hot-air

balloon reared up above the ground, with the balloon-ist's assistant shouting out an invitation.

'Come on now, ladies and gents. Make a daring ascent into the heavens, and see London as none of your friends have seen it. Leave your worries behind you and take a thrilling air ride——'

'Do you dare, Rosie?' Felix challenged.

She looked at him, startled.

Aunt May was more alarmed. 'Good gracious, I should think not. You keep your feet on the ground, my love——'

Felix smiled crookedly at Rosalind, and she knew he was remembering her own words: 'My feet are firmly on the ground. . .I'm perfectly content to be who I am. . .'

But who was she, without him. . .?

He was holding out his hand to her, and the nearby crowd sensed a taker for the balloonist's cries. They pushed them forward, clapping and cheering, and before she could even think what was happening a set of steps was put beside the basket beneath the balloon, and Felix and several more assistants were helping her clamber inside. The basket was large and deep, and the portly balloonist reassured her, saying it was perfectly safe, and the flight would last ten or fifteen minutes.

To the roar of the flames inflating the balloon, and the gasps and cheers of the crowd, the ground assistants released the safety ropes and the contraption left the ground quite gently. Rosalind clung to Felix's hand in sudden terror, wondering just how she had arrived in this situation.

She had an extraordinary feeling of weightlessness, and the people below them were quickly assuming miniature proportions. She tried to pick out Aunt May and Lady Lydia, but they were lost in the crowd. But after a few petrified moments she realised she was starting to revel in this strange new freedom as she saw the green of the park and the flags and bunting of the celebrations.

The balloonist began his rapid patter. 'You'll see buildings like you ain't never seen 'em before, lady and Captain. You'll see the twisting old Serpentine living up to its name——'

'And I'll see that you're paid double if you keep quiet and let me talk to the lady,' Felix said.

The man shrugged. 'It's your money, Captain, sir. If that's what you want, you won't even know I'm 'ere.'

Rosalind's heart jumped as the balloon hit a small pocket of turbulent air and the basket rocked slightly. She felt Felix's steadying arm around her, and was glad to let it stay there.

'I never seem to be alone with you, and I said last night I had something to tell you,' he said, almost aggressively.

They weren't alone now, but the balloonist was too busy concentrating on keeping his craft steady than bothering about them. Rosalind's heart was hammering by now, and not only with the novelty of feeling as if they were floating on a cloud.

'What is it?' she said huskily, sure that she already knew, and not wanting to hear again where his future lay.

'I'm going to resign my commission,' he said.

Her eyes widened, and she felt his arm tighten around her. She had never expected this. She didn't know what to say, but, in any case, she got no chance to speak.

'Let me finish. I've thought of nothing else since we returned from Yorkshire, and I finally made the decision the night before last. Yesterday's ceremonial occasion seemed a fitting end to a career.'

Rosalind swallowed. 'But Felix, you were so ada-mant—what will you do?'

'What do you think? Take up the reins of the family

business, of course. It's what you said I should do, isn't it?'

They were drifting over the park now, and neither of them saw any of it. The balloonist gave up worrying about this strange couple who didn't want to be educated into the rare delight of seeing London by air, and sent another blast of flame into the balloon, to the roaring applause of the crowds below. Rosalind clung to Felix in sudden alarm at the noise. But there was something far more important to discuss.

'You're not doing this because of me?' she said. 'Felix, you must only do it because you want to——'

'I do want to. I know it's right. I've always known it in my heart, and when you and I spent time together going around the mill I felt it in my soul. But why shouldn't I do it because of you? Don't you know you're the most important thing in my life?'

'Am I?' she said faintly.

He turned her into his arms, regardless of who might see.

'Good God, woman, you must know by now how desperately I love you. I've loved you, since the day I first saw you—my dear deceitful Widow Wood.'

The words were too spectacular for her to take in properly, and she found herself stammering.

'I didn't know—you never told me——'

'Would you have believed me? Wouldn't you have thought I was merely following my aunt's instructions?'

She stared at him, all the hope returning to her heart.

'Perhaps. But I should have known you weren't the kind of man to marry on such terms.'

She caught her breath, knowing it was true. She should always have known. Felix wasn't a man to be swayed by money or position, only by the dictates of his own heart. So far he'd said nothing about marriage, but now she felt his arms pull her into him more possessively. She could feel his breath, warm on her cheek, close to her mouth, and the sensation of floating was as much in her heart as due to the contraption in which they so effortlessly sailed the sky.

'So I'm asking you to marry me on *my* terms, my darling girl. Will you be content to be the wife of a Yorkshire mill owner? I can't promise you all of this. . .' He swept his arm around to encompass the illustrious panorama of London into which they were gently descending now.

'I don't want all of this,' she said, with a catch in her throat. 'I only want you, Felix.'

Dimly, she could hear people all around them cheering and clapping. It was encouraged by the balloonist, the obvious *amour* giving an extra fillip to the attractions of his balloon ascent. But neither she nor Felix cared if the applause was for the successful return of the balloon, or for the spectacle of the two people inside the basket who were kissing so passionately. All that mattered to them was the future they were going to share.

The other exciting

MASQUERADE
Historical

available this month is:

TANGLED REINS
Stephanie Laurens

Miss Dorothea Darent was quite content to remain on the shelf, but for her younger sister's sake she was happy to have a Season in town with their fashionable grandmother. The Marquis of Hazelmere had other ideas. One look at Dorothea's vibrant expressive face was enough, but their first meeting had put him at a disadvantage.

Careful planning was required if he was to win her to wife, but the Marquis found Dorothea couldn't be manipulated quite so easily, once she understood what he was about!

Look out for the two intriguing

MASQUERADE *Historical*

Romances coming next month

FAIR GAME
Sheila Bishop

Miss Olivia Fenimore was happy to spend the summer
months with her relatives in Parmouth, Devon, though she
was disturbed to find the family in an uncomfortable
situation. Mr Tom Brooke had apparently led her young
cousin Hetty somewhat astray, something not easy to hide in
a small community. It was Olivia's misfortune that she also
found Mr Brooke deeply attractive, but a man who appeared
to consider women fair game was not for her. . .

MASTER OF TAMASEE
Helen Dickson

Clarissa Milton's life fell about her ears, not once, but twice,
and she had no alternative but to accept when Christopher
Cordell offered marriage, even though this meant moving
from London to his plantation near Charleston. But no
sooner had the ceremony taken place, than Clarissa's past
reared its head—what chance did their marriage stand now,
particularly when in this year of 1812, England and America
were to go to war?

Available in October

An irresistible offer for you

Here at Reader Service we would love you to become a regular reader of Masquerade. And to welcome you, we'd like you to have 2 books, a cuddly teddy and a mystery gift - ABSOLUTELY FREE and without obligation.

Then, every 2 months you could look forward to receiving 4 more brand-new Masquerade historical romances for just £2.25 each, delivered to your door, postage and packing free. Plus our free Newsletter featuring special offers, author news, competitions with some great prizes, and lots more!

This invitation comes with no strings attached. You may cancel or suspend your subscription at any time, and still keep your free books and gifts.

It's so easy. Send no money now. Simply fill in the coupon below at once and post it to - Reader Service, FREEPOST, PO Box 236, Croydon, Surrey CR9 9EL.

- - - - - - - NO STAMP REQUIRED - - - - - - -

Yes! Please rush me 2 FREE Masquerade romances and 2 FREE gifts! Please als reserve me a Reader Service subscription. If I decide to subscribe, I can look forward to receiving 4 brand new Masquerade romances every 2 months for just £9.00, delivered direct to my door, postage and packing free. If I choose not to subscribe I shall write to you within 10 days - I can keep the books and gifts whatever I decide. I may cancel or suspend my subscription at any time. I am ove 18 years of age.

EP30

Mrs/Miss/Ms/Mr _____

Address _____

_____

Postcode _____ Signature _____